Cornwall on the Rocks

Grace Tremayne

PublishAmerica
Baltimore

ISBN: 1-4137-9955-8
PUBLISHED BY PUBLISHAMERICA, LLLP
www.publishamerica.com
Baltimore

Printed in the United States of America

To Goona

Our much-loved pet
and the inspiration for
Topsy

Acknowledgements

The author wishes to express his thanks to the following relations and friends who helped in the creation of this novel. To:

Valerie Simmons for her encouragement to me to write the novel and then reading multiple versions of it. Valerie also helped me choose my pseudonym.

Mandy Simmons, who suggested the characters and let me develop them the way that I wanted and in the setting that I chose.

My friends *Simon Cook and Dave Rolfs*, who both read the script, found inconsistencies and recommended many improvements that appear in the final version.

Chapter 1

Pharmacy college, 6th September 1994

Laura ran as fast as she could toward the Blimford bus stop, waving frantically. The bus driver had already closed the doors and signalled, ready to move off, when he saw her. He cancelled the signal and opened the door just as she arrived. He smiled, commenting, "It's either set the alarm five minutes earlier or no breakfast tomorrow."

Laura got her breath back sufficiently to thank him as she showed him her brand new pass.

"Penzance College, is it?" the driver observed as he pulled out into the traffic.

"Yes," Laura replied. "It's my first day today. I will be studying pharmacy."

The driver's face beamed as he continued the conversation with a teasing response. "My word, that sounds posh for one so young. So you are going to be one of my regulars then?"

Laura nodded as she settled into the front seat.

"That'll be nice; I'll keep an eye out for you."

The bus completed the short journey to St Ives in ten minutes, leaving Laura a five-minute wait before the Penzance train departed. It was already waiting on the platform. She said goodbye and thanked the driver again as she left the Blimford bus and crossed over to the station. As she boarded the train, Laura saw her two old friends from Hilary Taylor School, both of whom were going to take the same course. Scarlett Robinson waved to attract Laura's attention. Laura joined her and Kyomi Taylor in the last carriage. They were deep in conversation by the time the train left and did not stop until it was pulling into Penzance station.

"This is us," Scarlett called out as she got up and gathered her bags together.

The three girls disembarked, left the station and stood on the path looking lost until Kyomi, who had been observing the general flow of students, called out, "It's this way."

Within ten minutes they found themselves sitting in a small classroom with three other girls and one boy. It was just before nine o'clock.

"This is a bit of a shock to the system," Laura commented. "Yesterday I was still in bed at this time."

A woman in her mid-thirties came in. She addressed all present. "Are you all here for Year One Pharmacy GNVQ?"

Everybody either responded with a positive "yes" or nodded.

"Good," she continued. "I am Mrs. Marlow and I am your first-year tutor. Would you just respond to the register so that I know who you are, please?"

As she read out the names, each of the class put up his or her hand.

"Right, this is the plan for the first day," she began. "During the next half-hour I am going to give you your timetable for the first term and get you to introduce yourselves to the teaching staff and your fellow students. Your lecturers for the first term are going to join me in about five minutes. After that we are going to give you a tour of the pharmacy block, which will include a safety demonstration that will be given in the undergraduate laboratory. Did you all bring lab coats and safety glasses?"

She looked around the class. The boy put up his hand. Mrs. Marlow, anticipating what he was going to say, added, "Okay, we can sell you what you need. See the lab steward at the end of the safety demonstration."

While she was talking, the four first-year lecturers had come in and joined her at the front of the class.

After reading out the lecture timetable, Mrs. Marlow started the students' introductions.

"I will call you in alphabetical order. Would you please tell us a little bit about yourself, including why you wanted to study pharmacy? Can we start with Nicholas Dean, please?"

The boy stood up. He was about five feet five inches tall with a slight build, dark hair and brown eyes. He was wearing a scuffed leather bomber jacket over a blue sweater and blue jeans.

"Hi, everybody," he began. "I'm Nick Dean. I'm seventeen and I live in Penzance. I took a year out after taking my GCSEs to tour Southeast Asia, Australia and New Zealand. I returned last May when my money ran out. I worked on an ice cream van in the summer and have an evening job at the cinema up the road. So see me if you want tickets because I can get them at a discount for you. Anyway, I was going to take chemistry, but decided to change to pharmacy when I realised that Penzance ran a specialist course. Looking around me, it seems that I made the right decision. Thank you." With that he sat down.

Mrs. Marlow came in, "Thank you, Mr. Dean. Now Elizabeth Goodheart, please?"

A short, plump girl with short dark hair, brown eyes and tanned complexion stood up. She looked nervously around the class before speaking.

"Good morning, Mrs. Marlow, fellow students, my name is Beth Goodheart. I am sixteen and completed my GCSEs this summer. I have always wanted to follow in my father's footsteps and become a pharmacist. I work in his pharmacy—Goodheart's Pharmacy in St Ives—on Saturdays and during the holidays. Some of you might know it. Well, I intend to take it over from my father when he retires."

Kyomi whispered to Laura and Scarlett, "I didn't see her on the train, did you?"

Both said no as Mrs. Marlow's voice came in again.

"Thank you, Miss Goodheart. That's some valuable experience that you received in the summer. I would recommend that to all of you. It is much better than bar work or selling ice cream."

Her gaze moved to Nick as she made her last statement. She went on, "Miss Goodheart's father is a guest lecturer in this department. He usually gives a couple of open lectures each year, which I have no hesitation in recommending to you. Now, to continue, may I have Laura Hamilton, please?"

Laura was keen to give a good impression at the start of term. She had eschewed her favourite jeans, choosing instead a skirt and blouse. Her long blond hair was freshly washed. It shone under the classroom lights as she rose to speak.

"Good morning, Mrs. Marlow; class. My name is Laura Hamilton. I, like Beth, completed my GCSEs last summer. I live in the old lighthouse at

Blimford. My father first got me interested in pharmacy when he helped me with my science GCSE. He introduced me to organic chemistry by explaining that there was a whole separate world of chemistry based around just one element, carbon, which I found fascinating. Originally I thought of studying biochemistry, but realised that pharmacy offered the greater opportunity. I plan to run my own pharmacy one day."

As Laura sat down Mrs. Marlow responded, "Thank you, Miss Hamilton. It's good to hear that I will have a choice of pharmacies when I come to collect my old-age pills and potions."

Beth Goodheart's face reddened at hearing this. Mrs. Marlow continued, "And now Angela Palmer, please?"

A tiny girl with mid-length dark brown hair and grey-blue eyes stood up. Laura guessed that she was probably only four feet ten, but in any case less than five feet tall. She wondered where she would be able to get her clothes. Size six would probably fit, but even they would be too long. Her question was partially answered when Laura looked down to see that her jeans were turned up about three inches. She was wearing a baggy sweater that was probably a size too large for her, but even this did not disguise how small she was. She began, "Hello everybody, my name is Angela Palmer. My family calls me Angie and my friends call me Angela. Not Tiny, Titch, Shorty or Quarter Pint, and yes, I am standing up to address you. Seriously though, I, like Beth and Laura, am sixteen and completed my GCSEs this summer. I spent the summer working for my parents in their boarding house in Penzance. I chose pharmacy because I have an interest in poisons. I am told that this college has a team studying the medicinal value of common poisons. After completing this course I should like to study for a degree in pharmacy and then join that team. So to anybody who was thinking of calling me Shorty, beware."

Angela grinned as she made the last comment to convey the message that she was not really serious, although clearly she did not want a nickname that reflected her size.

Mrs. Marlow also smiled as she replied, "Thank you, Miss Palmer, very amusing. Miss Palmer is correctly informed about our research into poisons here at Penzance College and it is something of which we are very proud. The research is led by Doctor Jones here, who joined us last year from Kuala Lumpa University. Doctor Jones will be lecturing to you this term. He will be talking to you later. You will also be taken on a tour of his laboratories. Anyway, to continue, Scarlett Robinson, please?"

Scarlett stood up and looked around the class. Nick checked her over. He was impressed by her, assessing her not as fat, but rather possessing a well-built, athletic figure. He concluded that she must work out in the gym a lot. He estimated her height at five feet ten and probably a size fourteen. Like most of the others she was wearing jeans, but hers were new. They were also very tight, giving him a view of a fine pair of long legs topped off by a delightful bum. He broke off before completing his review to make sure that he was not seen to be staring.

Scarlett began, "Good morning, Mrs. Marlow, fellow students, I am Scarlett Robinson, which shows how much my parents liked old films. I am seventeen. I completed my GCSEs a year ago and continued at Hilary Taylor School studying chemistry, physics and mathematics. After a year in which I struggled, especially in physics, I decided that A levels were not right for me and that I should specialise in something that I would really like to do, hence my choice of pharmacy. I should like to complete this course and then go on to university. After completing a degree, I plan to use my acquired skills to help in a developing country, probably with VSO. I spent the summer working at Blakes, the chemist in St Ives, but unfortunately spent more time selling make-up and skin care products than I did in the pharmacy. I am hoping for more success when I go back there during the Christmas vacation."

Mrs. Marlow smiled as she replied, "Thank you, Miss Robinson. You have expressed some very noble sentiments there. If you would come back to me just before the end of term I shall write a note to Blakes to ask them to give you some time on the pharmacy counter. That will be very valuable experience for you."

She looked down at her register and then called, "Next it is Kyomi Taylor, please?"

Kyomi stood up and followed the same routine as the others. She stated that she was seventeen, had completed one year in the lower sixth studying English, French and Art but had not enjoyed it. She wanted to work in the cosmetics industry, but believed passionately that products should not be tested on animals. Her objective was therefore to learn how the industry worked so that she could speak knowledgeably about the subject. She was aware of the work on poisons being undertaken at Penzance but was not prepared to comment on the morality of it until she understood the work better and saw how the animals were treated.

Mrs. Marlow appeared to be taken aback by her candour but thanked her for it. She also praised her approach of coming to the subject with an open mind. Rushing quickly on from there, she called for Claire West. A girl, five feet five inches tall and of medium build, with short, mousy hair and glasses, stood up.

She was wearing a tight red sweater and faded blue jeans. She began, "The problem with having a surname toward the end of the alphabet is that everybody has said it all before it comes to your turn, so I will be brief. I am sixteen and I completed my GCSEs this summer. During the summer I worked as a temp in Penzance, which is where I live. I chose pharmacy because I find the subject interesting, particularly the medicinal properties of plants. I should like to do research in this field."

Mrs. Marlow thanked her, declaring that the introductions had now concluded. She then introduced the lecturers for the first year and took the class to the coffee bar where they were all provided with a drink. She explained that the drinks this morning were funded by the college, but from then on the students would have to pay for them. From there she took them to the undergraduate laboratory where a tall, bald steward in his mid-forties showed each of the students to a pre-allocated bench. He then gave them a safety demonstration that covered the use of the fire extinguishers, disposal of waste solvents and use of protective clothing, particularly safety glasses. After that, one of the lecturers that had been accompanying them, a tall, well-built man in his thirties, came in to address the class. The class fell silent as they waited for him to speak.

He started speaking with a strong Australian accent, "Good morning, ladies and gentlemen, I am Doctor Adrian Jones, and as those of you who are sufficiently wide awake will have deduced, I am from Australia, Sydney to be precise. May I have your full attention for what I am about to tell you now, please, even if I never get it in the lectures that I will be giving you. If you fall asleep during my lectures then you will probably fail the course, but if you fall asleep now you could end up being poisoned."

The power of his message, delivered in a strong, clear voice, had the desired effect. Everybody in the class sat up, waiting on his next words. Dr. Jones continued, "Mrs. Marlow has already told you that we run a Poisons Research Unit at this college. I am in charge of that unit. Our work requires us to hold stocks of some of the deadliest poisons known to man. There are some classics amongst them, as well as others, equally deadly, of which you may not have heard. You will be taught about them all in my lectures, but for now I should like to tell you about the procedure for the issuing and tracing of poisons in this college. Firstly, all poisons are kept under lock and key in a steel cupboard, and it requires two keys to open the cupboard. There is only one copy of each key held within the department. There are second copies of each, but they are for emergency use only. Their location is kept secret, with only Mr. Edwards here and me knowing that location. The staff key is held by me or a nominee of mine when I am away from college. The steward's key is kept by Mr. Edwards, who also nominates a deputy when he is on holiday."

He gestured toward the lab steward who had given the safety demonstration.

"Anybody requiring to use a poison must fill in the poisons book, stating how much of which poison is required and for what reason. The requester and both key holders must sign the book when the poison is issued. The same procedure is required for the return or verified destruction of the poison. This may seem to be overkill, if you will pardon the expression, but we know that the procedure works and we have not killed anybody yet!"

There was a faint ripple of laughter around the laboratory. Dr. Jones continued, "Having said that, I do not expect you to have any need to request poisons, at least during the first year of the course. I shall be giving lectures on these poisons, which will include some demonstrations, but those will be run by me. Incidentally, the first lecture will be in this laboratory at ten o'clock on Thursday. I will soon be taking you for a tour around the labs, but before that, are there any questions?"

Two girls raised their hands. Dr. Jones continued, "Since I have not yet learned who you all are, would you please give your name and then ask your question. The young lady over there, please?"

"Kyomi Taylor. Will you be using any live animals in your demonstrations, and if so, will they be harmed?"

Dr. Jones appeared both pleased and surprised by the frankness of the question. He replied, "No, Miss Taylor, in answer to both questions. We do test poisons on our rats, but never more than is strictly necessary. Apart from the obvious point of avoiding unnecessary suffering, the animals are expensive. All our tests are filmed so that we can share the results with other researchers and show them to our students. I will be showing you the videos, but I will keep them until the end of the lecture so that you can leave beforehand if you would find it too distressing to watch. Now the young lady over there, please?"

"Angela Palmer. Which poisons are you studying here at Penzance, please?"

"There are quite a number. We have for some time been looking at the common rat poisons, strychnine, arsenic and the cyanides, and more recently at some snake venoms used by African tribes. I will give you a complete list at the first lecture, where strychnine will be the first topic."

He looked around the room to see that no other hands had been raised.

"Since there appear to be no more questions, I will start the tour of the laboratory. Please do not touch anything and do not attempt to handle the rats because they bite. Now follow me, please."

Doctor Jones took the group down the corridor to his research labs. He used a swipe-card and numeric code to open the door into a large laboratory area that was illuminated by sets of fluorescent lights. Two girls in white coats were observing rats in a bank of cages on the far wall. They broke off as the group came in. "These are my researchers, Mary Wells and Diane Fielding. You will see a lot more of them around the campus, no doubt."

Dr. Jones proceeded to describe the laboratory and the work of the researchers, after which he took questions. Nick Dean asked, "Where do you keep the snakes then?"

His question was not so much to find out where any snakes might be housed, but more to see if any of the class would react with fear to the thought of seeing snakes. The ruse worked as he watched both Claire West and Beth Goodheart blanch and take a small step backwards.

Not appreciating the motive of the question, Dr. Jones answered it at face value. "We do not keep snakes here. Snake milking is a highly skilled and dangerous practice, which we leave to the experts. We buy in the snake venom as we require it. If there are no more questions, I will conclude the tour."

Angela Palmer came in, "Before we leave, would you show us the poison cupboard, please?"

"It is not in these labs. It is in a locked room within the apparatus store. There is nothing to see, so for security reasons we do not allow any unauthorised persons into the room. Okay, thank you, everybody; that concludes the tour. As a routine precaution would you all please now wash your hands in case you picked up any traces of poison from the benches? After that, follow me back to the undergraduate laboratory to collect all your belongings."

Once back in the undergraduate laboratory, Dr. Jones handed the class back to Mrs. Marlow. She explained that the morning briefings were complete and that lectures would commence in the afternoon at two o'clock. The students were free until then.

Chapter 2

Party night, 29th June 1996

Kyomi looked at herself in the full-length mirror. For any red-blooded, heterosexual male, this was a sight to behold. She had long legs supporting a perfect size-eight figure. Her wavy, shoulder-length dark hair fell around a face with a flawless ivory complexion and big blue eyes. As if that was not enough, tonight Kyomi was going for it. She had decided to shake off the gloom of Peter's death and announce to the world that her life was going to continue from here. She was wearing an electric blue backless mini-dress that dipped teasingly at the top and just about covered the essentials at the bottom.

"Is that all you are wearing?" her mother had asked, in a somewhat disapproving way.

"Of course not, Mother!" she had replied. "I shall be wearing my blue stone necklace and the silver ankle chain as well."

She was pleased with that remark. It had struck just the right balance between making it clear that she would do what she wanted and using humour to reduce confrontation with her mother. It would have been the remark that Peter would have made for her. He would then have given her a big hug and said, "Knock 'em out, sis."

Oh! how she missed those hugs. Peter was the big brother that all girls wanted, who became increasingly important to her after her parents separated. That was ten years ago and she had now lost touch with her father. She thought back to that moment on last New Year's Day when she had heard the news of Peter's death. She was sleeping in late when there was a knock at the door. She had ignored it, letting her mother, who had been up for some time, answer it. She assumed that it would be one of her mother's friends first-footing. All of her friends would have been in bed at that time.

As she turned over to go back to sleep, she heard her mother cry out, not once but time and again. Something was clearly very wrong, so she got up, put on her dressing gown and left her room to go downstairs. She was met by a uniformed policewoman who asked her to come into the lounge. In the lounge a policeman was sitting with her mother. He explained that Peter had had a motorcycling accident. He had been found on a country road by a milkman making early morning deliveries. The police had concluded that he had collided with a car that had not stopped. No other driver had reported the accident. Although Peter had been drinking and was over the limit, there was no evidence that his riding had caused the accident. It appeared that the other driver was to blame.

Kyomi had wondered at the time why they had bothered to tell her the details. The only thing that mattered was that her beloved Peter, her brother, friend, mentor and pillar in her life, had gone. With time to reflect, the manner of his death had begun to prey on her mind. Someone had killed Peter and not even bothered to stop to see if they could help. That someone had not been punished and that was wrong.

Enough, she thought. *Peter has been dead for nearly six months now and I have to get over it. I will not let it go and I will try to find the driver of the car that hit him, but not tonight. I know that he would not have wanted me to stay in and grieve over him. I shall just have to use my memories to carry me through.*

She could almost see him propped against her bedroom door as she put the final touches to her hair and eyes. He would have asked, "What poor guy are you going to drive wild tonight then?"

Peter was never the sort of brother who would talk about his ugly sister. Not even in jest. It was he who had seen her through those awkward teenage years when she felt gangly and spotty. He had given her the confidence to realise that she would, and indeed did, develop into a very pretty girl. Well, who was she going to go for tonight? That was an interesting question.

"David is here, Kyomi," her mother called up from downstairs, disturbing her concentration. David would certainly have been a candidate had he not been Laura's steady boyfriend. He was handsome, easy-going and very much devoted to Laura. Laura did not really deserve him and certainly did not treat him properly, but nonetheless they were going steady and Laura was a good friend. Maybe the party would yield other possibilities. She called down, "Just coming," sprayed on her favourite perfume, picked up her handbag and skipped downstairs. David was waiting in the lounge. His jaw dropped and she could see his eyes fix on her bust as she entered the room. *That's the impact I wanted*, she thought. *It's going to be a good night.*

It was a glorious June evening so, rejecting her mother's protestations that she should wear a coat, she left taking only a shawl. As she was getting into the car, her mother came running down the path waving a small, brightly coloured parcel. She had taken the trouble to wrap the silver brooch that Kyomi had bought for Laura. With a quick "Thank you" to her they pulled away.

She settled back into her seat, tugging at the hem of the dress to ensure that it provided at least minimal cover. David seemed a little embarrassed, which probably meant that he had already seen more than he should have. He said nothing and attempted to concentrate on the road ahead. Kyomi noticed, however, that his eyes stole quick glances at her legs and bust. She too said nothing, sitting back in the knowledge that her dress had created the image that she had intended. After several minutes of silence, and more to hide his embarrassment than out of genuine curiosity, David asked what was in the parcel.

"It's a little silver brooch that I got in St Ives. Laura told me that she prefers silver to gold and I know that she does not have many brooches so I thought I could not go wrong with that. What have you got her?"

David flushed but did reply.

"Well?" Kyomi persisted, "Come on, I told you what I bought her so you have to tell me what you got."

Goaded by her persistence, David eventually responded, "It's a secret."

Kyomi detected that the present was something a bit out of the ordinary. She was taking an impish delight in trying to tease it out of him and had no intention of letting him off that easily. She turned on all the charm in her voice as she attempted to demolish his protestations.

"Well, I can keep secrets, David."

David stayed silent as he struggled for a reply. He exaggerated his attention to the road by increasing the number of times he looked in the mirror and even threw in a couple of hand signals for good measure. The final hand signal was to indicate a left turn that took them into the lane leading down to the Lighthouse Inn. Only then did he give his final reply. "You will have to wait for the party," and then, with a great deal of relief in his voice, he added, "Anyway, we are here now."

Kyomi gave up on her quest of discovering what David's present was, but was still in a mood to tease him. Although David had a sports car that sat low on the ground, she could have got out of it easily without assistance, but decided to wait inside instead. David's good manners were legendary amongst her fellow students, so she knew exactly what would happen next. Right on cue, David came around to open the door and offer her a hand out. She took his hand, swung her legs out of the car and was standing beside him all in one smooth movement. Not content with that, she took hold of David's arm as they walked up to the Sou'wester Room of the Lighthouse Inn. It was just after seven and the sun was still shining brightly in the western sky.

Chapter 3

Welcome drinks and unwelcome surprises

Doctor James Cross felt very pleased with himself. His team had just won its rugby match, in which he had scored a try, to go top of the Summer Sevens league. He could now look forward to the rest of his free weekend. He had begged, borrowed, traded and done extra shifts to get it and now he was going to enjoy it. He turned off the beeper that was such a part of his normal life and placed it carefully in his dressing room drawer. It was Saturday night and he was going to a party with his new girlfriend. Well, not really new, since he had been dating her for a few months, but because he was a hospital doctor, he had seen so little of Carole Young that the relationship felt new. It did not help that she worked in a hotel, so did not get a lot of free time either. Tonight he was going to be one of the lads, instead of the one who patched them up after the accidents, fights and overdoses.

He reflected on his relationship with Carole. They had met late last year at a friend's Christmas party, which had been held on a Monday night because that was the time that most of them could get off. It was already late in the evening. He had been drinking with a friend in the front room of the house where the party was being held when the doorbell rang. Nobody answered it, so the bell rang again. "Well, I am going to answer it if nobody else is," James called out. "It might be Santa Claus."

With that he got up, realised that he had had a lot more to drink than he thought, stabilised himself and headed for the door. He opened the door to find a tall, attractive girl with an athletic figure wearing a black trouser suit and red chiffon scarf. She was holding a wrapped bottle in her left hand and a small black handbag in her right. He stood looking at her in admiration. She had short dark hair, big brown eyes and well-developed breasts. Before he could continue his examination she said, "Wow, the bouncers are getting more attractive, but what does a girl have to do to be allowed in round here? I'm freezing."

James was both pleased and taken aback at the same time. Admittedly he was six foot three and, thanks to his rugby training, had broad shoulders, but he never thought of himself as big enough to be taken for a bouncer. On the other hand he was pleased that this pretty girl found him attractive. The drink gave him the courage that he might not otherwise have had.

"Password or fee," he replied, making it obvious that the fee he had in mind was a kiss.

The girl stepped forward and planted a kiss full on his lips. He slipped his arm around her waist and pulled her toward him to prolong the moment. He found to his pleasure that she did not resist.

"I'm Carole," she said. "You will just have to wait a little longer for Santa Claus."

They had spent the whole night talking together. That was the start of something good, James reflected, and with a bit of luck it might get better tonight. Since then Carole had come to watch two of his rugby matches, including his debut for Cornwall, and they had been to the cinema three times. Those were all in the afternoon, he mused; this would be their first evening date. With that thought in his mind he slipped a packet of condoms into the pocket of his sports jacket. He put on the tie that she had bought him for his birthday, gave his shoes a quick polish, picked up his overnight bag and walked to the car with a distinct spring in his step.

The party did not start until seven-thirty, but Carole had said that he could come any time from six, which is exactly when he arrived. Following the instructions given on his invitation, he headed for the Sou'wester Room. Two girls, both in their twenties, whom he did not recognise, were working behind a small bar in the corner of the room. They were setting out glasses, arranging bottles and getting together bowls for crisps and nuts. The taller and, James judged, the elder of the two was about five feet eight, with short blonde hair cut into a bob. She was well-built without being overweight and had fair skin and green eyes. She was wearing a flowing blouse over tight black trousers. She looked up, saying, "There is a private function in here tonight. The Cliff View bar is open, though."

James replied, a little uneasily, "Yes I know, I am invited. I am James, Carole's boyfriend."

"Oh James, I am sorry," the girl replied, coming out from behind the bar to greet him. "I'm Jenny, Laura's cousin, and this is my sister Sarah. Carole is upstairs; I will go and get her." With that she left the room via the entrance behind the bar.

Sarah was about five feet six with curly mid-length blonde hair, hazel eyes and a slim build. James judged her to be the more attractive of the two and also the more appropriately dressed, wearing as she was a light green summer dress with a pale green cardigan draped over her shoulders. She came forward, offering her hand to James, who shook it gently. "Hello, James, it's nice to meet you," she said.

"And you too," James replied, looking around at all the preparation in the room, "but I thought that the party was in the lighthouse."

"Oh, it is," Sarah responded, "but we are all going to gather here first. Jean, that's Carole's mother and the owner of the hotel, has let us have this room for a pre-party drink. Uncle John, Laura's dad, said he would like to welcome everybody, so he is going to greet us all with a drink and then he is off to Truro to play chess with a friend."

James had never found it easy to talk to strangers unless he was wearing a white coat. He decided to try to make conversation.

"That's nice of him," he replied. "How many is he expecting?"

"I'm not quite sure," Sarah replied, trying to count guests in her head. "I know that Alicia, that's Carole's sister who also works here at the Lighthouse Inn, said that she was catering for twenty."

James remembered that Carole had mentioned Alicia, but not in very pleasant terms. He recalled Carole calling her the "galley slave" and a "nasty little swot." He also remembered that Carole had said that Alicia was her half-sister.

Sarah went on, "Now let me see, there's Laura and David, Jenny and me, our boyfriends are both working so they cannot come, Carole and James, that's you of course. Then there is Laura's old school friend, Scarlett Robinson, and her boyfriend Todd Mitchell. Todd is also Alicia's cousin by the way—very confusing when you are trying to sort out friends and family. And Kyomi Taylor. Then there are Laura's friends from the pharmacy college. I think there are seven of them. I remember Laura saying that there were seven in the class with only one boy. Nick, I think his name is. Kyomi and Scarlett are also at the college, so that makes three other girls excluding Laura. Yes, together with their boyfriends that makes seventeen in total, if they all come."

Sarah looked pleased with herself for having completed a set of cerebral gymnastics that involved memory and mental arithmetic at the same time. James felt the onus was now on him to speak. *Come on, James,* he rebuked himself mentally. *If this was a patient lying on a trolley, conversation would come easily to you.* He thought what he might say in those circumstances. "And what do you do, Sarah?" just came out. It seemed right because Sarah responded quickly and clearly appeared pleased that he cared to ask.

"I'm a primary school teacher in Penzance," she said with a smile. "That's how I learned to remember names. And you, James, didn't Carole say that you were a doctor?"

"Yes," James replied, not used to getting a coherent answer and even less to that answer being a question. "I'm a junior doctor at Penzance General. I have been there for nearly a year now."

James was struggling for a little more conversation when Jenny returned with Carole behind her. Carole was dressed in a tee shirt and pair of old jeans, with her hair tied back.

"Nice outfit," James commented dryly just before Carole kissed him.

"Silly, I have been helping to get things ready," she replied. Her arms lingered around his neck after they had kissed. "I have got to go and have a shower now. Will you help Jenny and Sarah for me, please? If you are a really good boy, I might let you come up and talk to me while I finish dressing. Come up in about fifteen minutes. It's the second door on the right and don't let Mum see you."

James decided that this was rapidly becoming a candidate for best day of his life. He forced himself to remember his manners. He removed his jacket and hung it behind the door. "Right, girls," he said with gusto, "how can I help?"

"Well, there is one thing," Jenny responded cautiously, "but I don't want you getting those nice clothes dirty. Follow me."

She led him out behind the bar and down the corridor. They went out the back of the hotel and into a shed on the left, which contained beer barrels. James heard a rustling sound from the corner of the shed. "Did you hear that?" he asked, suspecting the cause and concerned that Jenny might be frightened. He need not have worried.

Jenny replied in a perfectly matter-of-fact tone, "They have mice in here, that's what those are for." She pointed to a couple of white boxes, each with one-inch diameter round holes in the ends, which were marked clearly in red *Poison for rodent control*. Jenny continued, "Would you give me a hand with this one, please?" She was pointing to a beer barrel sitting on top of another amongst a set of about two dozen under the label *Bitter*. "I need to put it on in the Sou'wester Room."

James was about to lift the barrel down when Jenny got hold of one handle with both hands, clearly expecting him to grab hold of the other. Between them they lifted it down and manhandled it back to the Sou'wester Room. James then helped the girls, but kept a regular check on his watch for the fifteen minutes to pass. After about the third check, Jenny broke in, "I'm sure that you can go up now, I'll just check that the coast is clear." She looked out the back and beckoned James to come out. James was out and up the stairs like a shot. He tapped gently on the second door and heard those delightful words, "Come in."

Carole had worked fast. She was sitting in a silk dressing gown finishing off her hair. She turned off the hair drier. "Take a seat," she said, motioning him toward the corner of the bed. She put her foot beside him and starting painting her toenails. The dressing gown fell away to reveal a very shapely leg and a pair of lacy black briefs. "You can look, but don't touch," she said provocatively. "I don't want to get varnish on the duvet." When she had finished her toenails she stood up, saying, "Turn around, and no peeking."

James obeyed reluctantly, saying, "Spoilsport" as he turned.

"You'll just have to wait and be a very good boy, won't you?" Carole retorted as she untied her dressing gown and let it fall to the floor. James desperately looked for any reflective surface, but with no luck. He could only imagine what she must look like. He shuffled uneasily, saying any drivel that came into his head to keep his mind occupied. Eventually Carole said, "You can turn around now." He turned to see Carole tying the belt of her red silk jacket. It was very low cut and revealed quite a lot of her very attractive breasts. Her outfit was completed by black silk trousers and red open-toed sandals.

"I'll just do my nails and I'll be ready," she said. James was sure that she was wearing nothing under the jacket and was dying to confirm his suspicions. He had an almost overwhelming urge to grad hold of her and kiss her, but disciplined himself, saying, "Wow, you look stunning. What a transformation."

"Thank you, James," Carole responded, appearing genuinely pleased with his reaction and at the same time shaking her nails to dry them. "Ready?" The two of them went down to the Sou'wester Room. It was now six forty-five.

Jenny and Sarah had finished and were getting ready themselves. "It's just you and me then," James said, moving to cuddle Carole.

"Easy, tiger," she responded. "Laura and Alicia will be over in a minute."

"That's a point, where are they?" James asked. He had never met either Laura or Alicia. He was keen to meet this galley slave. Could she really be as bad as Carole had made out? What was she like? Was she fat and spotty from all the grease in the kitchen? As his mind wandered, two young girls came into the room. The first was a slim natural blonde with blue eyes, about five foot three with shoulder-length hair. She was wearing a midnight blue full-length dress that was high at the front and plunged deeply at the back. *Pretty*, James thought, *but she knows it*. He looked at her face, which, although attractive, appeared very harsh. He concluded, on this the flimsiest of evidence, that she was probably a bit frosty, if not the ultimate spoilt brat.

Carole began the introductions. "This is Laura, our birthday girl."

"I'm James, many happy returns," James responded, taking the proffered hand and shaking it gently.

"Pleased to meet you," she responded with no warmth at all in her voice. Carole then gestured toward the second girl, who had held back, allowing Laura to be introduced first. She too was slim, about an inch taller than Laura with shoulder-length copper hair and hazel eyes. Her face and arms were a mass of freckles. She was wearing an emerald green three-quarter-length dress with matching wrap. "And this is Alicia," Carole said icily.

"I am very pleased to meet you at last, James, Carole has not told us much about you," Alicia replied with genuine warmth.

So this is Alicia, thought James. She was nothing like he imagined from Carole's descriptions. She was not stunning, but she was not plain either. She was rather just a shy country girl who appeared to have a sweet nature. She did not have Carole's looks, but then again, he thought, not many girls did. James took an instant liking to her. "And I you," he replied, taking her hand and making to kiss her. Alicia appeared surprised by the warm response but immediately offered a cheek to receive the kiss.

"I hear that you have been busy all day preparing the food for tonight. I'm looking forward to that."

"Well, not exactly all day," Alicia responded modestly, "but I did want to do something nice for Laura. It's my birthday present to her."

By this time Laura was busy talking to her cousins and did not react. The gentleman in James was coming to the fore. He was not going to see all Alicia's hard work go unrecognised. It was obvious that Laura was not going to say anything and, it appeared, neither was Carole. She had already drifted over to talk to the other girls, leaving the two of them together The adrenaline was flowing and conversation was becoming easier. "And a very nice present too," he responded. "You must be dying for a drink. What can I get you?"

"Thank you, James; a small gin with lots of tonic, please," Alicia replied, getting herself comfortable on a barstool.

James prepared the drink for her and poured himself a beer. Meanwhile Sarah got drinks for Jenny, Laura, Carole and herself.

Todd and Scarlett arrived just before seven. Scarlett went straight across to greet Laura. Todd came across to Alicia and clapped both arms around her, taking her off her feet as he kissed her. "Todd, put me down and let me introduce you to James, will you," Alicia exclaimed, trying, but completely failing, to put any rebuke into her voice. She was clearly delighted to see him. She turned to James, who was smiling and thinking, *At least somebody appreciates this girl.* "This is my cousin Todd. His best friend David is Laura's boyfriend."

Todd extended a huge hand toward James, who took it. They shook hands very firmly. "Ah yes," James replied, "Sarah was telling me about you."

"Nothing too incriminating, I trust," Todd said, smiling.

Scarlett came over to introduce herself. Todd did not give her the chance. "This is Scarlett," he said, "the girl who keeps me under control."

"As much as anybody can," Scarlett replied, "and with a lot of help from Alicia. Still, he's not a bad lad really."

For some unknown reason James looked up and was transfixed by a vision of beauty in an electric blue mini-dress who had just walked in, followed by a tall guy wearing a suit. James's mind ran back to the thought he had had earlier: that not many girls matched Carole for looks. Being honest with himself, and even allowing for being prejudiced because he was dating Carole, this girl did. He was sure that he had seen a girl as pretty as her before, but he just could not remember when. The girl and the guy in the suit went over to Laura, who broke off to give the guy a big kiss, full on the lips. The girl did not seem to mind. James was struggling to work this out when Jenny turned to the guy, saying, "Hi, David, how are you?" So that was David Stevens, Laura's boyfriend, James deduced. So who was the girl in the blue mini-dress? That was answered a minute later when Laura addressed her as Kyomi.

"She's pretty, isn't she?" Todd's comment broke James's train of thought, bringing him back to the present with a start.

"Sorry, was I staring?" James responded, somewhat embarrassed.

"Just a bit," Alicia came in, "but I promise not to tell Carole."

"That's the famous Kyomi Taylor," Todd remarked. "Dream date for all the boys in Simon Baker School she was. Known as the orgasm on legs."

25

Scarlett slapped Todd playfully on the arm. James was not sure if it was for the thought, the putting of the thought into words or, more likely, both.

"I was at Simon Baker too, but I don't remember anyone like that," James replied.

"I know you were, James, you gave me a couple of prefect's detentions, if I remember correctly. Oh, don't worry, they were well-deserved. In fact there were several others that I got away with," Todd responded, continuing, "Kyomi was a bit after your time. She would have just been a scrawny second year when you ruled the roost."

"I thought I recognised your face," said James. "You have filled out in the chest a bit since then though."

Alicia came in, "It's all those engines he keeps lifting that's done it. He and David Stevens have got quite a business going."

By now it was nearly seven-thirty. A group of three girls and four boys arrived. Alicia explained to Todd and James that one of the boys and all the girls were Laura's fellow students at the pharmacy college in Penzance. The other three boys were the girls' boyfriends. She knew that the male student was Nick Dean and that the girls were Angela Palmer, Beth Goodheart and Claire West, but she did not know who was who. They all went up to Laura to wish her a happy birthday and to introduce themselves to Kyomi, Carole, Sarah, Jenny and David.

Carole came back over to reclaim James. "I hope that Todd and Scarlett have been looking after you," she said.

"Yes indeed," James responded, "and Alicia as well. She has been telling me who's who, but we are stuck on the pharmacy students."

Carole began to explain, in her own way, "Well, the short dark guy in the leather jacket who fancies himself is Nick Dean. He's the only male student in that class. Laura said that he only took that course because of the girls. Apparently he's not very good at it…and his pharmacy needs some work as well. She said he looks okay but he's pretty shallow. I can't even see the looks myself."

James did not like Carole's habit of running people down. She had been particularly unfair about Alicia, whose company he was enjoying, but with Nick she was confirming what his first impressions had told him. He would not get on with Nick.

John Hamilton and Jean Young came into the room and started mingling with the guests. After a few minutes David Stevens moved over to John, with Laura following closely behind him. He asked if he and Laura could have a private word. Jean took the four of them into her office.

John turned to David, asking, "Now what can I do for you?"

David appeared nervous as he began, but his voice grew in confidence as he spoke. "I would like to ask for your blessing for me to marry Laura. We are deeply in love."

John's eyes narrowed and his face reddened as he responded. He did not care who heard as he raised his voice and replied angrily, "Love?" and then with more venom, and raising his voice even more, so that it carried outside the office, "Lust, more like. I notice that you did not mention that she is pregnant."

He paused for a moment as a deathly hush fell over the office. David stood there dumbfounded. Laura was forcing back tears. Alicia heard the disturbance from the Sou'wester Room but mistook it for trouble in the bar. Realising that her mother was busy, she asked Todd to come with her in case there was trouble in the bar and particularly that anybody might became violent. Carole and Scarlett followed them as they traced the disturbance to the office. They came in to see what was going on, but John was by then so tense that he did not notice them enter.

John continued, "She is far too young."

This time David did not hold back. "Yes, I know she is young, but I love her and, as you say, she is pregnant. I don't care if her friends know it. I should like this to be her engagement party as well," he replied.

John was still determined, replying, "No, I cannot agree to that. She has her studies to complete. She must have an abortion."

It was only at this point that he became aware of his enlarged audience. Even so he continued, "If you still want to marry her after she graduates, then I will give my blessing." His voice was more measured this time, but there was no less determination.

Laura was shocked and silent, but David was by now running totally on adrenaline. "She is eighteen," he retorted. "We could have just gone ahead without telling you."

John was ready for that. His voice was much lower, measured and more intimidating. "If you do, then I will cut her out of my will and neither of you will be welcome at the lighthouse," he argued. Having made his point, he then tried to appeal to David with a more logical argument. "Now be sensible, lad. If you really love her you can wait."

The rest of the people in the office had listened to this conversation in stunned silence. After a moment's hesitation, David was about to respond again but only got out a word before Todd came in. "What a hypocrite you are, John. David was facing up to his responsibilities, unlike others I could name."

John's face reddened again. The measured tones had gone, to be replaced only by anger. He did not even question why Todd was there, but instead challenged Todd's assertions, "What do you mean by that, lad?"

Todd was quite ready to answer that question. "You weren't prepared to marry the girl you got into trouble, were you?" His anger was unrestrained. He continued, "My aunt had to struggle to bring up a child on her own."

John's anger had not subsided yet. "That's none of your business, and you have no right to be here. However, despite the fact that I do not have to justify myself to you, I will tell you that I did support Jean and Carole."

Alicia had been listening to this conversation with increasing trepidation. The originally cheerful countenance had been replaced in turn by shock, worry, and finally total disbelief. She burst into tears. She had not known that John was Carole's father.

Scarlett did not understand what was going on, but her instinct told her that Todd was getting himself into trouble and needed her help. She tried to be as calm as much as possible as he turned to Carole. "Carole, what is this? Is Mr. Hamilton your father?" she asked.

Throughout the whole of the revelations Carole had remained totally dispassionate. Even though Laura did not know the truth, she did. Jean had told her some time ago, but had made her promise not to tell either John or Laura that she knew. Her response was initially cold: "Yes, which makes Laura my half-sister," she replied, adding in a more contemptuous tone as she looked toward Alicia, "At least she is better than my other half-sister."

Up until this point Todd had merely been angry, but now he exploded. The bond between him and Alicia was stronger than most brother-sister relationships. He had always looked out for her, and there was no way that he was going to stand aside now. He was fuming as he broke in, "You are a heartless creature, Carole; can't you see how upset Alicia is?"

Of that there could be no doubt. Scarlett had already moved over to comfort Alicia, who was by now in floods of tears on Todd's broad shoulder. Scarlett showed no sign of jealousy toward Alicia, who was in her boyfriend's arms. Instead her concern was to calm Todd and protect Alicia from further damaging exchanges. Touching Todd gently on the arm, in as loving and calm a voice as she could muster, she came in, "Todd, leave it, don't spoil the evening."

Todd was in no mood to stop, though. "I have not finished yet," he went on, but then John broke in.

"You have said too much already, my lad." His tones became more measured again as he continued, "Anyway, now that it is public knowledge, I want you all to know that Carole is my daughter. I had been meaning to tell her for some time, but it appears that her mother has beaten me to it. Carole is just as much my daughter as Laura is, and I will recognise that in my future actions."

Todd was a long way from being satisfied by this. He had long wanted to have it out with John, and now he played his trump card. The anger in his voice showed through even more as he went on, "Not content with ruining my aunt's life, you had to wreck my parents' marriage as well by sleeping with my mother."

Once again Scarlett tried to cool the situation. Mustering all her charm, she said, "Calm down, Todd, and stop making wild accusations."

Todd drew breath for just long enough to allow John to continue, but this time John's mood was completely different. With an air of both admission and conciliation, he continued, "No, it's all right Scarlett, Todd has a right to be angry. What he says is true and I am not proud of it. That is why I do not want to see Laura's life ruined in the same way."

Scarlett hugged Todd to ensure that he would not continue, but Todd appeared satisfied. He had the public admission and consequent humiliation that he had been seeking. He broke away from Scarlett, kissed her gently, whispered something in her ear and left the room.

The office fell silent as everybody assessed the information that they had received. Scarlett continued to comfort Alicia while David and Laura stood in stunned silence. Jean Young was the first to speak. "Scarlett, would you take Alicia to her room for a while and rejoin us all when she is ready? Don't worry about Todd, I will see to him. Carole, please tell our hotel guests that it was just a minor disturbance and that everything is under control."

Scarlett, Alicia and Carole left to do as Jean had instructed. Jean then turned to those who remained in the office. She had assumed the mantle of a mother sorting out a set of squabbling siblings. "Well, this is a fine start to Laura's party, isn't it?" she stated in a tone that made it clear that an answer was not required. "John, you and David will have to sort this out and soon, but not tonight. We have guests to entertain and a birthday to celebrate." She then turned to Laura, asking in her best maternal manner, "Are you all right, dear?" Laura nodded, but did not speak. Jean continued, "Then you had better go and entertain your guests. Now run along you two, and for heaven's sake smile. It is your birthday, after all." Obediently, Laura and David left to do as they had been instructed.

Jean poured two glasses of scotch and took one for herself. She took some ice out of the small office fridge and placed it in the other glass before passing it to John. She then returned to her maternal role to admonish John, "Oh, John what am I going to do with you? Will you never learn to control that temper of yours? Don't you remember that we were young once and making exactly those mistakes? Can you not remember how we reacted to our parents when they told us what we should do? Are Laura and David so very different?" She hesitated for a moment before adding, "Anyway, are we fit parents to tell them what to do?"

The "we" was clearly directed at John, but also leant upon the parental bond between them to which Carole was testament. John was too drained for further protest. He knew that both Jean and Todd had exposed his shortcomings, not only as a parent but also in his relationships with the opposite sex. David and Laura had been foolhardy, but not to the extent that he himself had been. Jean did not give him the chance to reply, saying, "Come on, go and rejoin our guests and get this party underway while I go and find Todd.

Jean looked around the hotel, but could not immediately find Todd. She checked the other bars and outside the hotel, including the car park, without luck. She asked around her staff until one of the barmen told her that he had seen Todd in the beer shed. She met him coming out of the shed a minute later. "A word with you, my lad, in my office if you please?" Todd followed her sheepishly back into the office where Jean began a severe dressing down. "Todd, I warned you about causing trouble with John Hamilton, didn't I? What did I tell you I would do if there was any trouble?"

Todd hung his head in shame but did not reply.

"Well?" Jean persisted.

Todd mumbled, "You said that you would sack me, Auntie Jean."

"Yes, quite," Jean replied, "and don't try getting around me with the auntie bit. I am quite prepared to sack you and would have shown no mercy if you had made that outburst whilst you were on duty. I know that you have been highly provoked but that is no excuse. Perhaps now that you have got it off your chest we can have some peace around here. Well, can we?"

Todd again mumbled his reply, "Yes, Mrs. Young."

Jean decided that Todd had been sufficiently scolded. "Well, make sure that we do then, because you will not get another chance. Now go and enjoy the party."

Chapter 4

Party time

Carole was the first to return to the Sou'wester Room. She reassured everybody who asked her that there had been a small disturbance that had been sorted out and there was no need for anybody to worry. James headed straight over to her, intent on catching up on lost time. Carole also felt in need of his company, so, having done her duty by calming all who came to her with concerns, she and James headed for a sofa in the corner where they could chat quietly with each other.

John was the next to return. He made an effort to be on his best behaviour, introducing himself to each of the guests and taking time to talk to them. He was proud of himself for the effort that he had made. A little later, Scarlett returned with Alicia, who was wearing fresh make-up and was ready to party. Scarlett made her a drink and, seeing that Todd had yet to return, continued talking with her at the bar. David and Laura were the next to appear, arm-in-arm, making a clear display of their unity. The guests flocked over to them for news, but they were not forthcoming. A semblance of normality soon returned with everybody chatting and drinking, and the evening sun shone through the wide, western-facing windows.

Seeing that most of the guests had returned, Sarah took the chance to get everybody's attention. Her schoolmistress training came to the fore as she clapped her hands and asked for quiet.

"If I can have your attention for a moment," she urged, and then turning to Carole, continued, "Carole, I believe you and Laura have worked out the sleeping arrangements for tonight."

Carole picked up from Sarah, "Yes, we have just been able to fit everybody in by using all the rooms. Scarlett and Kyomi, you are in the Penzance Room; David, Todd and James, the Truro Room; Alicia is in the Bodmin Room; Angela, Beth and Claire, the Mousehole Room; Andrew and Chris are in the St Austell Room; Brian and Nick, the Looe Room; and I am in the St Ives Room. Sarah and Jenny are, by special permission, in John's room. Nobody else is allowed in and we are not allowed to play with his train set in case we get drunk and damage it. To make it easier I have written it all down." Carole handed out copies of the room arrangements.

John tried to forget his earlier problems by following on with the party theme. "Now please, everybody, charge your glasses so that I can toast Laura on her eighteenth birthday."

Sarah and Jenny were at the bar, so they began serving the others. Carole brought drinks over for John and Jean. "The bar's a bit crowded," she commented as she handed them over. "Mum, I knew that you would have a gin and tonic, and John...sorry, Dad—I must get used to that—I know that you like scotch and ice."

John took the glass and raised it, saying, "To Laura on her eighteenth birthday."

After the toast, the conversation started to return to normal. A few minutes later Todd returned. He was intent on being unobtrusive, making his entrance quietly and heading straight to Scarlett and Alicia. Only they, together with Laura and David, noticed him come in, since conversations had recommenced following John's toast. Having spent a couple of minutes talking with the two girls, he went over to Laura and David, with whom he exchanged words. He then shook David's hand and kissed Laura on the cheek before returning to the bar, where he made some drinks. He took away a tray full of drinks, which he distributed to Scarlett, Carole, Alicia and Jean Young. This left a glass of scotch and a pint of beer on the tray. He then left the Sou'wester Room, going into the hall where John was standing on his own, staring out to sea. Todd handed John the scotch, taking the beer for himself. "Peace offering," he said as he passed the scotch to John, adding, "I cannot, indeed I would not, take back what I said, but

I apologise for saying in front of everybody and nearly spoiling Laura's party. I have apologised to her and David, who have both forgiven me. Perhaps now we can share a glass to Laura's health."

John was clearly taken aback, but responded positively, "Neither of us has behaved well, Todd, and I guess I owe Laura an apology as well. As I said earlier, you have a right to be angry with me, and I regret treating your mother the way I did. You peace offering is gratefully accepted." With that he raised his glass, saying, "To Laura." They drank their drinks together before returning to the Sou'wester Room, where Todd rejoined Scarlett and John went over to Laura.

Todd looked into Scarlett's eyes as he whispered to her, "I have done as you asked, my darling."

Scarlett beamed with pride as she listened to what he was telling her. As soon as he put down his glass, she hugged and kissed him. After that she turned to Alicia, who was still mulling over the earlier events. "Come on, Alicia, cheer up," she urged. "You look like you have seen a ghost."

Carole could not resist the chance for another dig. "Don't say that, Scarlett; she is always seeing ghosts."

Alicia, provoked by the taunting, responded, "I have seen the ghost, I tell you."

Detecting that she had got Alicia going, Carole was in no mood to let go. "No you haven't, that was Laura playing tricks," she replied icily.

Alicia, by now close to tears again, shrieked, "I did see it, I tell you!"

Todd was prepared to stand no more of this. He said firmly, "Leave her alone, Carole," then turning to Alicia he continued cheerfully, "Come on, Al, let's party."

Scarlett added, "Yes, come on, Alicia; you can tell Todd and me about it."

The whole group stayed drinking in the Sou'wester Room for another half-hour, with Jenny and Sarah serving drinks behind the bar. Carole brought John another whisky while Jean was called away by one of the barmen from the Cliff View bar to handle a small disturbance in the car park. Alicia left with her.

After ten minutes, Alicia returned. Looking at David, she began, "Eh, excuse—"

Before she could continue, David broke in, completely misunderstanding what she was about to say, "Don't ask, Alicia; you don't need to know."

Alicia was somewhat surprised, but retaining her manners, continued, "All I was going to say was that Mum is ready to take us all over to the lighthouse."

Kyomi said, "But I thought the tide was out?"

"Yes, she is going to take us across in the Land Rover. We should be able to do it in two or three runs," Alicia replied in a slow, deliberate tone, designed more to help her stay composed rather than to add any extra clarity to the message.

Kyomi still questioned her, asking, "Isn't that dangerous? I thought the last person to try it got stuck on a sand bank."

Again Alicia retained her composure, responding firmly, with the intent of ending the conversation and getting everybody moving, "It's okay if you know what you are doing. Mum knows her way through the sand banks but she would not let anyone else try it. Even she would not cross in the dark."

Since the Land Rover could take eight passengers in sufficient comfort for a short journey, it was agreed that the immediate family would go across first to make sure everything was ready. This group comprised Jenny, Sarah, Laura, Alicia, Carole, Scarlett, Todd and James. The latter two were dragooned into manhandling a beer barrel on to the Land Rover. As they were loading it Todd was heard to comment, "We'll take it into the lighthouse, but there is no way we are carrying it up all those stairs. If they want beer they will have to come down to the ground floor."

David was left to organise the remaining trips.

Jean returned to collect the next group to go across. David asked Angela, Andrew, Beth, Brian, Claire, Chris and Nick—the "pharmacy set," as he described them—to go next. Realising that he could not fit two more in, he asked Jean to come back for Kyomi and him. The devil in Kyomi came to the fore. "Don't put her to that trouble," she interjected. "We can walk across. You will hold my hand, won't you, David?"

David, seeing the chance to combine good manners with what was not going to be an unpleasant task, replied, "Yes, of course."

Jean agreed and left with the pharmacy set. John wished them well and headed for his car, which he had left in the inn's car park. As John headed across the car park, his unsteady gait told him that perhaps he should not have had that last scotch, or in all truth the previous two as well. It did not help that he dropped his keys as he attempted to open the door of his Jaguar.

"Pull yourself together," he said to himself as he picked up the keys and tried again, this time with more luck. "It's only Truro." He slid into the driver seat. He started the engine, engaged first gear and was away in one smooth motion.

As he was waiting at the top of the lane for a gap in the traffic on the main road that would allow him to turn left, he mused to himself, "That's better, told you that you could do it. You have always been able to handle your drink. It doesn't affect you as much as it does the youngsters, because you have become accustomed to it. It's a bit like the snake charmers who become immune to snake bites, only in your case it's whisky."

His train of thought was rudely interrupted by the siren of a police car as it sped past him heading for St Ives. John decided to use the country lanes just in case. He had learned his way around them after spending his first summer in Cornwall stuck in traffic jams with the tourists. He was confident that he had sufficient time to take it easy. Forty minutes, probably twice as many turns and several villages later saw him entering Truro.

As he drove past the church hall that housed the Truro Chess Club, he mused, "Richard Brown, my friend and keen adversary, thank you for providing my alibi for tonight, but you will have to use your undoubted skills against some other willing combatant; for I have a different challenge to overcome."

A quick call at the petrol station for flowers and chocolates followed by three more turns and he had arrived. He parked under the lamp post opposite 35 Penswick Drive. He was particular about ensuring that the Jaguar could be seen at night, since he did not want his pride and joy damaged by any careless or drunk drivers.

He flew up the stairs on wings of alcohol and, in anticipation of the pleasure of the evening to come, rang the bell of flat 3 and cheerfully announced into the intercom, "John Hamilton at your service, ma'am." The door buzzer sounded for just enough time for John, complete with flowers and chocolates, to enter. He skipped up the single flight of stairs to find the door to flat 3 ajar.

As he entered, a voice called out, "Go into the lounge and make yourself a drink. I'll only be a couple of minutes." John placed the flowers and chocolates on the lounge table and did as he was instructed. He was sitting with a large whisky and ice in front of him when a lady in her late thirties came in. She was of medium height, slim with shoulder-length chestnut hair and tanned complexion. John attempted to spring to his feet, but finding the soft leather sofa seat difficult to get out of, fell back in the process. He managed at the second attempt, but the result what not the smooth greeting that he had planned. To make matters worse, as he approached her, arms outstretched, he slurred his greeting, which came out, "Julia, how *nishe* to see you again."

Julia allowed him to kiss her on the cheek before gently removing his hands from her waist and persuading him to sit down again. Noticing the chocolates and flowers, she replied, "John, you really should not have. Are you trying to fatten me up? That will mean another ten minutes on the exercise bike for each of those chocolates." She added, "The flowers are lovely, though. I will put them in water straight away."

With that she picked up the flowers and headed for the kitchen. John called through, "Can I fix you a drink while you are doing that?"

Julia's reply, delivered with some criticism in her voice, came quickly, "Yes, but make it just orange juice and ice please, because it's clear who is going to be driving tonight."

John was about to protest, but, deciding that this might not be wise, he settled for a simple, "Yes, darling, but we could take a taxi if you prefer."

Julia returned complete with flowers in a cut glass vase, which she placed on the coffee table. Taking the offered drink, she replied, "No, I do not mind driving, but you are going to have to let me take the Jaguar as a treat."

John winced at the thought, but decided that it was best not to object. He had already been persuaded by Julia to insure the car for her for precisely this situation, so there seemed no logical reason to refuse. His reply was a model of diplomacy: "That's fine. I have booked the Ship, by the way, because I know that you like it."

Julia's face beamed with delight. The Ship was indeed her favourite and they were always treated very well because John knew the manager, who was a fellow model railway enthusiast.

The five-minute drive to the hotel passed with little conversation and no incident. At the Ship Hotel they were greeted by the manager. "John, Miss Rowntree, how good to see you again. Please do come through." He showed them through to the lounge, where both were soon served with a drink and the menu. After ordering their meals, John excused himself for fifteen minutes to, as he put it, "Do a little bit of business with the manager," before they sat down to eat. Julia was more than a little unhappy as she watched John walking away to the manager's office with a stiff, unsteady gait. He returned after fifteen minutes as promised, this time with a steadier gait, but looking very pale.

Julia's concern was genuine as she asked, "Are you all right, John? You do look very pale."

"I don't feel at my best," John replied. "I feel really stiff and I ache all over, but let's hope it's nothing that a good Ship Hotel steak will not cure."

They were just finishing their main course when John complained to Julia that he really did feel unwell and suggested that they might return to Julia's flat. Although this was achieved with the minimum amount of fuss, John became worse in the car, sweating and shaking uncontrollably. Julia had to support and at times almost carry him up the stairs to the flat. Once inside, she left him in the lounge for a moment to call the doctor. Before she even reached the telephone Julia heard a load thud and rushed back to the lounge to find John collapsed on the floor. Blood was oozing from a large gash in his head. She did not panic, but instead checked John's breathing and pulse and ensured that he was unlikely to come to any further harm if she left him to call for help.

The ambulance arrived after twenty minutes, by which time Julia was getting very concerned about John. She had dressed his head wound, but he was unconscious, his breathing was shallow and his pulse irregular. The paramedic also looked concerned. He called down to his colleague for oxygen and a stretcher. The two men worked on John where he was as Julia looked on anxiously. They decided that he was not responding and had to be given specialist treatment immediately, so took him to the Trelawny Memorial Hospital.

Julia was left outside the cubicle as John was whisked behind the curtains with a whole medical team to work on him. She sat there in disbelief for about twenty minutes, hardly touching the tea that a nurse had bought her. A doctor approached her, his head bowed. "Mrs. Hamilton?" he enquired.

"No, I am his girlfriend, Julia Rowntree; John is divorced from his wife. How is he, Doctor?" she replied nervously. She looked again at the doctor, whom she decided could not be more than twenty-five.

He began nervously, "There is no easy way to say this, but…." Julia did not need him to finish the sentence, because she knew what was coming. Her father had died of a heart attack at the same hospital less than two years previously.

Chapter 5

Tragedy, 30th June 1996

It was eight-thirty on a bright June Sunday morning. Edward Hamilton sat in the back of the Land Rover with a heavy heart as Jean Young drove him and Sven Ffolkes across the causeway to the lighthouse. He could not believe the news that he would have to give. His twin brother John had died suddenly during the night of a suspected heart attack. How was he going to break the news to John's daughters, Carole and Laura, or to his own daughters, Jenny and Sarah? He had already told Jean Young, who had insisted on driving them across personally even though she herself was shocked. She protested that the causeway was too dangerous for anybody who did not know it and she would not see them walk across.

Sven was a Norwegian long-time friend of Edward's who worked for the Oslo police force. They had met at an Interpol conference twenty years previously, establishing a friendship that had proved very enduring. Two years ago, Edward had been invited to spend three weeks with the Oslo police, learning their techniques. Sven had now come over on a similar mission with the Cornwall and Islands police. Today, neither was here in any official capacity. Sven had come to be with his friend on this difficult mission. Knowing that it was Laura's birthday party the previous night, they had left it as long as they dared before coming across, but despite this, they expected everybody still to be in bed.

The three sad figures entered the lighthouse and began ascending the stairs when they came upon a group of teenagers milling around on the second floor landing and in the Truro Room. Several girls were crying and one of the boys was nearly hysterical. Alicia was the first to speak to him. "Edward, what are you doing here?" she asked him in a faltering voice. It was clear that she had been crying.

Summoning up all his reserves of control that twenty-five years as a policeman had taught him, Edward said calmly, "Would everybody please come into the lounge? I have something to tell you." The teenagers all obeyed quietly. Edward recognised the hysterical boy as David Stevens. Todd Mitchell and Scarlett Robinson helped him up the stairs. They all seated themselves in the lounge, looking toward Edward and Sven. Jean Young had remained downstairs in the kitchen making tea.

Edward briefly introduced Sven and was about to tell everybody about John when Todd broke in. "How did you get here so quickly?" he enquired.

Edward was taken aback by the question. "What do you mean?" he asked, adding, "Jean drove us across, but where is Laura?"

There was a moment of silence before David blurted out, "Laura is dead!"

Edward did not appear to comprehend. "Dead? What are you talking about, David?" he asked.

David broke down in tears again. Carole, in a faltering voice, continued the explanation. "There has been an accident."

Before she could continue, James broke in, "Laura *is* dead; it looks like she fell over the balcony."

Sven's face showed a mixture of surprise and alarm. He realised that he would have to take control of the situation. This second shock had left Edward dumbfounded. He was considering what to say when Alicia asked, "But how did you know to get here so quickly, Edward?"

Edward replied, his voice drained of emotion and almost mechanical, "I did not know. I came on another matter."

Todd immediately came in, "What do you mean?"

Sven knew that he had to act immediately. He was sure that something was seriously amiss and his mind was working overtime to determine what it was. He said calmly, "Let's just leave that for a minute. Please everybody just sit quietly where you are for the moment." Several people tried to speak at once but Sven raised his hand to stop them. He continued, "Please, we must take it one step at a time." He looked desperately around the room for somebody to help him control the situation.

At that point Jean Young came up the stairs with a large pot of tea on a tray. "Ah, tea. Let's all have a cup while we take stock of the situation. For the moment would nobody say anything about this matter, please? Mrs. Young, would you be so kind, and perhaps, Sarah, you might help?" Both accepted their tasks willingly. Sven then turned to Edward, who was beginning to regain his composure. "My dear friend," he began, "you are far too deeply involved in this emotionally. Will you permit me to take charge temporarily until we can get your colleagues over here? Just a precaution at this stage, you understand."

Even in his emotional state, Edward picked up that something was not right. He had heard Sven use the term "just a precaution" before. It had always amazed him how Sven did not only have complete mastery of the English language, but had also acquired the peculiarly British use of the understatement. Sven was seriously worried about something and his fears were normally well-founded. "Please continue, Sven. What would you like me to do?"

Sven's response was immediate and clear: "Would you ask three of your fine CID colleagues to come across and take some statements, please?"

"Yes," Edward replied, reaching for the phone. He called Penzance CID and was pleased to find that his sergeant, Peters, was on duty. "Would you come across immediately, George, and bring Constables Jenkins and Orchard over with you as well, please? You will have to arrange for the Coast Guard to provide you with an outboard and driver, as the tide will cover the causeway soon." He turned back to Sven, saying, "I was lucky that my sergeant, George Peters, was on duty. He is one of the best. He has bags of experience. He joined us after doing twenty years with the Metropolitan Police in Walthamstow. He decided that he wanted to bring his kids up in a safer environment. Anyway, that's arranged, so now what?"

Sven asked him to take control in the lounge, to make sure that nobody talked about what had happened until he could arrange for CID interviews to be started. "Perhaps you could get all their names and addresses and make sure that all their parents are informed that they may be late back. In the meantime, I should like to see Laura's body." He turned to the assembled group, asking, "Where is she, please?"

James responded, "I can show you if you wish."

"No, just tell me, please," Sven responded. "I do not want anybody to leave the lounge."

"If you would like to step out on to the balcony, I can show you from there." James motioned toward the French windows. Sven nodded and followed James on to the balcony. He led him around to the seaward side of the lighthouse and pointed downwards A sheet, weighted down by stones, covered Laura's body.

"Down there," James said, "and look at this." He pointed to a couple of railings immediately above where the body lay. Sven looked at them. Each was rusted at the base and was bent outward at about thirty degrees from their correct position. "I reckon that she was leaning against those railings when they gave way and she fell," James commented, showing some satisfaction with his powers of observation.

Sven hid his own conclusions, replying, "Thank you, young man. I must now go down to see for myself."

Sven scrambled across the rocks to where the body was lying under the sheet. He removed two of the stones and lifted the sheet carefully. He could see Laura lying on her left side on the rocks. She was wearing pyjamas. Without touching them Sven examined the position of the pyjamas. The coat was unbuttoned, but the buttons were still present and the buttonholes were not torn. The coat had been pulled clear of Laura's shoulders, which showed extensive but shallow scratches. The trousers were down on her knees. Sven could see more shallow scratches on the exposed parts of her stomach, abdomen and thighs. Her face was pasty white and her feet blue. There was a deep contusion that had oozed blood on the right side of her skull, above and behind her ear.

Before going in, Sven looked up from where Laura lay. His eye followed a line past the windows of Penzance and Truro Rooms and Laura's room to the balcony. He could see the broken railings sticking out awkwardly from the balcony. The railings were in line with Laura's body, so maybe she had fallen from there as James had suggested. Sven did not want to move the body, so he decided to wait for the post-mortem to determine what other injuries there were on the parts of the body that he could not see. He carefully replaced the sheet and returned to the lounge.

Almost immediately after he had returned to the lounge, three men entered. Edward greeted them, "Sergeant Peters, Constable Jenkins, Constable Orchard, I think you all know Inspector Ffolkes, don't you?"

They replied smartly, "Yes, sir."

"Please do as the inspector requests. I am too deeply involved personally to take charge of this investigation, so he is handling it for the moment. We are lucky that he happened to be visiting us, so observe carefully, gentlemen, and I am sure you will learn a lot. Peters, I want you to make sure that the correct administration procedures are followed and that the proper authorities are informed. Inspector Ffolkes, please?" Edward gestured to Sven to ask what he wanted.

Sven began, conscious of the need for some formality, "Thank you, Inspector Hamilton. Firstly, who amongst you has been out to see the body?"

Jenny was the first to respond, "David Stevens found the body. He was the one who woke us up. Kyomi Taylor then fetched James Cross to examine Laura. James is a doctor. When James told me that she was dead, I took a sheet out to cover her up. Todd helped me. I think that is everybody." She turned to the rest of the group for confirmation. They nodded in agreement.

Sven responded, "Thank you, Jenny. That was good thinking to cover the body. Just one point: where did you get the sheet from?"

Jenny replied, without needing to reflect on the question, "From the airing cupboard in the kitchen."

Sven continued, "Sergeant Peters, would you take statements from each of the ladies who did not go out to help with Laura's body, please, and perhaps, Constable Jenkins, you could do the same for the gentlemen? If Sergeant Peters will use the St Austell Room and Constable Jenkins the Mousehole Room, then I will use the Looe Room to interview those who helped with Laura's body. Edward, would you and Constable Orchard arrange for interviewees to be sent from the lounge to the relevant room and for those who have completed their interviews to be taken back to the Lighthouse Inn and then collected? I do not believe any of them should drive after this shock."

Everybody set about their tasks, with Orchard taking control in the lounge while Peters and Jenkins started work in the basement rooms. Edward took Sven out on the balcony. "What is worrying you, Sven?" he asked. "Is this not just a tragic accident?"

Sven's forehead creased as he started his reply, "Edward, my friend, there are several things that concern me. One: two members of the same family dying within twenty-four hours without foul play is extremely unlikely, although not totally impossible. In my career I have seen no parallel. Two: I cannot explain some of the injuries on Laura's body, particularly the scratches. Three: if Laura did fall from the balcony as has been suggested, why was she out there by herself in her pyjamas? Four: if she was on the balcony in her pyjamas by herself, then why did she unbutton the coat, for it was certainly not torn open? These things I must investigate for you. For the moment, I would also like to treat the death of your brother as suspicious."

Sven allowed Edward to take this in before he continued, "There are three other things Edward. Would you make sure that those who have given statements are sent to the Lighthouse Inn without speaking to those who have not? I want their individual recollections before they have a chance to discuss the night's events."

"Certainly," Edward responded, now sufficiently convinced that Sven's concerns merited investigation, "but you said three things. What are the other two?"

"Yes," Sven confirmed, "could you tell me where I might find a copy of the tide times for last night, please?"

Edward responded, "There is a copy on the lounge table." He moved across to the table, picked up the booklet and checked it. He continued, "Yes, here we are, June 29th, causeway clears fifteen forty-one, causeway floods twenty-one eleven. It did not clear again until four twenty-one this morning." He replaced the booklet, asking, "And the third thing?"

Sven's head bowed and with his voice dropping to a whisper he added, "They do not know of your brother's death. Are you up to telling those who were interviewed by Peters and Jenkins? I will of course tell those whom I interview."

Edward's heart was heavy, but he nodded his acceptance of this task. With that, both men set about their respective duties.

Chapter 6

Finding Laura

Sven sat back in the armchair with the whisky that Edward had given him just before he had retired to bed. It had been a long day and they would have another long one tomorrow. The strain had got to Edward and it showed. He clearly wanted to be involved in any investigation but knew that his personal connections would debar him. Sven would be his only contact and he was not going to let Edward down. He wanted to go over the statements he had taken while they were still fresh, particularly the events leading to the discovery of Laura. He could not bring himself to call his friend's niece "the body." He had seen her several times as she grew up. She should not have died so young. If her death was not an accident, then somebody was going to be bought to justice. The events of the night of the party before Laura left to go to bed could be gone over with the other detectives tomorrow. For now he wanted to piece together the morning's events at the lighthouse.

David said that he woke up at eight-thirty with a thumping headache. He had gone to the kitchen to look for an aspirin but could not find one, so decided to get some fresh air instead. As he walked outside he saw something on the rocks. It was a woman. He had rushed over to find to his horror that it was Laura. She was lying there motionless. He felt sure that she was dead, but had gone to get James just in case. He ran into the lighthouse and banged wildly on the door of the Truro Room, calling out for James. It was not James but Todd who came to the door. At the same time that Todd had answered at the Truro Room, Kyomi, hearing the disturbance, came to the door of the St Ives Room and Nick came down the stairs.

Kyomi had said to Todd that she would get James and that he should see to David. Nick said he would get the people in the cellar. David added that Todd had taken him into the Truro Room where he had sat him down on the bed. By this time, David claimed that he did not know what to do and was very distraught. Scarlett Robinson was already in the room. She had put her arms around his shoulders in an attempt to comfort him. He had then dissolved into tears and remembered little else until the police had arrived. Todd's and Kyomi's statements both confirmed his version of what they had done. Sven made a note to check Nick's and Scarlett's statements in the morning.

James's statement confirmed that he had been woken by Kyomi just after eight-thirty. Still drowsy, and with his head thumping, he had gone to answer the door. Kyomi had dragged him out and pulled him downstairs, where he found the front door open. He said that she was so insistent that he only had time to put on a pair of trousers and shoes before he left the room. The cold air had had a sobering and reviving effect on him. James said that he could see Laura lying on her left side on the rocks. She was wearing only pyjamas, with the top unbuttoned. He thought that she was dead and his examination soon confirmed it. James and Kyomi had agreed not to disturb the body, but to go back in and tell the others. They found them all in the Truro Room, with Todd and Scarlett trying to comfort David. Jenny, Sarah, Carole and Alicia were standing there not saying anything. Angela, Andrew, Beth, Brian, Claire, Chris and Nick had come up from the cellar. Kyomi's statement confirmed what James had said.

Jenny had reported that she and Sarah had been woken by Carole banging on the door of John's room, where they had been sleeping. That was just after eight-thirty. Carole had told them that David had found Laura dead outside on the rocks. They had gone with Carole up to the Truro Room where Todd and Scarlett were comforting David. On the way up they met Alicia, whom Carole had awoken just before she woke her and Sarah. Jenny's statement also confirmed that Kyomi and James came in to report that Laura was dead. James had conjectured that she appeared to have fallen off the balcony and fractured her skull. Jenny then said that she thought that the body should be covered, both for decency and also to preserve any evidence that might be required for an inquest. Sven thought to himself how Jenny, who was just a rookie WPC, had already learned a lot from her father and could go far in the police force. She had collected a sheet from the airing cupboard and asked Todd to help her cover Laura. Todd's statement confirmed this.

Todd, Jenny, James, Kyomi and David were all clear that none of them had moved Laura. Their descriptions of how she was lying were all consistent and fitted with his own observations of how he had found her. He was less persuaded about James's explanation of how she had fallen. Although feasible, it did not convince him. It would not explain the contusion on the right hand side of her skull or the scratches on her body. He concluded that he had done all he could for the day and that sleep would be the most beneficial aid for future analysis.

Chapter 7

Routine police work, 1st July 1996

Edward and Sven were back at their desks early the next morning. They were immediately called in to see Ron Graves, the Chief Inspector. Graves began by offering Edward his condolences and suggesting that he should take some compassionate leave. Before Edward could respond, Graves broke in, saying, "Before you answer that, hear me out fully, please." He then turned to Sven. "Sven, thank you for the highly professional way you began the investigation into Laura Hamilton's death yesterday. It is nothing less than I would expect having come to know you as we have over the past two weeks, but it is nonetheless very welcome. As you will know, much as I should like to I cannot allow you to lead an investigation for the Cornwall and Islands police, as you are officially on a fact-finding visit. You have not been invested with the formal powers of a policeman in the force. Clearly I cannot give this case to Edward as he is far too closely involved, and I expect him to be taking some compassionate leave anyway."

Edward was about to break in, but Graves raised his hand to stop him and continued, "I have, therefore, assigned this case to Inspector Pinks and would ask you to work with him for a while. I know that you enjoy working with

Edward, but it would not be right for us to restrict you to seeing the work of just one of our inspectors, would it now?"

The tone of Graves's voice and the little smile with which the remark was delivered made it clear to Sven that this was not the main message and did not require an answer. Graves was merely obeying the rules in the way that only the British could. Sven remained silent, as did Edward, who had picked up the same subtext. Graves continued, "Sergeant Peters, Constable Jenkins, and Constable Orchard will remain on the case reporting to Inspector Pinks. They have all told me that they would welcome the chance to work with you, Sven, to understand how the Norwegians do it. I rather think that they mean how our particular Norwegian guest does it." Sven smiled, nodding his appreciation for the compliment that he had just been paid. Ron Graves then drew breath before continuing, "There is one difficulty that I need to make you aware of, Sven. Peter Pinks is currently very heavily involved with a complex murder case, which is occupying most of his time. I do not believe that it is worth your while trying to catch up on that. Would you be content to work with DI Pinks and Sergeant Peters concentrating on Laura Hamilton's case?"

Sven marvelled at the way the British could manipulate their own rules. He would be pleased to run the case, although formally to be shadowing Peter Pinks. "But of course, Chief Inspector," he replied.

"Thank you, Sven, most kind of you," the chief inspector replied, "and now, Edward, I will put you down for a week of compassionate leave then? I know that you will have lots of things to sort out: wills and funeral arrangements, that sort of thing. That's agreed then?"

Edward nodded. He knew that Ron was giving him the chance to be involved and that Sven would discuss the case with him. Ron could not have done more. He replied, "Thank you, Ron, that is very kind of you." With that the two left the chief inspector's office.

"A quick cup of coffee before I go then, Sven?" Edward asked, meaning coffee and a chat. They headed toward the cafeteria via a route that would take them past the incident room. As both men had hoped, they ran into Sergeant Peters and Constable Jenkins. Edward asked, "Fancy a coffee, George, Eric?" Both immediately accepted the invitation. Over coffee, Edward was the first to speak. "George, the DCI has granted me a week's compassionate, so I shall be off soon. I need to go to the solicitors to get my brother's will sorted out, and Laura's, if the poor kid made one. I should be able to get a copy for the police, which I will pass to Inspector Ffolkes for you. I know that you three will enjoy working together, but don't expect much help from DI Pinks. Just make sure that he is kept informed and signs the right bits of paper, will you please?"

Peters's reply was crisp and immediate, "Will do, guv." With that Edward left. Peters turned to Sven. "Poor man, he must be shattered. The lads want to get this one right for him."

Sven recognised that there was genuine warmth in Peters's comments. "And I too," he responded. "If you have not done so already, would you and Constable Jenkins please go over the statements that you took yesterday and give me an account of the events of the party from the time that everybody first arrived at the lighthouse to the time when Laura was last seen alive? If you can sort out the bits where everybody's statements agree and then any anomalies, we can compare your statements with the ones that I took. Shall we meet in half an hour?"

"Will do, guv." Peters's response showed clearly that he was prepared to give Sven the respect that his Oslo rank conferred.

Sven was, however, following the carefully crafted words of the chief inspector, still concerned that the protocol be observed. He replied, "Thank you, Sergeant. Oh, by the way, it was very kind of you, but perhaps you should just call me Sven and save the 'guv' for Inspector Pinks?"

Peters smiled, replying, "My pleasure, Sven."

Half an hour later, Sven met Peters, Orchard and Jenkins in the incident room. He began immediately, "Well, gentlemen, what do we have so far? Sergeant Peters, what do they all agree on?"

Peters looked at his notes and began, "It appears to have been quite a party. We are told that everybody had a lot to drink and at least one person suffered for it during the night. Taking it from the start, they arrived in two trips of the Land Rover belonging to the Lighthouse Inn, which was driven by Mrs. Young. David Stevens and Kyomi Taylor walked across. They were all at the lighthouse by eight-twenty. They assembled in the lounge at the top. Sarah Hamilton helped Alicia Adams to unwrap the food while Jenny Hamilton got drinks for everybody. After he had been served a drink, Nick Dean offered to help Jenny. The rest of the party appeared to want to change Mrs. Young's carefully crafted sleeping arrangements."

Sven gave a knowing smile as he observed, "To a more paired arrangement, I take it?"

"Yes, quite." Peters continued, "The girls from the pharmacy college and their boyfriends were the first. They had three rooms in the basement between the seven of them. Nick Dean, who was on his own, agreed to sleep in the lounge. The remainder paired off into the three rooms, with Angela Palmer and Andrew Pitman in the St Austell Room, Claire West and Chris Fisher in the

Mousehole Room and Beth Goodheart and Brian Whitehead in the Looe Room. They each corroborated those arrangements. That was all arranged before nine o'clock, which was the time that Nick Dean took over the bar from Jenny Hamilton. Jenny then left the party, saying that she was going to John's room to do some studying for her sergeant's exams. She was without her boyfriend, so was more there to keep an eye on things than to party the night away. The same was true for her sister Sarah. She was going to do some marking, but agreed with Jenny that there was no point in them both going to John's room, because they would just talk and neither would get any work done. Sarah asked Laura if she could use her room. Laura agreed, but Sarah cleared away the party food and washed the cutlery instead. We could not corroborate this without Jenny's statement. Is that consistent with what Jenny said?"

Sven confirmed that it was entirely consistent, so Sergeant Peters continued, "Sarah said that she and Jenny were quite happy to ensure that the party was orderly, but were not prepared to enforce a moral code. They therefore agreed to turn a blind eye to the room shuffling. Sarah asked that we did not let that get back to Inspector Hamilton. Anyway, it seems that the pharmacy students were not the only ones who were planning room changes. Todd Mitchell and Scarlett Robinson also agreed to spend the night together, which is why David Stevens got the wrong room when he was trying to find James Cross the next morning. Scarlett got Carole to agree to share with Kyomi in the Penzance Room. They both agreed, but then fifteen minutes later Carole asked Kyomi if she would sleep in the St Ives Room instead."

Sven broke in, "Yes, I can confirm that from Kyomi's statement. She was quite amused by it. It seems that Todd asked James to sleep in the St Ives Room instead of Carole. James worked out what was going on and after a few drinks tried his luck with Carole, who agreed to spend the night with him. James was very honest about it. He said that he had been trying for some time and the hints he got earlier made him 'go for it,' as he put it. Did Carole confirm this?"

Sergeant Peters continued, "Yes. That appeared to end the room reshuffle, at least for then. The next big event was the present-opening, which was scheduled for nine-thirty. Just before then Carole and James went out on to the balcony to 'look at the moon.' Although there was a full moon on Saturday night, this really meant to have a snog." Peters hesitated, believing that Sven might not understand, then added, "Sorry, kiss and cuddle."

He need not have worried, as Sven came in, "That's all right, Sergeant; I am familiar with the term 'snog.'"

Peters nodded and continued, "They came back for the present-opening at nine-thirty. Jenny also returned especially for it. Sarah remembered that she had agreed with Laura that Laura would open her presents at twenty-one thirty. Laura did not understand the twenty-four-hour clock, so Jenny had to explain that it meant nine-thirty. We made a note of all the presents and have been able to account for each of them. David gave her a gold watch; Carole, two Boyzone CDs; Kyomi, a silver brooch; Alicia, the evening's food and a silk scarf; Todd and Scarlett, a portable CD player and a Take That CD, James, a gold pen and pencil set; Angela and Andrew, perfume and shower gel; Beth and Brian, a large Paddington Bear cuddly toy; Claire and Chris, set of *Friends* videos; Nick, a silver St Christopher and chain; and Sarah and Jenny, a cheque for £100 to buy clothes. We have been able to account for all the presents."

Peters paused to allow his audience to digest that information and then continued, "Alicia said that David had saved for months to get that watch. It would have set him back a few hundred pounds at least and possibly more. Laura showed very little appreciation for it. Either she did not know the value of the watch or just did not care. It seems that she was not very appreciative of any of the other presents either, from what the guests said. 'She went around thanking people in a showy, insincere way,' and that is quoting her own cousin, Sarah. Scarlett was more reserved, but she said that Laura expressed little gratitude for what had been done for her, in particular the effort that Alicia had put in to do all the party food. She made all of it herself in the Lighthouse Inn kitchen. Not just sandwiches, but the full buffet works. I would not have minded being there for that myself."

Sven had been thinking deeply. He stopped Peters to confirm his thoughts. He began, "So everybody was in the lounge and accounted for while the presents were being opened. The causeway floods at twenty-one eleven, so nobody would have had enough time to get away after that. That puts them all in the lighthouse overnight, and unless anybody else came across by then and hid from the whole party, it must be one of them that killed Laura." After a further moment's thought, he added, "Unless, of course, it was an accident or even suicide. Not by any means conclusive, but a good indicator at this stage. Anyway, please continue, Sergeant."

Peters returned to his notebook. "Well, the present-opening and thanks took until ten o'clock, by which time most of them seem to have drunk quite a bit, so to beat the tide would have been very difficult if not impossible. Also it would have been getting dark, which would make any return to the mainland very risky. The exceptions to my heavy drinking statement were Sarah and Jenny Hamilton, who were just there to keep order. They agreed that things were going on all right, so they decided that they could safely withdraw to let the youngsters get on with it. Sarah said that she had had a couple of drinks, but that she felt up to doing an hour's marking. This time she did go to Laura's room. She said that Jenny decided to do some studying for her police exams. She went to John's room. Does Jenny's statement confirm that?"

"Yes it does," Sven replied, "which takes those two out of the party and makes them unaccounted for. Did Laura stay in the lounge?"

Referring again to his notes, Peters continued, "She did to start with. After the presents, some of the guests started dancing. That was Angela and Andrew, Beth and Brian, Chris and Claire, Alicia and Todd, Kyomi and David and Carole and James. That left Nick serving at the bar, talking to Scarlett and Laura. There is an interesting point here. David had picked up Kyomi and walked across the causeway with her. Kyomi is a bit of a stunner and it seems that she was flirting with David. He was enjoying it, lucky lad. After they had been dancing for about half an hour, Laura finally cottoned on. She accused David of flirting with Kyomi, although the rest of the statements suggest that it was the other way around. That did not help David. Laura went off to her room in a huff. David was angry, presumably because he was not the one who started it and because of Laura's reaction to his present, so he did not try to placate her but instead just let her go. Laura came back twenty-five minutes later."

Sven broke in, "We must be careful not to presume anything. What we know is that he was spending a lot of time with Kyomi and he was prepared to let Laura leave without trying to follow her. And this is the man who asked Laura's father if he could marry her not more than three hours before. So now we have Laura away from the rest of the party for twenty-five minutes, but returning apparently unharmed. Do we know what happened to her in that time?"

"According to Sarah, Laura went to her room, bursting into tears as she arrived. Sarah managed to comfort her, told her not to spoil her own party and to go back and try to enjoy herself. That seemed to do the trick. We only have Sarah's word for this, but the times she gave do stack up with those given by the others for her return to the party."

Sven checked his notes and nodded, asking, "Did anything interesting happen while Laura was away?"

Peters responded, "More of the same really: drinking, dancing and snogging. Angela and Andrew stopped dancing and started kissing on the sofa, Alicia and Todd joined Scarlett and Nick at the bar and the rest kept on dancing. It got more interesting when Laura come back. Carole and James stopped dancing. Carole went down to the toilet while James went to the bar to get some drinks.

Remember that the toilets are at the bottom of the lighthouse, so she was gone for a few minutes. While Carole was away, Laura dragged James away for a dance and started flirting with him."

Sven asked, "What was Carole's reaction when she came back?"

Peters turned to Jenkins, who had interviewed Nick. Jenkins answered, "To start with she did not seemed too bothered. She went over to the bar to pick up her drink, which James had left at the bar. She chatted away with Alicia, Todd, Scarlett and Nick. Even when Laura took James out on the balcony she did not react initially, but when they were not back after five minutes she went out there as well. They all came in again a couple of minutes later."

Peters took up the story, adding, "Carole said that she explained to James that Laura was just using him and he had better stop if he wanted to sleep with her. She does not mince her words, that girl. Anyway, it seemed to do the trick. By now it was gone eleven and nothing of interest occurred until half past, when David started dancing with Alicia. He took the opportunity of breaking away from Kyomi when she went to the toilet."

Sven cut in, "Yes, David told me that. He said he did it partly because he felt that she was being left out and partly to keep himself away from Kyomi, whom he was beginning to fancy quite strongly. He stayed chatting with Alicia for well over an hour."

"So he wanted to get away from Kyomi, but rather than go back to Laura he picked another girl to flirt with," Jenkins observed.

Sven responded, "That thought crossed my mind too, so I asked David why. He said that he was very drunk by this time. He was not proud of what he did, but that he felt he would be safe with Alicia because he did not fancy her. He was still angry with Laura, so was not prepared to go back to her. He wanted Laura to make the first move. Typical young love, I suppose." Sven paused for a moment, then apologised to Peters for interrupting him, requesting that he should continue the story from when David started dancing with Alicia.

Peters thought for a moment before starting, "That was at about the time when Sarah decided that she was too tired for marking. She told me that she went up to the lounge, collected a bottle of wine and two glasses and took them to John's room, intending to have a night-cap with Jenny before going to bed. Jenny seemed happy to break off her studies, so the two of them sat on the bed with the wine and started talking. She told Jenny about how Laura had come back to her room crying after the altercation with David."

Sven got up to draw some notes on the incident room whiteboard. He then asked Peters to continue. "Sarah said that the wine made her tired quite quickly, so she got into bed and drifted off to sleep. The next thing she remembered was being woken by Carole banging on their door. Jenny confirmed that Sarah was asleep by about eleven forty-five. She popped up to the lounge at just past midnight to check that all was well. Apart from Angela and Andrew, who had gone to bed, everybody else was there, either drinking or dancing. Happy that all was well, she returned to John's room and went to bed. She heard some things during the night, but to keep the chronology right, I will leave that for later. Anyway, Todd and Scarlett went on to the balcony at about twelve-fifteen. They stayed there for about fifteen minutes, during which time the party numbers started thinning out. Nick admitted that he had far too much to drink. He felt sick, so went to the toilet. That was at twelve-twenty. He said he was sick and passed out in one of the cubicles. Although we cannot definitely confirm that, Alicia went to the toilet at twelve forty-five. She reported that the other cubicle was locked and that she could smell vomit."

Peters paused for breath while turning the page of his notebook. Realising that there were no questions, he continued, "At about twelve twenty-five Claire and Chris left for the Mousehole Room and Beth and Brian for the Looe Room. Angela and Andrew confirmed that they heard their voices at that time. David passed out on a sofa in the lounge at the time Alicia went to the toilet. Not much then happened until about one-thirty, when Alicia, who admitted feeling mildly vindictive toward Laura, jokingly suggested that they give Laura the bumps. She was surprised when they all took her seriously and agreed to do it. David was asleep and Nick was still absent, so the bumps were given by Todd, Scarlett, Alicia, Carole, James and Kyomi. James insisted that they should be careful because Laura was pregnant, so it was just a token gesture. They held her along her whole length and let her down very gently, just once, from a height of no more than thirty centimetres. Nonetheless, as you might have guessed, Laura was not pleased and went off to bed in a huff again. That is the last time anybody reports seeing her in the lounge."

Sven sat back and thought for a moment. He asked Jenkins to check on the post-mortem results for both Laura and John, Peters to follow up with forensics and Orchard to check police records for any activity by any of the suspects. Just as they were about to leave, Sven added, "Do any of you lads do any sailing?"

Peters and Jenkins both turned to Orchard, who replied, "I do a bit when I get the chance, sir."

"*A bit!*" Peters interjected. "He is only the star of the St Ives club. Got placed in the Fastnet once, didn't you, lad?"

Orchard blushed, but was clearly pleased to have his talents recognised. Sven came to the point of his question. "Then you will understand the winds and tides around Blimford Lighthouse. If anything was thrown out seawards from the lighthouse, would it be washed ashore, and if so, where? Would you work that out for me and then check with the beach cleaners and beachcombers to see if anything was found? If anything might still come ashore, then get a team to search the beach, please."

"What are we looking for, sir?" Orchard enquired.

Sven responded after consideration, "I am not sure, and it might be nothing, but please check for anything."

"Will do, sir," Orchard replied, and with that he left.

Sven decided that he needed to know more about both his victims and his partygoers. Now was the time to use his informal status to obtain some background on them. He made up his mind to ask Edward about both John and Laura, but he would also need to talk to somebody who was closer to each. Turning first to Laura, he asked himself who had known her the longest. Both Scarlett and Kyomi fitted the bill, but he chose Scarlett because she appeared to be closer to the other guests as well. He wondered what her reaction might be when he phoned, but was pleased to find her quite willing to meet him. She said that she had been staying with Todd at the Boatman's Cottage since the tragedy and would be happy to meet him there that morning. Todd was out with David working on a friend's car, so she would be pleased to have the company.

Chapter 8

Recollections of a friend, 2nd July 1996

Scarlett placed two cups of coffee on the small table. She sat in one of the two chairs that faced out of the bay window overlooking the sea, motioning Sven to take the other. Sven explained that he was trying to understand the relationships that Laura had with the rest of the pharmacy students.

"Can you provide me with some background on how you got on and any particular incidents that would give me some background, please? Were there any stories that might shed light on anything?" Sven asked, trying just to get Scarlett talking.

Scarlett sipped her coffee and then began cautiously, "Well, since I have known Laura for such a long time, there are a wealth of stories that I could tell you. For example, there is the story of our first day at college. Laura used to have me in fits of laughter whenever she told it, but I am sure that you have already heard about that."

Sven recalled that he had been told that story by Laura herself when he had last visited Edward. "Actually I have. Laura was clearly quite a raconteur, and that was certainly a good tale," he replied, adding, "but I am sure there are other stories that you can tell me. Do you have a favourite of your own?"

Scarlett sat back and finished her coffee. She looked very coy as she replied, "Well, I do, but it does not involve Laura, so I doubt that it will interest you."

Sven was not about to let her off that easily. Any background information would be useful, and he could return to Laura later. The important thing from his viewpoint was to get Scarlett relaxed and talking. "Please tell me what it is about," he said.

Scarlett responded as Sven had hoped she would. "Well, it's about this cottage actually, or more precisely about the dinner that we had to celebrate its completion, in August last year."

"Pray do tell; I would be fascinated to hear it if you have the time."

Scarlett nodded and then began. She told it in the third person, with the full gamut of face and hand gestures.

"It was a typical English summer evening. David had the wipers going at double speed as the rain lashed down outside. He had hoped that for once he could come to Todd's cottage without wading ankle-deep in mud. He prayed that the concrete drive and path that they had only finished that afternoon would have dried sufficiently not to make his shoes dirty. Worse still, he feared that both might be partially washed away. He parked at the bottom of the lane and waited for the rain to ease. Looking across to the cottage, he saw that Todd had laid some planks across the mud where the lawn was to go. *Well done, Todd*, he thought as, reaching down into the passenger foot well, he grabbed the pot plant and the bag containing three bottles of wine. As the rain eased, he sounded his horn. Todd opened the door and he made a dash for it.

"'Nice evening,' he said to Todd as he wiped his feet and handed over the wine. 'This is a little house warming from me…oh! and something from mum.' With that David handed over the pot plant. 'She says that you are to put it in a sunny window and keep it moist.'

"Todd smiled and thanked David, saying, 'You should not be bringing the gifts. It's for me to thank you for all the hard work. Please thank your mum for this, it is really kind of her. I will have to ask Scarlett what to do with it, but we will put it on the windowsill for now. Time for a quick one before the girls arrive?'

"David nodded as Todd pulled a couple of cans of lager from the fridge. 'Since it is a special occasion, you can have it in a glass this time.'

"'Who else is coming?' David asked.

"'Only Scarlett and Alicia,' Todd replied. 'I just wanted those who had made this possible.'

"The two of them sat in the single downstairs room looking out over the inlet. Todd put on some music. The sun was now breaking out from behind the clouds. A few minutes later there was a ring on the door. Scarlett was outside holding two carrier bags. Todd moved to kiss her, but she moved past him, saying, 'No time for that now, Todd, I have got to get this into the kitchen for Alicia. Would one of you two give her a hand? She has got loads of stuff.'

"Todd and David went to the car where Alicia was busy unloading bags of food from the back seat.

"'Alicia, you have done enough to feed an army here,' Todd observed as he started picking up bags and passing them to David to take in.

"Between them they got all the bags into the house in one trip. Alicia headed for the kitchen to get everything under control, as she described it. Todd opened some wine and poured a glass each for Alicia and Scarlett. David was despatched to get a couple more beers."

Scarlett blushed at this point before continuing. "I will tell you the next bit as I once heard David recount it. Todd was not going to miss out on his kiss. He headed over to Scarlett, swept her off her feet with a bear hug and planted a smacker on her lips as he did so.

"Scarlett made an obviously insincere protest, exclaiming, 'Todd, put me down! We are in company.'

"'Aah, so's we are, my luv'ly, but us Cornishmen does nots worry 'bout that sort of thing, does we?' Todd replied as he playfully bit her ear.

"Scarlett giggled as Todd knew she would because she always did when he put on his 'accent for the Grockles.' She struggled, protesting that she should be helping Alicia.

"'Seems that my little cousin and David have things well in hand,' Todd replied. 'What's say you and I check out the bedroom?'

"Scarlett was about to protest more earnestly when Alicia called out from the kitchen. She immediately rebuked Todd in a sisterly way, saying, 'No time for that now, the dinner is almost ready. Todd, will you help David with the hors d'ouvres and let Scarlett powder her nose, please?'

"Todd somewhat reluctantly released Scarlett, who made a beeline for the stairs, as much to cover her embarrassment as to attend to any other needs. Todd stood smartly to attention, made a mock salute and barked with clipped military precision, 'Roger, will co. Ma'am, over and out.'"

Scarlett added, "Of course, David told it much better."

Scarlett then continued the story from her own viewpoint. "Anyway, as I escaped, David came out of the kitchen, shoved two plates into Todd's hands and rebuked him by saying, 'Take these and make yourself useful before you upset both the girls in your life.'

"One glance at Alicia's eyebrows was enough for Todd to realise that David was probably right. 'Sorry, Al, I'll behave,' he called back as he placed the plates on the table. He then picked up the bottle of wine, took it to the kitchen and filled Alicia's glass, kissing her on the cheek as he did so.

"Alicia smiled, gave him a playful punch in the chest, handed him the sauce boat that she had just filled and motioned him back out of the kitchen area. 'You're forgiven this time, and be careful of that because it's hot. Now come on and let's start this dinner.'

"I came downstairs at the same time so Todd motioned us all to our places. The late evening sun poured through the window as we all sat down. It shone straight into my eyes. 'You will have to get a blind for that window, Todd,' Alicia observed, seeing that I was in some discomfort.

"'You're right,' Todd responded. 'I have to pull the curtains for now.' With that he pulled the curtain across and turned on the lights.

"David, observing the cosy scene, added, 'All we need now is the candles.'

"'I almost forgot,' said Alicia, heading for the kitchen. 'Where are the matches, Todd?'

"Todd began, 'You're kidding me, aren't you?' but immediately followed it with, 'Oh! you're not; you really have thought of everything,' as Alicia produced a pair of wine bottles with candles in them.

"'Mum says that you can have these, but she wants her catering manager back. That's me, by the way, she made it official today.' Alicia beamed as she placed the candles on the table.

"Todd said, 'Oh, well done, Al! This deserves a celebration.'

"'That's a good job, isn't it, Todd, because that's exactly what we are having, aren't we?'

"Todd was not expecting such a response from Alicia, and for once that evening he was lost for words. I could see that Todd looked embarrassed, so I said, 'Well done, Alicia, and well-deserved.'

"'Yes, well done, Alicia,' David added.

"Todd, recovering his composure, decided that this time a compliment really was required. 'We all know that you deserve it, and it's something that Auntie Jean really should have done a while ago. What finally made her do it?'

"Alicia thought for a second and, appearing a little coy, looked down, saying 'Well…there is a reason.'

"'Well, tell us, Al, don't keep us all in suspense.' Todd was not putting it on; he really did want to know of his cousin's successes. He was her big brother-figure and she was the little sister he would always have liked.

"Alicia replied, her voice getting more excited as she spoke, 'I got my A level results today and I passed.'

"Todd was pleased, although he clearly did not comprehend how significant the results were to Alicia. 'Well done, Al, I always knew you would. All those hours of doing my homework for me were not wasted.' Todd had never been very academic, preferring to work with his hands. The cottage was testament to that. When they were at school, Alicia did quite a lot of Todd's homework for him, despite Todd being two years above her. He would repay her by looking after her in awkward situations, especially where boys were concerned.

"David was not particularly academic either, but he detected from Alicia's voice that there was more to be told, but that Alicia was waiting to be asked. 'Well done, Alicia. What grades did you get?'

"Alicia face beamed with triumph as she replied 'An A and two B's.'

"I realised, even if the boys did not, how well Alicia had done. 'Will you go to university?' I asked. 'With those grades you could go almost anywhere.'

"Alicia's face showed pleasure in being recognised as having done well. She had taken jibe after jibe from her mother's other daughter, her half-sister Carole, for being a nasty little swot. Carole had never said that to her face, but Alicia knew that was what she had told others. Now Carole had to recognise that she was a force to be reckoned with at the Lighthouse Inn. She was not about to offer Carole the chance to steal a march on her. 'Well, not *Oxbridge*, but it would get me into one of the good Red Bricks, or I could do a catering course. I thought I would leave it for a year or two to get some real experience behind me first. I can't have Carole taking all the plaudits with her front-of-house charms, now can I?'

"There was venom behind those remarks about Carole. Carole had been made staff manager a year earlier because she was good with the guests. Alicia was prepared to admit this and also that Carole was good at handling the staff. She had seen Carole have the courage to really tear a strip off a burly porter for being rude to a guest. But Alicia wanted recognition for her catering skills. Now that she had got that recognition, nothing was going to stand in her way.

"Dinner was an example of Alicia's skills in action. She had gone to great lengths to make Todd's first Boatman's Cottage dinner a memorable occasion. Previous dinners had been single-pot casseroles eaten on our laps while sitting on the stairs dressed in overalls. This one was going to be different. The hors d'ouvres were followed by Poullet de la Maison, a special dish that she had developed for the Lighthouse Inn.

"Alicia was about to get the dessert when Todd raised his glass. 'Thank you, my dear friends, without whom the Boatman's Cottage would still be a crumbling shell rather than this excellent one-bedroomed bijou residence so beloved of estate agents.' When he put his mind to it, Todd could be good with words. He intended to make a short speech that showed his appreciation for what those around the table had done for him. He continued, 'To David, who gave up many an hour as a deck chair attendant in St Ives to help me complete this project. Mind you, he had the worst paid job in Cornwall, so this excellent dinner, beautifully thought-out and prepared—not by your host, I hasten to add, but by my little cousin Alicia—should easily compensate for that.

"'To Alicia, not only for tonight's feast but for many a delicious supper prepared under less-than-perfect conditions while we were working on this place. Also congratulations to her on both her A level results and being appointed catering manager of the Lighthouse Inn. I see Michelin stars raining down on Cornwall.

"'Last, but not least, to my beautiful Scarlett, who spent many an evening cleaning, clearing and acting as our handy-girl. She spent so many days wearing old jeans and a head scarf that I thought this was the new fashion. Call me a male chauvinist if you like, but I prefer the dress that she is wearing tonight. Please raise your glasses to the creators of the new Boatman's Cottage.'

"Everybody drank the toast. Alicia then rose to cheers from the other three. She began, 'Thank you, Todd, for those kind words. I certainly am very happy, with both my exam results and with Mum's reaction to it. I thought that she was never going to give me the title, but no matter, it's all the more sweet for that. But still enough about me, this evening is about christening the Boatman's Cottage. There were a lot of people who said that Todd had wasted his inheritance on a broken-down building that he would never live in. We knew better. We knew that the Cornish Likely Lad had a lot more depth and determination than the doubters gave him credit for. He had both the vision to realise what it could be and the determination to see it through. And that is where the other Likely Lad, David, came in. We have seen a completely different pair of Likely Lads. I am sure that the two of you know of your reputation at Hilary Taylor—likely to get a girl into trouble, that is. It is now likely to help each other to finish something that they have started, whether it is your car or this fine cottage. And let us not forget who has brought about this transition in my big cousin from teenage tearaway to responsible, property-owning adult. I refer, of course, to Scarlett, who has worked tirelessly to ensure that this project has been a success. All we need to do now is to find another Scarlett to weave the same magic on David. So my toast is to the Cornish Likely Lads and their very own Thelma, Scarlett.'

"All the glasses were filled and this second toast drunk. A few more followed for good measure. David blushed at the mention of his going steady with a girl in the same way as Todd had.

"By midnight we had all drunk quite a bit. Alicia looked at the clock, which showed twelve-fifteen. 'I have got to go,' she said. 'I am on breakfasts from six o'clock.'

"'I'll drive you,' said David, trying to appear the gentleman.

"'Absolutely no way…after what you have drunk tonight?' Alicia responded 'We will call for a taxi. You can leave the car here and share the cost of the cab with me if you like.'

"David retorted, 'How are you going to do that? Todd is not on the phone yet.'

"'From the box just up the lane; now come on and get your coat.' Alicia was in no mood to argue. She had seen too many customers of the Lighthouse Inn drive after having too many to drink. She knew of at least two who had lost their licences, and she was not about to have the same fate befall David. 'Scarlett, will you come with us?'

"I blushed, replying, 'Er…er, no, I'll be okay. I would like to stay a little longer.'

"As Alicia put it, 'Her eyes moved to Todd, who was almost grinning with delight.'

"Alicia loved her cousin and with good reason. He was like that big brother all girls really longed for…but oh, was he transparent? Alicia knew what he was planning and I realised that she knew. It was so obvious that even David had probably worked it out. Alicia wondered why we could not be open about it. *It's the nineteen nineties and everybody is doing it,* she thought, instantly correcting herself within her own mind by adding, *except me, that is.* As she put it to David, 'They are so right for each other that they were bound to end up getting married even if they had not yet realised it themselves.'

"What Alicia did not know was how devout my parents are. I would never want them to know, but I am sure that I can trust to your discretion on that one."

Sven nodded before Scarlett continued, "Todd and I waved goodbye as David and Alicia walked up the lane to the phone box. After about fifty yards both of them simultaneously looked back at the cottage. The upstairs light was on and the downstairs light had been switched off. Alicia's comment reflected that dry sense of humour of hers. David told me that as she pulled open the door of the telephone box, she said, 'It does not look like the washing up is going to get done tonight then. It's a good job I put the hotel dishes in soak before we started dinner.'"

Scarlett finished her story and then blushed as she realised how much of her own feelings she had given away with it. Sven realised it too and sought to reassure her, "Thank you, Miss Robinson, for being so open with me. You have given me some good insights, not necessarily of Laura, but of some of those close to her. I appreciate that and I will use the information carefully. For now I must take my leave of you. If I may take one more liberty with your hospitality, would you kindly call a taxi for me, please?"

Chapter 9

Recollections of John

On his way back in the taxi Sven thought about how he might get the same insight into John Hamilton's life. One person he would have to talk to was Edward and he knew that that was going to be difficult. When he got back to the office he telephoned Edward to suggest some lunch, which Edward incorrectly, or at least incompletely, interpreted as an opportunity for Sven to tell him what was going on. Edward did not feel like going out and was keen not to be seen discussing the case, so he suggested a take-away at his house.

Sven had completed his account of progress to date and he and Edward had finished their pizza. Sven knew that he had to ask his difficult questions. "Edward, my friend," he began, unconsciously wringing his hand together.

Edward, a trained policeman, picked this up immediately. He knew that Sven was struggling. He was not about to make his friend suffer. Sven had not brought this pain upon him. Moreover he was trying his very best to understand the events that had led to John's death and, if foul play had occurred, to bring his murderer to justice. He began calmly, "You have to ask me some difficult questions, don't you, Sven? That is not your fault. You are a policeman doing his job and what is more you are doing it to help me and my force. So ask away and I will answer as truthfully as I can."

Sven did not need to be invited a second time, but still he was going to be as gentle as he could. "Edward, as you know, murder is not a popularity vote for the victim. It is about somebody believing that the victim should die, either because they are in the way of what the murderer requires or there is a real or imagined grudge against them. Do you know of anybody who had any grudge against John?"

The response from Edward came quickly: "I have asked myself that question over and over again since Sunday and I can still think of nobody. So the next question that I asked myself was whether he had any bad traits that might generate such bad feeling in somebody that I do not know. There I did come up with two things. The first is that John was never good with his relationships with women. Jean Young and her sister Gill could probably shed more light on that than I can." Edward stopped and hesitated.

Sven just had to probe. "You said that there were two things?"

Edward took a deep breath and began, "John liked his drink. Nothing wrong with that, but he was far from careful when it came to driving after drinking. A good example was when he came to us for the evening of Christmas Day in 1992. He and Laura had just finished lunch with Jean Young and her daughters. You might want to talk to Jean about that. I will pick up the story as John told me finally when I put it to him that he had driven to me over the limit."

Edward's voice dropped as if he wished to ensure that any unseen observer could not hear him. He did not want to recount what he was about to, but knew that he had no choice. "John took the back road around St Ives to avoid the police. As he was heading down the B3311 toward Penzance, he felt fairly safe. He had got away from St Ives on to a road that was clear in both directions. He glanced in his mirror; nothing. Another glance two seconds later revealed what he most dreaded. The white police car closed toward him and then stayed back at a respectable distance.

"*Keep calm,* John had told himself. *They will not stop you if you are not doing anything wrong.* He checked his speed: fifty. That was fine, and now to take real care around all the bends. A left-hander, down to third gear, then a right, third gear again and then a sharper left. He considered second would be appropriate on this occasion, although normally he would have stayed in third. The police car had kept a respectable distance all this time. As he accelerated along a long straight section, the police car turned on its lights, including the blues and twos, and started speeding toward him. John's heart raced as he prayed that he had left it long enough for the alcohol to disperse. He saw a lay-by ahead, signalled left and pulled in. The police car sped by, with the policeman in the passenger side waving his thanks as they passed. John sat there for a moment to allow himself to relax.

"'Are you all right, Dad?' Laura had enquired with seemingly genuine concern.

"'Fine, Laura, fine,' he replied, 'just a bit of indigestion. It's passed now.'

"The rest of the journey back to their house was uneventful."

Having recounted the incident, Edward paused, but then decided to continue the story. "He tried to hide it from me by taking the car home and walking to our house. That really upset Laura. 'Dad, I though we were going to Uncle Ted's,' she had protested as John pulled the Jaguar on to the drive.

"'We are, Laura, but I wanted to drop the car and the presents off first and pick up a couple of bits for Ted and Rose.'

"Laura gave him hell. 'I don't want to walk,' she complained, 'I've got my best shoes on.'

"John was not going to risk it again. He knew that I would never let him have much to drink if he had the car and it would be difficult to leave it at our place. Laura would just have to walk. He did his best to reassure her. 'It's only ten minutes and you can put some trainers on and carry those shoes.' He could see that Laura was about to complain further, so he added sharply, 'We either walk or we do not go. If you stop complaining I will order a taxi to bring us back.'

"John mused over what he thought to be a nice combination of stick and carrot as he watched Laura weighing up her options. She decided that he meant it before she finally agreed to the arrangement. Laura, bless her, noted that the walk took seventeen minutes, but she decided that it was best not to say anything to John, although she made a lot of it when she told Jenny and Sarah. She was able to spend the rest of her Christmas day with her cousins, which she had wanted to do all along. The three of them were more like sisters. Since she was the youngest they always let her have her own way, which suited Laura fine.

"They had hardly finished ringing the doorbell when the door was thrown open. Rose greeted them cheerfully with a hearty, 'Come in, dears, you must be frozen. Come and warm yourselves by the fire.'

"It was not that cold, but the fire was welcome."

Again Edward could have stopped talking, but instead he continued to reminisce about a good evening that his family had spent together. Sven knew that he would have no more of them, so he let him continue. "Rose and I had a full house. Jenny and Sarah were accompanied by their boyfriends, Andy Watson and Colin Smith. Our elderly neighbours Frank and Mabel Joyce were also there.

"Jenny and Sarah came down to greet them. Jenny began, 'Hi, Uncle John, Happy Christmas.' With that she planted a peck on his cheek. As Sarah was greeting John, Jenny turned to Laura, saying, 'Come up, Laura, we are playing Monopoly. You can join in. Andy has to go on duty soon so you can take over from him.'

"In an instant Laura was rushed upstairs. John looked slightly bewildered, holding the bag of presents that he had brought for the family. Realising his dilemma, Rose said, 'Just put them under the tree, John, we can get around to them after supper.' She called into the kitchen where I was getting some drinks, 'It's all right, Ted; they walked round so John can have a drink.'

"Little did either of us then know the truth. I remember saying to John, 'Best way; we don't want Andy having to deal with you professionally, do we?'

John looked a little perplexed, so Rose explained, 'Oh, of course you would not know, would you? Andy has joined the Force. Ted's been influencing him with all the career possibilities. He did not mention the Christmas Day duties, though.'

"'That's a point Ted,' John observed. 'I did not expect to see you yet. How come you have managed to get Christmas Day off?'

"That was a laugh. 'Not all day off, old boy,' I responded. I had been in from six to twelve that morning clearing up some stuff. 'That's CID for you, and I'll be there again at six tomorrow,' I told him, 'but at least I managed a good chunk of Christmas Day off. Poor Andy was on from six until two.'

"I poured John a scotch on the rocks. I did not have to wait for confirmation, pouring a generous measure over a couple of ice cubes. John sat down to enjoy that one, safe in the knowledge that the Jaguar was now back in his garage where it belonged."

Edward came out of his reminiscences with a start. "Sven, you should have stopped my rambling. Anyway, I have got to see John's solicitor. I'll leave you to it." With that he made his excuses and left.

Chapter 10

More routine police work

Sven headed for the armchair that was now becoming integral to the investigation. It was a place away from the bustle of the incident room where he could sit back, relax and think. Rose had gone shopping and both Jenny and Sarah were out and, he presumed, at work. Edward had gone to see John's solicitors, leaving him alone in the house. He tried to piece together the movements of all those left in the lounge after Laura went off to bed. What had they told him and what did he believe?

David had a vague recollection of a commotion and cheering soon after he fell asleep in the lounge. He was very drunk, but remembered Kyomi offering him some food to soak up a little of the alcohol. As he put it, even with his dulled senses he could recognise that beautiful face and her soft vocal tones. She gave him a couple of seductive kisses and whispered to him to come to the St Ives Room when the others had gone. She then left, telling everybody that she was going to bed. He had no idea what time it was, but most of the others appeared to have already left and the room was by then in semi-darkness.

A little later James came over to ask if he was all right. He felt David's pulse, lifted an eyelid and, deciding that he just needed to sleep, put a blanket over him. Later still and somewhat to his surprise, because he was sure that she said that she was going to bed, David heard Kyomi tell James that she would look after him and that James could go to bed. He heard Kyomi tell James that the St Ives Room was free.

David recalled that when James left, Kyomi was alone with him. She had snuggled up and started kissing him. Despite the amount of alcohol he had consumed, David could not resist her advances. His words again: he kissed her forehead, then her pretty little nose, and then each cheek before finally their lips met. Why was it, then, when the whole of his body sought to enjoy a most wonderful night of passion with this highly desirable girl that his brain engaged and asserted itself?

No, he said to himself, *I must not do this. It is Laura whom I love and Laura I must be with.* "I must go to Laura," he told Kyomi as firmly as he could. The firmness was more for his benefit than for hers. As his brain began to take control again, he sought to extract himself with dignity and preserve his friendship with the girl he was about to desert. It was true that she had tried to seduce him but he had been a willing partner. He thanked Kyomi for bringing him around and ensuring that he was okay. She smiled at him but said nothing, clearly realising that further attempts at seduction would be pointless. He then gave her a gentle hug, kissed her on the cheek and was gone.

David knocked on the door and called, "Laura, Laura, let me in." He prayed that she would come. His heart leapt as he heard footsteps coming toward the door. As the footsteps stopped he awaited the opening of the door and the chance to be in Laura's arms again, but then he heard the key turn in the door lock. The footsteps started again, then faded to silence. Surely Laura had gone back to bed to wait for him? He tried the door, expecting it to open and allow him to rush over to her, but no, it was locked. A realisation that Laura was not ready to forgive and forget came to him like a hammer blow. Why not? She was as much to blame, and he was prepared to forgive her. Perhaps a little more persuasion would do it? He called to Laura again, but there was no reply. His love for Laura was turning back to anger. At that moment he felt Kyomi brush past him as she came down from the lounge and continued on down stairs. He was getting angrier. Was Laura trying to teach him a lesson? Well, if she was, it was about to backfire.

His mind relived the previous moment. Why had Kyomi brushed passed him? She was a slim girl and had enough room to get past without making contact. For no reason that he could identify, two facts came into his head. The first, told to him by his aunt, was that a woman would never touch a man accidentally. If she touched him, then she meant to touch him. The second fact, which came from a book that he had read on body language, was how men and women would pass each other in tight spaces. Whereas men would turn to pass face-to-face, women would turn to pass back-to-back, instinctively protecting their breasts. Kyomi had turned to face him as she passed, allowing her breasts to brush against him. Was this girl still offering herself to him?

He put the thought of Kyomi to the back of his mind and waited for Laura, but nothing happened. Crestfallen, he returned to the lounge and settled down on the sofa to sleep. As he was falling asleep he heard somebody in the lounge. Was it Laura? Had his patience and fidelity been rewarded? He did not dare look. If it was Laura, she would come over to him. He heard a door open and felt a draught as somebody went out on to the balcony. He concluded that this was a clandestine rendezvous and decided that he would rather not know who it was.

It was now clear that despite all his pleas and allowing her time, Laura was not going to come to him. It was time for him to teach her a lesson. If she did not want him, he knew somebody who did. He was going to confirm his deductions on body language one way or the other. He went down to the St Ives Room, knocked on the door and whispered, "Kyomi, are you there? Can I come in?"

There was a long silence before he heard her say, "Come in." He crept in and went across to the bed. "I should send you back to your precious Laura," she said, trying to appear cross, but he worked out that she wanted him to stay. He undressed quickly and pulled back the duvet. To his surprise and delight Kyomi was naked. Her beauty took his breath away. This time he was not going to talk himself out of the pleasure that he knew awaited him. He surveyed her all over: her big blue eyes, pretty little nose, luscious lips, dimpled chin, fine white neck, delightfully proportioned breasts with erect nipples and flat stomach running down into a gorgeous little mound of silky black hair between long, shapely legs. He intended to kiss every part of her.

"Get in then, I'm freezing," Kyomi protested. He slipped into the bed beside her, pulled the duvet over them and cuddled her. She was right: she was cold— but not for long, he thought.

David said that he stayed with Kyomi for an hour. They agreed that it would be better if the others did not know that they had been together, so he left and went back to the lounge.

During the time that they were together, David heard footsteps coming up the stairs, pass the landing of the St Ives Room and continue going up. When he returned to the lounge, he could see somebody in a sleeping bag behind the sofa, but did not know who it was. He or she did not wake as David settled back on to the sofa. Just as he was drifting off to sleep he heard a door open, and an icy blast came up from the stairs. Was this the famous ghost? He snuggled further down under the blanket.

A while later he heard the sound of somebody being sick. Even the ghost must have had too much to drink. He drifted off to sleep. He woke up again at eight-thirty with a thumping headache. He went to the kitchen to look for an aspirin but could not find one, so decided to get some fresh air instead.

As he went outside he saw something on the rocks. It was a woman. He rushed over to find to his horror that it was Laura. She was lying there motionless. Her face was pasty white and her feet were blue. He felt sure that she was dead, but had to get James just in case. He ran into the lighthouse and banged wildly on the door of the Truro Room, calling out for James. Todd came to the door at the same time as Kyomi, hearing the disturbance, came to the door of the St Ives Room and Nick came down the stairs. He blurted something about Laura having fallen and needing a doctor. He heard Kyomi tell Todd that she would get James and that he should see to David. Todd agreed. Nick said he would get the pharmacy set from the rooms in the cellar.

Todd took David into the Truro Room, where he sat him down on the bed. David did not know what to do. He became very distraught, feeling this was a punishment for his unfaithfulness. Scarlett put her arms around his shoulders in an attempt to comfort him. David just dissolved into tears.

Kyomi's statement confirmed all that David had said about their interactions during the night. Because she had had less to drink, she could fill in more of the detail. It was two o'clock when she left David on the lounge sofa, telling him to join her when the others had gone to bed. She waited expectantly in the St Ives Room. The party died down to silence within twenty minutes, but David did not appear. After another ten minutes she went back to the lounge to find James checking David to make sure that he was all right. There was nobody else there. She told James that she would look after David and that he could go to bed. James looked at his watch and stood there bewildered. She concluded that he was on a promise but that he had been told to give Carole some time before going to her. She told him that the St Ives Room was free.

After David left her for Laura she went back to the St Ives Room. She confirmed that she had brushed past David when he was knocking on Laura's door. She was surprised to find James in the St Ives Room nervously pacing around when she had expected that he would have been with Carole. James had looked at his watch. "What time is it?" she asked him rather sarcastically. James, who had not picked up the sarcasm, replied that it was two forty-three. It was useful for Sven that she had remembered that incident. James stayed chatting with Kyomi until three o'clock, when he made an excuse to leave.

Kyomi decided that she might as well go to bed, since the drink was making her feel very tired. She confirmed that David then came and stayed for about an hour. During that time she heard footsteps coming up the stairs, pass her landing and continue going up.

After David left, she had only slept fitfully, with her sleep being disturbed three times. On the first occasion she heard footsteps outside her room, which gradually faded as whoever it was moved farther away. She was too drunk to tell if they were above and going up, or below and going down, or starting from the same level and going either up or down. All that she could be sure about was that they did not pass her landing, either from above going down or from below coming up.

The second disturbance was a few minutes after that when she felt a very cold draught. Perhaps it was the ghost, she thought. The final disturbance was a little later, after she had fallen asleep. It was already light outside. Again it was footsteps going away from her room. She also heard the extractor fan from one the toilets, so she knew whoever it was went downstairs.

Alicia went to bed by herself in the Bodmin Room at one-thirty. She told a weird story about drifting off to sleep, but then being woken with a start. It was getting light, but the room was semi-dark, apart from a shard of light coming through the gap in the curtains. She sat up feeling freezing cold and looked across the room. She said that she felt terrified, although she did not know why.

Now here was the weird bit. There was a tall, bearded man beckoning to her. Although the door was closed he appeared to be standing in the doorway. For reasons she could not explain she looked at her watch. It had an LED display so she was able to read it clearly as four thirty-eight. She looked back to the door, but the man had gone. She turned on the light to look around and went over to the door, where she felt even colder. Her concentration was broken by the sound of somebody being sick in the bathroom below. She heard footsteps on her landing, then a door open and close.

She settled back into bed, trying to warm herself. Although she was successful, the cold had given her the need to relieve herself. She went to the toilet where she could smell disinfectant. At least whoever was sick had had the manners to clear up after him or herself. She then went back to bed.

The next thing she heard was Carole banging on her door. Carole told her that David had found Laura dead outside on the rocks. She went with Carole up to the Truro Room, where Todd and Scarlett were comforting David. Kyomi and James came in and confirmed that Laura was dead. James explained that she appeared to have fallen off the balcony and fractured her skull.

Todd and Scarlett were the next to leave the group at just after two o'clock. They said that they had gone to bed together in the Truro Room. Todd said that the music went off soon after they left the lounge. The two of them had made love before he had drifted off to sleep. He reported hearing various sets of footsteps going up and down outside the room but paid little attention to them. The next thing he remembered was being woken at eight-thirty by David banging on the door.

Scarlett also talked about the footsteps, but her story was no more illuminating than Todd's. Sven found it most frustrating that he had no independent corroboration or proof of their stories, which separately had been quite consistent.

Carole left the party at ten past two to go to bed in the Penzance Room. She told James to follow her at three o'clock and to make sure the coast was clear so that it was not obvious that they intended to spend the night together. She remembered that she had not got a dressing gown, which she might require in case she needed to go to the bathroom. She therefore went to see Laura to borrow something, asking for something sexy for James to take off. Laura was too worried about her Japanese silk dressing gown to lend it, so Carole was given her bathrobe instead.

When she got to Laura's room, she found her to be very upset about how things had gone with David during the evening. She was crying and chastising herself for being mean to him. She did not know what to do. Carole stayed talking to Laura for a little less than half an hour, going over the evening with her, listening to her views of what should have happened, trying to explain how David might feel, agreeing that Kyomi was the real culprit but still blaming David for giving in to her. By the time Carole left, Laura was much calmer and resolved to deal with the issue in the morning. She was even beginning to blame David again.

Carole got back to the Penzance Room about twenty minutes before James arrived. She wanted to appear sexy for him, but did not want to risk her new silk outfit by lying around in it. She decided on a compromise. She removed the trousers, hung them up carefully in the wardrobe and sat cross-legged on the bed. She checked herself out in the mirror. Yes, that would have the right impact. James tapped gently on the door at one minute past three. Clearly the boy was keen. She called softly for him to come in.

James came in and quietly shut the door. He was carrying his jacket over his shoulder and his tie was loosened around his collar. He hung his jacket in the wardrobe and carefully removed his shoes, taking care not to make a sound as he placed them in the wardrobe.

"Not undressed and in bed yet," he observed.

"I thought you might like to do that," she replied provocatively.

Carole decided that it was time to excite him a little. She called him over to the bed, where she removed his tie and unbuttoned his shirt and gently removed it. Before he could start on her she undid the belt of his trousers, unzipped them and allowed them to fall to the ground. As he stepped out of his trousers and stood there in his boxer shorts, she thought that she would then give James a chance to undress her.

"You can examine me now, Doctor," she whispered seductively as she passed him the end of her belt. He took it and pulled gently. The belt untied, coming away in his hand as the red silk jacket fell open.

James looked in awe at the deep cleavage he saw before him. He had been asking himself ever since he first saw her in that outfit, back in her bedroom, whether or not she was wearing a bra. His conclusion, which was that she was not, reached after an evening of deliberation, was proved correct.

He pushed the jacket gently off her shoulders to reveal those wonderful breasts that he had been so itching to see ever since he met her. He did not care now that he had not found a mirror seven hours earlier. She slipped out of the jacket, laying it carefully on the chair beside the bed before moving across the bed to him. She sat on the edge of the bed and put her arms around his neck. He kissed her full on the lips as he forced her back on to the bed and knelt across her. He made as to give her breasts an examination for lumps, but there was no need. The texture was firm and healthy and very much to his liking. He squeezed them, kissed them, sucked them, bit them and then went back and did the same all over again. He had waited a long time for this moment and was going to take the maximum pleasure out of it, in the knowledge that she would be enjoying it as well.

"Will I live, Doctor?" she enquired seductively.

"I will need to make a more extensive examination," he replied as he started sliding her knickers down. She lifted her buttocks so that he could pull them right down her legs and remove them. He added, "I might need to give you a course of injections."

"A course!" she replied in mock surprise as she pulled at his boxers. "That confident, are we?"

As James lay there exhausted, drifting into sleep—or had he already fallen asleep?; he could not be sure—he heard Carole pick up and put on the bathrobe. She got up quietly and left the room without turning on the light. It was already dawning so she had enough light to get around. Carole returned ten minutes later. She slipped off the bathrobe and slid into the bed with her back to James. Her feet were freezing and he could smell disinfectant on her.

"Are you all right?" he enquired.

"Too much to drink; serves me right," she replied.

"Come for a cuddle," James suggested, pulling her into him and wrapping his arms around her. One hand fell on to her breasts while the other slid down her abdomen, coming to rest between her legs. Although tempted, neither of them had the energy for further love play. They both fell asleep.

They were awakened by frantic knocking on the door and Kyomi shouting, "James, James, wake up! It's Laura."

Still drowsy and with his head thumping, James grabbed his trousers, slipped them on and went to the door. Kyomi dragged him out, pulling him downstairs to where the front door was open.

James's and Carole's accounts of their night together had been totally consistent. James also described the time from when he left the lounge until he arrived at the Penzance Room at three o'clock. At two-thirty he had been left alone with David and was checking that he was all right. He concluded that David had just had too much to drink, so he had to sleep it off. James had found a blanket and thrown it over David.

He was intending to wait there until three before going to see Carole, but Kyomi had come back. She said she would look after David and that he could go to bed. He was a bit dumbfounded and did not know what to do. Kyomi had said that the St Ives Room was free. He decided that she had guessed what was going on, so he just followed her suggestion. She came back to the St Ives Room at about a quarter to three. He knew because he was checking the time to make sure that he did not spoil the plan he had prearranged with Carole. He made small talk with Kyomi until three before he made his excuse to leave, just as Kyomi had said.

Sven noted to himself that James was probably the only one who had spent time with Kyomi who had not observed how pretty she was. Clearly he had his mind on somebody else. Carole explained that in the ten minutes that she was away from James she went downstairs because she was feeling unwell. She had opened the door to get some fresh air in an attempt to stave off the sickness, but it had not worked. She rushed to the toilet to be sick and cleaned up with disinfectant. She then returned to James, who confirmed that he had smelled the disinfectant.

Nick confessed that soon after midnight he realised that he had had far too much to drink. He staggered downstairs to the first of the toilets, where he had been sick and passed out. The next thing he remembered was waking up when everything was quiet. He felt awful, but had enough presence of mind to wipe around the toilet, flush it and then clean himself. His head was thumping. It was still dark, but other than that he had no idea what time it was. He staggered back to the lounge, found the sleeping bag under the sofa and crawled into it. He placed himself behind the sofa, which shielded his eyes from the moonlight.

His headache eased sufficiently to allow him to drift off to sleep. He vaguely remembered hearing somebody coming into the lounge, but did not bother to stir to see who it was. He was woken at eight-thirty by the sound of somebody banging on a door downstairs. An hysterical voice was shouting that Laura was dead and was calling for James. He went downstairs to see what was going on. He found David outside the Truro Room talking to Todd, who was standing just inside the open door. Kyomi was standing at the door to the St Ives Room. He observed that she looked just as good in the morning. What was it about this girl that made every man comment on her looks?

That accounted for all those present when Laura went to bed. Sven's mind then turned to the three female pharmacy students, Angela, Beth and Claire, and to their boyfriends. What could he draw from the recollections of three couples who had drunk copious amounts of alcohol and were more interested in each other than what they had heard go bump in the night? He turned over in his mind what they had said. Andrew and Angela were awakened during the night by what sounded like the door opening. It was already getting light. They spoke of a cold draught coming under the door, which they put down to the outside door being opened. The two of them snuggled together and went back to sleep. Beth said that she had opened the window before she and Brian went to bed. Soon after she had fallen asleep she was awakened by what sounded like a thud outside. She sat up, but did not turn on the light for fear of waking Brian. He did not hear anything. Claire also reported being woken by a thud, which Chris did not hear. Her sleep was also disturbed at dawn by somebody being sick in the toilets. Whoever it was sounded really ill. Chris had also slept through that.

Sven turned the statements over in his mind. He knew that at least one of them was not telling the truth. Whether by accident or intent, the responsibility for Laura's death lay with one or more of them, but with whom, and why? What of John's death? Was that natural causes or was it linked to Laura's death? He could surmise as much as he liked, but what he really needed was some more evidence to go on.

Chapter 11

Yet more routine police work

Sven had not noticed time pass as he had been turning things over and over in his mind. He heard the door unlock. It was Edward returning from the solicitors. Edward came into the lounge armed with two cups of tea.

"What news, my friend?" Sven asked as Edward settled into the armchair opposite him. Edward explained that he had been trying to deal with John's affairs. The Trelawny Memorial Hospital, where John died, had requested a post-mortem but had not yet released the results, so the solicitor could not get a death certificate.

Edward observed, "You are more likely to get the results, since they said they would release them to the detective in charge. Just ask Peters to get a note of authority from Peter Pinks. There is not much else to report. John's solicitor said that he would phone tomorrow to give me more details. I asked him to get the will ready for the police. I assume that you will want to send somebody to interview him about that? Now what news do you have for me?" Sven took Edward through the statements and the lack of any conclusions he had been able to reach. "Seems like we need some more facts," Edward observed, confirming Sven's conclusions. With that Sven left to attend a meeting of the detectives that he had arranged for that afternoon.

Peters, Jenkins and Orchard were working away in the incident room when Sven arrived. As they gathered for their meeting, Peters observed the formalities that Chief Inspector Graves had put in place, saying, "Inspector Pinks sends his apologies, asks that we should carry on without him. Over to you, Sven."

"Thank you, George," Sven replied, "then let us do just that. Perhaps you would like to start?"

Peters described his morning at the College Hospital in Penzance, where he had obtained preliminary reports from the doctor conducting the post-mortem on Laura Hamilton. James Cross had formally certified Laura as dead where she was discovered, at eight thirty-three on June 30th. There was a fracture at the right rear of her skull caused by a single blow, either from a blunt instrument or impact of a rock. From the width of the depression in the skull, twenty-one millimetres, and the length, one hundred and two millimetres, the examiner thought it more likely that the blow came from a fashioned piece than a jagged rock. There was a second fracture, to the left cheekbone, fifty-five millimetres long in an irregular line, which was probably caused by a fall. There were further fractures: two to the left upper arm and one to the left collarbone. Her body had multiple bruising on the upper left side. There were abrasions on her breasts, stomach, abdomen and fronts of her thighs consistent with the body having scraped against a hard metallic surface. Tiny fragments of paint and rusty metal were found in some of the abrasions.

The cause of death was internal bleeding from multiple injuries. The injuries on the left-hand side of the body were consistent with a fall, with impact on the upper left, probably face-first. The blow on the right side of the skull was inconsistent with the fall. The amount of blood around this wound was greater, which strongly suggested that it was made first. The examiner had summed up his preliminary finding by saying that although he could not be sure, it was likely that the blow to the right rear of the skull preceded the injuries from a fall. He believed that the blow knocked her unconscious but did not kill her. The fall did not kill her either. She died later from multiple injuries, between two and four-thirty on the morning of 30 June 1996, with his best guess being that she died fifteen minutes to an hour after she fell. The pathologist also said that Laura Hamilton was about twelve weeks pregnant.

Peters then turned to Jenkins, saying, "Constable Jenkins went to Trelawny

Memorial Hospital in Truro to get some preliminary findings from Dr. Brian Davidson, the pathologist who is conducting the post-mortem on John Hamilton." Constable Jenkins summarised these findings. The only evidence of external injury was bruising to the right temple. This was superficial and did not cause death or serious injury. The bruising was consistent with a fall as John Hamilton fainted, which was described by Miss Rowntree in her statement to the police. Death was caused by heart failure induced by the intake of strychnine poison. Blood analysis showed a level just above that normally considered lethal for a healthy adult. The poison would have been ingested between two and four hours before death. A significant volume of alcohol and a meal taken around the same time that the strychnine was ingested would have slowed the effect, so the examiner estimated the latest time of ingestion to be two hours before death, with three hours before being the most likely. Blood analysis revealed an alcohol level of one hundred and fifty milligrams per millilitre of blood, which is equivalent to having eight to twelve standard drinks. The pathologist also observed that the condition of the liver and analysis of the liver cells indicated that Hamilton was a heavy drinker, but that this condition was not life-threatening and did not contribute to his death.

After Jenkins had finished, everybody looked to Orchard, who began his report. He had been searching the records for any evidence of criminal activity by any of the guests at the party or either of the victims. Orchard began to recount his findings: "Well, there are four of them with form, but it does not really amount to much. When he was eighteen, Todd Mitchell was convicted of causing actual bodily harm when he got into a fight outside a pub in Penzance. He got a fine and a six-month suspended sentence for that. He was cautioned a couple of times for affray when he was sixteen. David Stevens was involved in the same incident that Mitchell was done for and he was convicted of affray. Both have stayed out of trouble since. Nick Dean has been cautioned twice for the possession of marijuana, both in the last six months. He was also convicted for supplying to a classmate last year. Alicia Adams was arrested for obstruction at a peaceful animal rights protest at Penzance College last year, but was released without charge."

That was the extent of the criminal past that he had found for any of them, but then his face lit up as he began to describe his other find. "You remember that cracker, Kyomi Taylor."

Sven came in wearily, "It would seem that all the men did." He looked around to see smiles from Jenkins and Peters and realised that they were with Orchard on this point.

Orchard continued, "I thought that I had seen her before. Well, you don't forget a figure like that in a hurry, do you? Anyway, I was right. I have only just moved into CID from traffic. Last New Year's Day at six-thirty in the morning we were called to the scene of an accident. A milkman had found a dead motorcyclist on a quiet road outside St. Ives. From his injuries we deduced that his motorcycle had been in collision with another vehicle that had not stopped. He had probably been there for several hours. If he had been treated immediately, then he would probably have survived. Instead he bled to death from his injuries.

"Well, the motorcyclist was Peter Taylor, Kyomi Taylor's brother. We had to go round to tell his relatives. That was where I saw her. She told us that just before the accident Taylor had been at a New Year's party with her then-boyfriend, Darron Anders. So I went to see Anders and he confirmed what she said and also that they were all drinking heavily. He said he had tried to stop Taylor from riding the bike but Taylor insisted. Despite this, Kyomi had blamed him for her brother's death and had dumped him. He was upset about that and had tried to get back with her."

Orchard then added with a smile, "Well, who wouldn't? Anyway, she had none of it, and as far as he knew she had not had a boyfriend since. He said she changed from an outgoing, fun-loving girl to something approaching a recluse. Anders did not stop there. He told me that Peter Taylor had been going out with Carole Young, but they broke it off when Taylor decided to tour the world. He offered to take Carole with him but she decided to stay working at the Lighthouse Inn. Something about not letting her half-sister Alicia gain an advantage over her at the hotel. Anders did not know the fine details."

Sven summed up what he had heard. "So we have John Hamilton, whom we know likes a drink and is prepared to drive over the limit. We also hear again of this tension between the two half-sisters who run the Lighthouse Inn with their mother. Orchard, you did well getting that information out of Anders. How would you like to find out more about John Hamilton and his drinking habits from some of the regulars at the Lighthouse Inn? See if you can get any of them to open up a bit. And please, gentlemen, not a word of this to Inspector Hamilton. If anyone is going to tackle that with him, it is going to be me. Jenkins, would you interview the manager of the Ship Hotel to find out what that bit of business was that Miss Rowntree talked about, please? You might also ask her if John Hamilton made a habit of drinking and driving. After that, would you get the will for John Hamilton and also see if Laura made one, please? Inspector Hamilton has already talked to the solicitor, so he should be expecting a visit from us. George, you and I will visit Penzance College tomorrow. I should like to understand how well the Poisons Research Unit controls its stocks. Oh, and for the record, also give Inspector Pinks a briefing on how things are going, please."

The meeting broke up, leaving Sven to plan his next day. Just as he was about to leave, Edward Hamilton telephoned him. "Just wanted to confirm when you were coming back tonight. Rose wants to know when to get supper. Don't try to say not to bother because she insists. I think it helps take her mind off things. Also both girls are home tonight, so we will make a bit of a family thing about it." Sven thanked him and confirmed that he was on his way.

After dinner, as she and Sven were clearing the table, Sarah asked Sven for a confidential word. She said that she had some information that she had told Jenny. Jenny had advised her that it was not appropriate to talk to their father, since he was not on the case. Jenny said that she could tell Sven, but it would be better if Sarah gave a first hand account. "I will be taking the dog for a walk after we have cleared up. Please volunteer to come with me." Sven agreed, and half an hour later found him walking along the beach with Sarah in the late evening sunshine.

"Well, what is on your mind, my dear?" he enquired in his best English, avuncular fashion. Sarah explained that out of respect for Laura's reputation, she had not told the police everything. She was now concerned that what she had held back might be relevant, so she really had to tell him. During the party she had gone to Laura's room to do some marking. She had been working for about half an hour when Laura burst in, in floods of tears. She said that the whole world was against her. As Sarah comforted her, she blurted out the whole story. She said that David was flirting with Kyomi and did not love her anymore.

Sarah told her that she was just being silly and that she should not spoil her own party. It was then that she dropped the bombshell. She confessed that she could not be sure that the baby was David's because she had a one-night stand with Nick at a party on the fourth of April. That was during the time when she might have conceived. Sarah had promised that she would not tell anybody and eventually persuaded her to go back to the party.

"Did you ask Laura if she had told Nick?" Sven asked. Sarah replied that she had asked and Laura said that she had not told Nick. She pointed out that he would have found out at the party, though, after the row that Laura had with her father.

Chapter 12

Poisons and Controls, 3rd July 1996

Mrs. Marlow extended her right hand to Sergeant Peters as she approached him and Sven in the foyer of the pharmacy building of Penzance College. "Sergeant Peters?" she began, waiting to see which of the two reacted.

Peters shook her hand and introduced himself and Sven, adding, "I trust that you have no objection to Mr. Ffolkes's presence during our discussions?"

Mrs. Marlow's reply was quick and firm. "Not a bit of it; the more brainpower we have to attempt to resolve this dreadful matter with poor Laura, the better." She escorted the two policemen to her office, sat them in chairs opposite her desk and said, "How can the college help you gentlemen?"

Peters turned to Sven, who said, "We should like to talk to you a little about Laura, and then perhaps you would allow us to inspect your facilities for handling poisons?"

"Certainly," Mrs. Marlow replied. "I can talk to you about Laura and arrange for you to talk to Dr. Jones the poisons. Let me see if I can arrange that straight away." She picked up the phone and began dialling, but continued talking as she waited for a response. "Dr. Jones is the head of our Poisons Research Unit. We set it up eighteen months ago. We were lucky to get Dr.

Jones. He is considered a leading authority on poisons. He came to us from the Hawks School of Tropical Medicine in Kuala Lumpa."

She broke off her explanation when the phone was answered at the other end. "Hello, Dr. Jones? Yes, I have the police with me now." With that she turned back to Sven. "In half an hour, will that be all right?"

Sven nodded as he replied, "Yes, thank you, that will be fine."

Mrs. Marlow returned to the telephone conversation. "Half an hour is fine, thank you; we will see you then. Goodbye."

With that she put down the phone, clasped her hands together over the desk and, looking at Sven, continued, "Now about Laura Hamilton, what can I tell you, Inspector Ffolkes, Sergeant Peters?"

Again it was Sven who responded, "How was Miss Hamilton doing with her studies?"

Mrs. Marlow turned to the screen on her desk, saying, "Well, let's have a look, shall we?" She then keyed in some instructions and waited for a couple of seconds before continuing, "Ah yes, here she is, Laura Hamilton. Attendance, very good. She did not miss a single class up until Easter, but has been a bit erratic since. She missed four 9 a.m. lectures in April, but has been back to normal since. Coursework, again very good, she got B+, B and B for the autumn term's work and A-, B+ and B+ in the spring term. There have been two pieces of work due for this term where she got C- and B. The first of those pieces was handed in late, which is why the mark was down."

Peters came in, "When was that piece due in, please?"

Mrs. Marlow checked the screen, hit a key and then relied, "April 21st, and it was handed in on May 6th." As she finished talking a printer behind her sprung into action, producing two pages of text. Mrs. Marlow turned around, picked them up, quickly checked them over and then passed them to Sergeant Peters, adding, "Here are the details for you to peruse at your leisure. Would you please give me a police receipt for them, because they are confidential and would not normally be given out to anybody other than Miss Hamilton or her parents."

"Certainly," Sergeant Peters replied. "I will do that right away."

While Peters was writing the receipt, Sven continued with his questions. "There appears to have been a sudden dip in her performance recently. Did you investigate that?"

Mrs. Marlow appeared surprised by the question. "No," she replied. "It would take a bigger fall in performance for that to have come to my attention. In terms of her marks, it could have just been a topic of which she was unsure. Our students cannot be expected to excel at everything, and all these marks are passes. Until now I had not made any connection between the timing of the poorer marks and these missed lectures. Clearly if she missed the lectures then it is probably not surprising that it took her a lot longer to get the work in. The lateness alone would account for the lower mark. Why, do you think there was anything that happened to her at that time, because her marks rapidly came back to normal?"

Sven did not answer the question but instead asked one of his own. "Did you or any of your staff notice any change in her at the time?"

Mrs. Marlow's response this time was more guarded. "Well, I did not, but that is perhaps not too surprising, because I have relatively little contact with the students unless they are failing, which Miss Hamilton certainly was not."

As she was speaking she turned back to her screen and typed in more instructions. "Let's see what her course tutor had to say. Ah, here are the two term reports from Dr. Jones." She perused the screen for a moment before declaring, "Nothing to worry about here. Both say how well she was doing and how interested she was in her work. Of course the report for the summer term is not due yet, and from what we have seen that is when the drop in performance occurred."

The printer sprang into life again, producing two further sheets of paper, which Mrs. Marlow handed to Peters. "Would that be the same Dr. Jones that we are going to meet in a short while?" Sven enquired.

Mrs. Marlow smiled, replying, "Yes, that would appear to be a fortunate coincidence. Why don't you ask him if he had any concerns for this term? Meanwhile are there any other questions for me, or should I take you to Dr. Jones now?"

Sven turned to Peters, who nodded to confirm that he had finished, and then replied, "Thank you, Mrs. Marlow, you have been most helpful. Would you take us to Dr. Jones, please?"

The two men found themselves sitting in a small office in front of a desk that was strewn with papers. Mrs. Marlow had left them there with the comment, "Dr. Jones will not be long."

A screensaver was playing on the computer screen that sat on the desk. As Peters put his notebook on the desk it happened to nudge the mouse, causing the screen to change display to a series of file names. They recognised the names of all the pharmacy students amongst them. Both men looked at each other in surprise at the apparent lack of security. Peters tried the file on Laura Hamilton, which opened, revealing her coursework marks, term reports and lecture attendance. There was a separate file entitled "TUTOR1" covering the students for whom Dr. Jones was the course tutor. Peters discovered that he was also the tutor of Nick Dean and that they shared tutorials at 5 p.m. on Tuesdays and Fridays. Peters had to abandon his examination when he heard footsteps outside.

Both men stood up as Jones entered the office. Sven made sure that his papers were seen to move the mouse to ensure that Jones would not expect to see the screensaver. Jones held out his hand to Peters and greeted both men. "Good afternoon, gentlemen. Adrian Jones. Please be seated. I believe that you have come to talk to me about Laura Hamilton. Such a sad business, and to happen to one so young is tragic. Now what can I tell you?"

Peters introduced Sven and himself and asked to be shown the poisons register and cabinet. "Surely you do not suspect our poisons were used. Anyway, I was told that Laura had died from a fall from the lighthouse."

Sven's reply was methodical. "Dr. Jones, I will answer all your questions, but not necessarily in the order that you proposed them. Yes, Miss Hamilton did fall from the lighthouse and indeed that was a tragedy. To make matters worse, her father has also died, and in his case we suspect that poison was the cause. We need to find the source of that poison, and for that we must look to all reasonable sources, of which your laboratory is but one. I have an open mind as to whether it is the source and would, if possible, like to eliminate it from our enquiries."

Jones was clearly shocked by this news. After taking time for the information to sink in, he replied, "Geez, that is a sad state of affairs. I had no idea that her father had died as well. What must her poor mother be going through? Anyway, I will show you our poisons procedure. I am sure nothing could have gone astray with our system. Please, come this way."

He motioned the two policemen to leave his office and led them down a corridor to a door that read "Poisons Research Unit." He swiped a card through the locking device and keyed in a number. Sven watched carefully as he went through the process. The three men entered the laboratory and proceeded past all the animal cages to the storeroom at the back of the laboratory. The two assistants in the laboratory continued with their work as Jones unlocked the door to the storeroom, again using his card and a keyed number. Inside the store a laboratory steward was unpacking a delivery of chemicals and placing them on shelves.

Jones addressed his opening remarks to the laboratory steward. "Mr. Edwards, these gentlemen are from the police. They have come to examine our poisons handling procedure."

Edwards smiled as he replied, "Well, that's good timing, sir. I have just received a batch of poisons from the snake-milking unit that I need to log and store. That should demonstrate our system quite well."

Jones turned to Sven, saying, "I will describe the process as we do it. This will show you the poisons receipt process, after which I can describe the difference for poison return and destruction. Will that meet your needs?"

Both Sven and Peters nodded, so Jones continued, "It requires both of us to be present before any delivery of poisons is opened. It fact, it requires both of us for most actions in relation to poisons. I will describe the steps that we take from initial receipt of a package of poisons from the courier. By the way, we never receive poisons through the post."

Jones began counting the steps on his fingers as he spoke. "Firstly, we check the package for any sign of damage or tampering. The person receiving the package, who is normally Mr. Edwards or myself, does this check. My assistants, Mary Wells and Diane Fielding, have been trained in the procedure and can sign for poisons in our absence, but as an additional precaution we require both of them to be present and to sign for poisons. If there is no sign of damage, then the received package is locked in this cupboard, which is separate from the main poison cupboard, until we are ready to unpack it. There are two keys to this cupboard, one held by me and the other by Mr. Edwards. If our assistants have to receive a package, then they will be issued with one of our keys, for which they must sign. The key is signed back to us when it is returned. The key-signature book is kept locked in the cupboard." Jones pointed to a single cabinet with a locked steel door located underneath the bench.

"If the parcel shows any signs of damage or tampering, then the courier's driver is made aware of it. The courier's office is advised by telephone at the time and the receipt is annotated before it is signed. We also contact the supplier immediately. Both the courier's staff and ours always wear disposable gloves when handling these packages in case of leaks. After use they are placed in the contaminated waste. Should we suspect that a damaged parcel might be dangerous, for example if there is fluid leaking from it, then we would immediately place it in an isolation bin like this, lock that in the cupboard and call the supplier."

Jones pointed to a thick cylindrical cardboard drum about twelve inches in diameter and eighteen inches deep, labelled "Isolation Bin," which was sitting under the bench. He took it out and removed the top to reveal about six inches of sawdust at the bottom of an otherwise empty container.

"Fortunately we have never had to use this procedure, as all the packages that we have received have been undamaged. The next step is to open the package, check and store the poisons and enter them all in the poisons book. We will demonstrate that to you now."

Jones and Edwards unlocked the poison cupboard locks with their separate keys and removed a book labelled "Poisons Register" from inside. Edwards opened the book at the next page, entered both his and Jones's names and signed the book. He then passed it to Jones, who also signed it. Before opening the package, Edwards removed the invoice from the front of the parcel and entered into the book the contents, by type and volume, that the package was purported to contain. He filed the invoice in a ring binder entitled "Poison Invoices." He then opened the package and removed the contents one at a time, checked each of them for loss and damage, confirming with Jones that they were undamaged, and placed them in their allocated positions in the poisons cupboard. Where poisons of the same type were already present in the cupboard, he made sure that the new stock was placed behind the existing stock. Both men then signed against the entry in the poison book. It was clear to Sven that they had performed this routine many times before. After all the poisons had been logged, Edwards drew a thick line under the last entry and drew diagonal lines across the rest of the page. He left just sufficient room for both men to sign at the bottom of the page, under the title "Final Check."

Jones then turned to the policemen, asking, "Before we complete this procedure, would you like to examine the book?" Immediately Sven took up this offer. Even before Jones could respond, Edwards opened a drawer and asked Sven to take a pair of disposable surgical gloves.

Jones came in to reassure Sven, "Just a precaution in case anything has rubbed off on the book."

"Very wise," Sven responded as he put on the gloves and then checked the book. Although not entirely sure what he was looking for, he flicked over the pages for anything unusual. Edwards's name appeared in virtually all the entries, mostly with that of Jones, but occasionally with Wells or Fielding. He was about to return the book when he noticed the name of Angela Palmer against an entry for 5th April 1996, for the withdrawal of strychnine. He asked Jones, "There is an entry here signed by Angela Palmer; is she the same lady who is doing first year pharmacy?"

Jones responded immediately, "Yes, she is very interested in the work of the Poisons Research Unit and asked if she could have some temporary work for the holidays. We gave her a trail this Easter and she will be coming back to work for us during the summer. She is a smart young lady and fitted in very well with the rest of the team."

Sven thanked him for the explanation, returned the book to Edwards and then asked, "Would you describe the poison destruction process now, please?"

Jones removed a file binder from the shelf as he replied, "Yes, certainly, this is the instruction book that describes the process for making each poison harmless. Again it takes two of us to sign the book confirming the destruction. Usually Mr. Edwards performs the destruction, witnessed by the person who originally signed for the poison. This is one way that they can demonstrate that they have properly dealt with what they have signed for. The other way is to produce notes of how the poison was used, and if on any animals then a video reference should also be included."

"What about poisons that are in use for experiments?" Sven enquired. "How are they kept overnight?"

Jones hesitated before replying, "We try to avoid withdrawing more poison from the cupboard than we intend to use on that day. I would much rather see several small withdrawals made day after day than see one larger one. We allow unopened packs, for example, sealed ampoules, to be returned, but opened material must be destroyed. No poison should be left overnight, but I know that there have been exceptions. Each member of the team has a dedicated drawer that he or she can lock, and I know that occasionally poisons are locked in drawers overnight. I have done it myself on occasions when I am working late. If Mr. Edwards has gone home, then I cannot return the poison to the cupboard and there may be nobody else around to confirm safe destruction."

Sven nodded as he turned this information over in his mind. Peters came in with his own question, directed at Jones. "Can you tell me what Angela Palmer was using the strychnine for?"

Jones did not need to think about his answer. "Yes, we have a programme that is looking at possible antidotes for common poisons, one of which is strychnine. We test them by mixing them with the strychnine and examining the effects. The more promising antidotes are tested on rats. As a byproduct we are also trying to find a way of destroying strychnine that does not require us to incinerate it. I will get the notes for that particular withdrawal for you." Jones noted on a scrap of paper the entry reference number and date from the poison register. He then placed the paper in his pocket, adding, "We will look at that back in my office where I have access to the computer. Is there anything else that I can help you with here?"

Sven asked, "Are there any keys to the poisons cupboard other than those held by Mr. Edwards and yourself?"

"Yes, there is a duplicate of each key held in a secure location known only to

Mr. Edwards and myself. Even the head of the pharmacy unit does not know that location."

Peters asked, "Will you tell me that location, please, sir?" Recognising that Jones was reluctant, he continued, "We have to know, sir, so that we can eliminate those keys as a potential source of exposure."

Jones still hesitated, but the replied in a whisper, "Yes, I understand. They are held in the safe at the Penzance branch of the college's bank. If ever they are required, which to date they have not been, then they would need to be signed for by either the college bursar or the principal himself."

Peters replied, "Thank you, sir, I understand the need for security, and you may rest assured that this information will remain confidential."

Jones responded with his voice showing a little impatience, "Thank you, Sergeant. Can we now leave Mr. Edwards to get on with his work?"

Sven and Peters checked with each other before Sven confirmed, "Yes, I think that is all for here. Thank you, Mr. Edwards. Perhaps we could return to your office then, Dr. Jones?"

Edwards replied, "Glad to be of help, sir. I hope you find out who committed this terrible crime. Just as a precaution, gentlemen, would you wash your hands as you leave the unit, please?" Jones also thanked Edwards as he showed Sven and Peters to the wash room and then back to his office.

Once in his office, Jones asked the two officers to be seated, removed the scrap of paper from his pocket and then turned to his computer. After a short search, he said, "Ah, here it is. Entry 171, dated 5th April 1996, used by Angela Palmer on the strychnine antidote and destruction sub-programme. Fifty-milligram unit withdrawn, ten milligrams mixed with each of agents A to E and the resulting mixtures tested, using infrared, nuclear magnetic resonance and mass spectrometry. In each case no reaction was observed. Residues placed in the poison waste container for destruction."

"Poison waste?" Peters questioned. "I do not recall your mentioning that in any procedure."

Jones appeared surprised. "Sorry, I thought I had. Waste from any tests is placed in a plastic-lined cardboard container, which is incinerated at the end of each day. Edwards does that, witnessed by me or one of the assistants. It is entered in the book. I thought that you had seen it."

Sven came in, "Yes, I did see those entries. Perhaps now we can talk about Laura Hamilton. I believe that you were her course tutor. How was she doing?"

"Yes, she and Nick Dean were assigned to me," Jones replied. "We had tutorials on Wednesdays and Fridays at five o'clock. She was a good student, always there on the dot, which is more that I can say for Nick. He attended when he felt like it, although there was a period of about three weeks when he attended regularly and on time. I think that Laura had something to do with that because they arrived and left together. Laura would nearly always get her work in on time as well. The piece due in after Easter was late, but that seemed to be a glitch. After that the work came in on time again."

"Did she seem upset recently or was anything out of the ordinary?" Peters enquired.

Jones gave the question due consideration before replying, "The only thing was around Easter and that piece of coursework. She did not appear to be quite her normal self. Although she attended all the tutorials, she did miss a couple of my early morning lectures. She apologised both times and asked for copies of the notes, which I ran off for her. She seemed to be over all that though and told me how much she was looking forward to her party. She even said that she would bring in a piece of her birthday cake for me. Yes, I would say she was right back to her normal self. I don't know what it was that upset her, but she seemed to have got over it."

Sven stated that he had completed his questions and thanked Jones for his time. Jones escorted the two men back to reception. As he was saying his farewell, Sven enquired casually, "If you do not mind my asking, would you be aged forty-one or forty-two by any chance?"

"My word, you are a good judge of age," Jones replied. "I am forty-two next week, and here is me thinking that I looked younger."

Peters and Sven discussed the visit as they drove back to the police station. Peters commented, "I know how you pulled that age trick. I was able to read his pass number over his shoulder as well. 1954, wasn't it? I wonder how many others have done what you and I did. I don't suppose that he changes it that often, either."

Sven agreed and also pointed out other ways by which poison could have been got out of the unit without the fact being recorded. He said, "While we were coming back to his office, I asked him when he last audited the contents of the cabinet against the register. It came as quite a shock to him. He said that he had never done an audit but would conduct one as soon as he could and telephone the results through to me. In the meantime would you check out with the bank whether those keys have ever been requested, or indeed how good their security is? I suspect that it will be much better though."

Chapter 13

Motive and opportunity

Sven's list of guests with a motive for killing either Laura or John was growing. He had no choice but to have the team interview all of them further about these motives. He asked Sergeant Peters and Constable Jenkins to organise interviews with Todd Mitchell, Scarlett Robinson, David Stevens, James Cross, Nick Dean and the three couples from the pharmacy class. He scheduled himself to interview Jean Young, Carole Young and Alicia Adams. Since he did not trust any of them to be objective about Kyomi Taylor, he also elected to interview her himself.

He telephoned Kyomi, asking her to come in to clarify a few points. She arrived at the police station with her mother and was met by WPC Deborah Hayes, who was to attend throughout. Sven listened to the conversation that occurred between the three of them before he met Kyomi. WPC Hayes showed her to the interview room.

Mrs. Taylor followed instinctively, but Kyomi turned to her, saying "It's all right, Mum, I can handle this by myself." Mrs. Taylor was worried and urged Kyomi to let her remain, but Kyomi was adamant. Her voice displayed both strain and insistence as she replied, "Mother, I agreed that you could come with me because you were worried, even though I felt quite happy coming alone, but please now leave me to get on with it." Since she was over eighteen, WPC Hayes did not insist, instead offering Mrs. Taylor a cup of tea and somewhere comfortable to wait. Mrs. Taylor, clearly upset, declined, saying that she would take the opportunity to do some shopping and return in about an hour.

Sven went to the interview room to find Kyomi sitting at the single table, with WPC Hayes sitting in a chair in the corner of the room. For reasons of protocol he asked Orchard to join him. Orchard may have been taken by her looks but he was a good detective and would also listen to what she had to say. Sven allowed Orchard to commence the interview.

Orchard began, "Good morning, Miss Taylor, thank you for coming to see us today. This is simply a fact-finding interview and I should like to confirm with you that your attendance is voluntary. Do you understand that?" Kyomi nodded to confirm that she understood. Orchard continued, "This is my colleague, Inspector Sven Ffolkes, whom I believe you have already met. Mr. Ffolkes is from the Norwegian police force. He is on an exchange programme with the Cornwall and Islands police. Would you have any objection to his attendance at this interview and to his asking you some questions?" Again Kyomi agreed, although she appeared a little nervous.

Sven looked her over before he began. She was wearing a pair of jeans and a white tee-shirt. Despite this casual dress, it was clear that she had taken some trouble with her appearance. The jeans, although faded, were clean and fitted well—very well—and the tee-shirt was new. She was wearing full make-up. He was beginning to understand why the team found her so attractive. He determined to put this to the back of his mind and treat her like he treated any other suspect in a murder enquiry, which was with respect, recognising that currently she was an innocent party who had come voluntarily to help, and if he thought that she was guilty of any crime, then he would build a case against her. He started, "Are you comfortable, Miss Taylor? Would you like anything to drink before we start?"

She responded, "Yes, thank you, I am comfortable, and no, thank you, I have already been given a cup of tea. Please call me Kyomi; Miss Taylor sounds so formal."

Sven thought for a moment. Was this girl just genuinely confident or was this bravado to hide worry, or worse still, guilt? There was no doubt that she was attractive, so there was every reason for her to be at her ease, especially with young men like Orchard, but what about with him? He was approaching fifty, and although he still had all his own hair, most of it was grey and he had acquired additional girth. Not exactly the sort that a teenager would fancy, although the converse would not necessarily be true. How did she view him? Would she see him as just another dirty old man or would she respect or even fear his experience and intellect? Her demeanour betrayed neither.

Having gained nothing through observation, he began his questioning. "Thank you, Kyomi, and firstly my apologies for taking you away from your studies."

He paused for a reaction and response, but it was not what he was expecting. "No problem," she replied. "The college has suspended classes to allow us all to get over Laura's death. All lectures have been cancelled for the next two weeks and we have been given more time to submit our coursework."

Sven wondered whether Kyomi was a cold fish or just somebody trying to get some semblance of normality back into her life. He decided that he could wait no longer before he broached the subject. "I know that you have told Constable Orchard about the events of the party, but I should like to ask you about your brother." He watched as her eyes began to fill with tears. Sven had suspected that this would be painful for her, so he tried to be as gentle as he could. "Please take your time in answering my questions, and if at any time you wish for a break, just let us know." Kyomi nodded but said nothing. The confidence had been replaced by sadness. Sven knew that this was no act. "Please tell me about him."

Kyomi wiped the tears from her eyes, and then her mood of sadness was replaced by pride as she began, initially in a faulty voice, but gaining coherence as she spoke, "Peter was a wonderful person. He was my big brother, my father figure and my friend all in one. He was training to be a lawyer and I know that he would have been brilliant as an advocate. He had all the natural ability to think an argument through logically and to present it with clarity. When he helped me with my homework he never just did it for me or told me what to write, but instead he explained what was important and let me present that. He was far better than my teachers. Even though he chose law, his grasp of chemistry and biochemistry was much better than mine, so I benefited from his help. I do not think I would have got to college without him, but I am determined to qualify to prove that all the time and effort that he spent with me was not wasted."

Kyomi stopped for a moment. Tears came to her eyes as she continued, the faltering voice returning, "He was taken from me through an accident that should never have happened and by a careless motorist who was more interested in saving his own licence than Peter's life." Her sadness turned to anger as she spoke. The words now came with more strength and clarity. Sven knew that he would not need to coax information out of her. She was ready to tell anybody who was prepared to listen.

Orchard was about to come in with a specific question, but Sven raised a hand to stop him. He wanted to hear it in her own words. He replied gently, "Please go on."

Kyomi continued, "Peter had just finished his degree and started his articles at Jones, McInally and Harbour in Truro. He was planning a trip around the world and had agreed a six-month sabbatical with his employer. He asked his girlfriend Carole Young to go with him, but she refused because she did not want to leave the Lighthouse Inn. Her excuse was something about not wanting to let Alicia steal a march on her. The stupid girl considered that more important than Peter. I have never seen a clearer case of bad judgement. Anyway, they agreed that since Peter was going come what may, they had little future together, so they split up. So last New Year's Eve, since Peter had no girlfriend, he and I were going to spend the evening in a pub with my then-boyfriend Darron Anders. I was not feeling very well so I cried off. Peter agreed to go anyway to make my excuses and to keep Darron company. He was like that. They did what boys do when they are by themselves. They drank too much and continued drinking until the New Year was well in and celebrated. Peter should have stayed the night or taken a taxi home, but he was sure that he was capable of driving home. Darron should have stopped him, but the wimp did not have the courage to tackle Peter. He let my dear brother drive off in the night to his death. Yet Peter did not kill himself. An evil man, who was probably also drunk, came around the corner on the wrong side of the road and hit him. To make things worse he did not even stop to see if he could help. He could have saved Peter's life rather than his precious licence."

Despite the tears rolling down her face, her demeanour was now much more confrontational. The venom in her voice betrayed a lingering hatred for the other driver, upon whom she heaped all blame. She wiped the tears from her face, sat back in her chair and composed herself. WPC Hayes poured her a glass of water from a bottle on the table beside her.

Sven decided that she had recovered sufficiently to be questioned. "Kyomi, you have now four times referred to the other driver as 'he' or 'him.' What makes you so sure that it was a man? The police were never able to identify the other driver."

"Because," she replied, "I took time to do some investigating on my own. I talked to the milkman and to a couple of the police who investigated the incident. It is amazing what a simple question and a smile will achieve."

Not from you it isn't! was the thought that went through Orchard's mind, although he decided that it was best not to state it. Concurrently the same thought and decision went through Sven's mind. Sven enquired, "So exactly what did you discover?"

A realisation dawned on Kyomi that she knew things that she should not know. "If I tell you, will you promise me that nobody will get into trouble?"

Her concern was genuine. Sven concluded that although this girl was quite prepared to use her charms to get what she wanted, she was not prepared to leave a trail of devastation in her wake. He admired that. He turned to Orchard, who nodded. Sven replied, "My dear, I am just a guest of the Cornwall and Islands police force, with no formal powers and no need to report everything I hear. Constable Orchard is investigating a murder and I am observing how he does it to aid the Norwegian police force. He has not asked you to name any names and I suspect that they would not help his investigation, so you need not fear. Pray tell me what you have discovered about Peter's death."

Sven amazed himself at how he was using his unique position to avoid difficulties in such a truly British way. Perhaps he really was learning something that would be of value in Norway. Kyomi began nervously, looking to Orchard for his assurance that he too would not cause problems for her sources. With those big blue eyes looking expectantly on him and having heard Sven's assurance, Orchard was not going to be difficult. He smiled and nodded his head to assure her.

"I talked to the milkman, who told me that he saw maroon paint on Peter's bike. He also described the two traffic policemen who attended the incident. St Ives is a relatively small community and most people know somebody who knows somebody. One of my old school friends has a boyfriend who is in Traffic Division. She was able to identify both of them from the descriptions and arranged a foursome with one of them, her boyfriend, her and me. We talked a lot that evening. From what he said I was able to piece together that the police were fairly sure that they had identified the car from the tyre tracks and the maroon paintwork. The paint was identified from shade and age testing to a type used by Jaguar between 1963 and 1964 on their Mark II range. To me a car is a means of getting from A to B. Some are bigger, faster and more comfortable than others, but according to Al...."

Kyomi's faced blushed and she hesitated as she realised that she had give away the name of the policeman. She then recovered quickly, "That's not his real name, of course. Anyway, according to Al, the Mark II is a real collector's car. He drooled over it. Apparently Inspector Morse has one? Anyway, they did a search for Maroon Mark II Jaguars of that age and visited all the owners. Most of them were undamaged and in pristine condition so could be ruled out. Ten had recent damage that might have been caused by that accident, but seven of them could account for their accidents by providing the names of the other drivers. Of the remaining three, one lived close by and the other two lived in Bristol and Manchester. None of them could prove conclusively where they were on New Year's Eve, so the police did not have enough evidence to charge anyone. The case was left open. Al was sure that it was the local man."

"Did Al tell you who the local owner of the Jaguar was?" Sven asked, being sure to keep up the pretence that Al was just a pseudonym.

"No, but he gave me enough information for me to work it out. He said that the owner's garage was on a piece of land opposite the Lighthouse Inn and right by the causeway leading to the lighthouse. I was pretty sure then who the owner was, but I confirmed my suspicions by spending an evening drinking in the Lighthouse Inn with my friend and watching the garage."

"And whose car was it?" Sven continued.

Kyomi's answer came back decisively, "John Hamilton's. He spent most of the evening drinking in the bar and then left and went straight to the garage. He drove away, although I am sure that he was over the limit."

The tone of Kyomi's voice made it clear that she was sure that Hamilton was the culprit. "Did you discuss any of this with Al?" Sven enquired.

Kyomi smiled knowingly, replying, "No, I never saw him again and I did not give him my phone number. Before you ask, no, I did not confront John Hamilton with what I knew and I did not discuss it with Laura. Whoever killed Peter, it was nothing to do with Laura so I saw no reason to upset a friend by telling her that I thought her father was a criminal."

Sven reflected for a moment on why had Kyomi volunteered that information. Was it just that an intelligent mind had followed the thinking behind the questions or was there something more sinister? Was she tackling the subject on her own terms to avoid difficult questions? He concluded that he would get little more information so determined to end the interview.

"Thank you, Kyomi, it was kind of you to take the time to come in and talk to us. Your information has been most helpful." With that WPC Hayes took Kyomi out to where her mother was waiting for her.

Sven looked over to Orchard, who responded before he could even ask the question. "Yes, Sven, I know Al. I will get all the details from him, and no, I will not shop him or let on that Miss Taylor put his name in the frame, or tell him why I am enquiring." Orchard added with a smile, "And I will not give him Miss

Taylor's phone number either. I don't really think he is her type, unlike me, of course." Orchard left the room, clearly intent on seeking Al out straight away.

The team came together that evening to discuss progress for the day. George Peters began proceedings in what was rapidly becoming a tradition: by presenting Inspector Pinks's apologies and turning the meeting over to Sven. Sven then asked him to describe how far he had got and what he had learned from the interviews that he had conducted that day. Peters began with his interview of Todd Mitchell, which he and Jenkins conducted at the Boatman's Cottage in Puddlewick.

"We took WPC Freeman with us because we knew that Scarlett Robinson was going to be there and we wanted to interview them separately. Scarlett understood and agreed to talk to WPC Freeman in the garden while we interviewed Mitchell. We concentrated on his relationship with John Hamilton and the cause of the outburst at the party. He said that John Hamilton was an evil influence on his family. He first met Hamilton when he was twelve and that was not a pleasant experience for him. It was at the time when Hamilton was having an affair with his mother. He surprised them at home on returning late on a Saturday night when he was supposed to be staying at a friend's house. He had had a fight with his friend and decided to leave. He left without telling his hosts and walked two miles through dark streets by himself. Even at the age of twelve he was independently minded and well capable of looking after himself. His mother introduced Hamilton as an old friend who just happened to be passing and dropped in to say hello. Since Mitchell's father was at sea fishing, he deduced that there was something more to it, taking an instant dislike to Hamilton in the process. Mitchell's parents separated a few months later and his father died a year after that. That cemented his hatred of Hamilton, whom he blamed for both his parents' separation and his father's death.

"He did not meet Hamilton again until he was seventeen, when Hamilton moved into the lighthouse and starting frequenting the Lighthouse Inn, which is run by his aunt, Jean Young, who is Todd's mother's sister. Todd started working part-time as a barman at the Lighthouse Inn when he was eighteen. He saw Hamilton quite regularly, but kept his peace because Jean Young warned him that she would sack him if there was any trouble. Laura's party was the first time that he had reacted, and he says he regrets his timing, although not what he said. He was very grateful to Scarlett for keeping him under control."

Sven interrupted to ask, "Did you believe him?"

Peters thought for a moment before replying. "Difficult one, that. Clearly the lad had harboured a grudge against Hamilton for some time and has now got it off his chest. He is not known for being verbally articulate so I suspect that it would have been difficult for him to lie convincingly, although again that could be an act. He also said that on Scarlett's request he tried to bury the hatchet and to some extent he succeeded. So, on balance, then yes, I think that he was telling the truth."

Sven detected that Peters was far from sure, so a second opinion would be of value. Turning to Jenkins, Sven enquired, "What do you think, Constable?"

Jenkins, who clearly was not used to having his opinion sought, stumbled on his reply, which he addressed to Sven. "Er, I agree sir, a difficult call, but I think that Sergeant Peters is right. It would have been difficult for him to fabricate that."

"Right," Sven began. "We will believe him for now, but would you please check the facts of his account with Jean Young and Gillian Mitchell? Will you arrange that in the morning, Sergeant Peters?" Peters nodded his agreement.

Sven then asked Peters if he or WPC Hayes get anything out of Scarlett Robinson. "I did not speak to her myself, but I have her statement taken by WPC Hayes," Peters replied, opening his file to obtain it. "She confirms all the points that she gave at the lighthouse last Sunday. She also confirms that she asked Todd to make his peace with Hamilton and was proud of him for having done so. WPC Hayes then asked her about the pharmacy students. The six girls get on very well together and they all attend the classes regularly. Nick Dean is struggling, not least because his attendance has been poor. He failed his mid-term exams and only scraped through at the end of the year. She said that Nick had tried to go out with most of the girls in the class, including her. She was not aware of his succeeding with any of them but could not be sure."

Sven turned to Orchard. "What have you found out today, Constable?" he asked.

Orchard got out his notebook and started, "You asked me to look at three things, sir. Firstly to check with the constable from traffic division who went out with Miss Taylor. He remembered the particular case. He was sure that Hamilton was the culprit but he could not prove it. There was damage to his Jaguar that had been cleaned off and primed to prevent it rusting. Hamilton told the police that he had hit a deer and that he had made the temporary repair to stop the bodywork rusting. Well, anybody who took as much care with an old classic like that Jaguar would, so in itself that was not suspicious. However, there were no reports of dead or injured deer that night, which, judging by the amount of damage, there should have been. It's always possible that somebody took the deer away and it ended up in a freezer. It has been known. Anyway, Hamilton had an alibi for the time. He said he was in the lighthouse asleep and that the tide was in. I checked and that is true, sir, the causeway flooded at twelve forty-five that night."

Peters came in, asking, "Who was the witness?"

"That's the point, Sergeant, it was Laura Hamilton. She said that they were both in the lighthouse that evening. Her father had insisted that she left her New Year party in time to get back over the causeway before it flooded."

Sven resisted asking the obvious question to allow Orchard to show that he had thought about his enquiry and asked the right questions. Orchard continued, "I asked him if he had told Miss Taylor that his suspect had an alibi. He said he thought he had, but he was sure that he had not said who it was or that the suspect lived in the lighthouse. So Miss Taylor might have worked it out, but she was not told it directly." Turning toward Sven, Orchard added in a note of triumph, "She did not tell us that she suspected Laura's complicity when we interviewed her, did she, sir?"

"Indeed she did not," Sven responded, making sure that his voice reflected admiration for a job well done by Orchard.

Orchard followed up, "Should we bring her in again?"

Sven thought for a moment before responding, "No, but keep her under observation for a while. Let's see how she is coping with all this. And spread the surveillance around a bit to make sure that we are not noticed. I am sure that you will get a few volunteers from the other teams to do a bit of that. Make sure WPC Hayes is also used because I want at least one objective report." Sven knew that all the young bucks on the team would enjoy that assignment and he was not the sort to deny enjoyable moments to them in what was a tough and demanding work with little reward, but also he wanted to make sure that the job was done properly. "Anyway, Constable, what else do you have for us?"

Orchard began, "You asked me to check with the drugs team if they had any more on Nick Dean. Quite interesting, that was. He is on their surveillance list. They were dead worried about our investigation affecting their work. They asked to be kept informed of anything relevant from our enquiries."

"Did they offer anything in return?" Peters enquired, clearly expecting the answer to be no.

"Actually they did, Sergeant," Orchard responded, also showing surprise. "They suspect that Dean is still doing it and might now be pushing more dangerous stuff like Ecstasy. He has been seen in the company of Big Porky Jewell, a known dealer."

Jenkins came in, asking with a snigger, "Why do they call him Big Porky, Dave?"

Orchard blushed, but Peters was on to Jenkins like a shot. "That's enough of that, lad, this is a serious investigation."

Turning to Sven, who was looking bemused, he explained, "Sorry, Sven, this is a joke amongst the lads. Orchard once asked if he was called Big Porky because he was big and fat, which is quite a reasonable assumption, but in this case not true. Jewell comes from the east end of London. He got called Big Porky there because he has a—"

Sven broke in before Peters could finish. "Thank you, Sergeant, I think that I understand now. That's another one for the book on English slang for foreigners that I intend to write when I retire.

Peters laughed, replying, "Actually, Sven, I was about to say because he has a habit of telling very unbelievable stories. It comes from Cockney rhyming slang, but I much prefer what you had in mind."

Sven blushed with embarrassment, which he tried to cover by saying, "Well, two for the book then. Now please continue, Constable."

Orchard took a deep breath to prevent himself from laughing and continued, "My contact said that there was probably some E going at that party. He even gave me the likely users. Dean himself, Angela Palmer, Andrew Pitman, Beth Goodheart, Brian Whitehead and guess who, Laura Hamilton. I phoned the pathologist to check if there were any drugs found in her body. He was still working on it, but was grateful for my telling him. He said he would not necessarily have checked when there was no suspicion of drugs. Just in case, I also phoned the pathologist dealing with John Hamilton. He said that he would check with the lab and include the results in his findings."

Sven responded, "Good work, Orchard. Clearly we shall have to add Mr. Dean to our list of interviewees. Please co-ordinate that with the drug squad. They might wish to conduct the interview with us in attendance. You said that you had a third thing to tell us?"

Orchard had being saving the best for last. He began with a note of excitement, "That was the challenge that you set me to find out where anything thrown out to sea might land. It would depend upon when it was thrown, but I guessed you meant during the time after Laura left the party. The tide was high early on and going out fast later, but with the help of the oceanography department at Plymouth College, I was able to predict it to a one-mile stretch of beach working out from the lighthouse. Anything would come to shore within twenty-four hours, so I checked it out with the beach cleaners. Apart from litter, they reported a wheel trim, a bin bag full of towels, a bikini top—thirty-four double-D—three buckets, two spades and a single flip-flop. I was lucky because I was only two hours ahead of the rubbish collection. I kept them all, but the one that caught my eye was the bin bag full of towels. I thought that they were too new to be thrown away and they all had a lot of red stains on them. There were two large, one medium and one small, all matching. I bagged them and sent them for analysis. I would put money on those red stains being blood. I don't know what made you suspicious, guv, but I think that you hit the jackpot."

Sven's face beamed with delight. He was pleased that his hunch had paid off. "Thank you, Constable Orchard, that was a good piece of detective work. I think that you might win your bet. If there is nothing more, gentlemen, I think that we will call it a night. We still have a lot of interviews to conduct, as well as a surveillance to organise and some facts to confirm. We will meet again tomorrow at the same time to compare notes. I will go to the Lighthouse Inn to see if I can talk to Carole Young and Alicia Adams. You can also leave it to me to speak to Jean Young about those points from the Mitchell interview. Until tomorrow then, and have a relaxing evening. Just one other thing, Orchard, if you find the owner of that bikini top, or the flip-flop for that matter, then you can be the one to return it."

Chapter 14

A family business, 3rd July 1996

Sven arrived at the Lighthouse Inn at ten sharp, carrying a parcel wrapped in brown paper. This time he had deliberately come alone so that he could put all his interviewees at their ease and, more importantly for the hotel, not have uniformed police traipsing around during the holiday season. Jean Young had suggested that time as there would be a break in the busy schedule for him to talk to her and her two daughters. She took Sven through to the office where a waitress brought them coffee and biscuits. Jean Young appeared totally relaxed as she poured the coffee and invited Sven to start. He asked about her relationship with John Hamilton.

"Now that is a big question," she responded. "John and I go back a long way. How much do you need to know?"

Sven smiled, replying, "Really as much as I can. I need to build up an insight into the man from somebody who knew him well. Will you talk me through from the time you first met, please?"

Jean sat back in her chair with her coffee. "This could take some time, but here goes. I met John on Christmas Day back in 1974. We were both invited to dinner by a mutual friend, Anna Martin. Her parents hated to think of anybody being on their own at Christmas, so their home was always open house over the holiday period. My parents had gone on holiday to Florida with my younger sister Gillian and her new fiancé Francis, so I was one of their lost souls. John had been on his own for some time. He worked for the same company as Anna. We were instantly attracted to each other, sharing interests in old cars, model railways and drinking. Men find it surprising that girls are interested in model railways and cars. I got into it when I was allowed to play with my dad's train sets. He only had daughters with whom to share them. John was always taken with quality cars and my dad had an old Mark II Jaguar. Dad even let him take me out in it a couple of times. John wanted to make love in the back but I would not let him for fear of damaging the leather. He said that one day he would have his own and then I would have no excuse. We were a bit old for that sort of thing by the time he got his, though."

Sven smiled as he saw the glint in Jean's eye and a little blush come to her cheek. Two things were clear: firstly that she was telling the truth and secondly that there was warmth in the memory of their first meeting. Did the relationship continue that way? he wondered. He nodded but kept quiet, hoping that Jean would continue, which she did.

"John invited me out the next day. I had an office job at the time so was off on Christmas Day, Boxing Day and the day after that, which I had saved from my meagre holiday entitlement. That was a Friday, so I got five clear days off. John had saved three days holiday so he was off right through to the New Year. That was only the second year that New Year's Day was a public holiday here in the United Kingdom. I remember it well, because I had to work the first New Year's holiday as a result of the three-day week."

Sven looked perplexed, so Jean explained, "It was during the miner's strike. The miners picketed power stations and the power workers would not cross the picket lines. That meant that power was in short supply and there were regular power cuts. The Prime Minister of the day, Ted Heath, declared that all non-essential industries would only receive power on either Monday to Wednesday or Thursday to Saturday of each week. My office had power on New Year's Day and they wanted everybody in.

"Anyway, we made the most of our time together. We spent our bank holiday playing with John's trains. I leave you to guess where that led. We were soon, in the current jargon, an item. It lasted for a blissful year, during which time we enjoyed foursomes and holidays with my sister Gillian and Francis Mitchell, whom she married in the following March. Gillian fell pregnant with Todd soon after that. It was three months later that I discovered that I too was pregnant. John was shattered. He really did not want to settle down to look after a child, but he said he would if that was what I wanted.

"We carried on seeing each other for a while but the spark had gone. John seemed to change and I was drawn toward Alan Adams, a friend from work. Alan did not seem to care that I was pregnant, so we just started dating. John and I drifted apart, and it was Alan who took me to the hospital when Carole was born. He treated her as his own daughter. We married six months after she was born."

Jean drank some coffee and pondered. As she was reflecting on that period of her life a small tear formed and ran down her cheek. She wiped it away and continued, "John offered to pay maintenance for Carole but Alan did not want it. He said that he would bring Carole up as his own and that he would support her, but John had to agree not to see her. John accepted this arrangement and I saw very little of him for a long time after that. He took an overseas contract with his firm and started living as an ex-pat in Bahrain. He wrote to me occasionally, sending the letters care of my sister so that Alan did not find out. He met Emma, a nurse who was working out there, and they got married in July 1977. That was two months after Alicia was born. Emma fell pregnant with Laura soon after they married, so she returned to St. Ives, where John had retained his flat. John carried on working three-month tours in Bahrain for another seven years, finally returning to St Ives in 1985.

"I met him again at a Christmas party that Gillian had arranged. He came on his own, explaining that they could not get a babysitter so Emma was staying at home with Laura. Alan did not speak to him, preferring to spend the evening drinking and talking to Francis. I think it was then that things started going wrong for the Young family. Gillian and John started an affair, which led to great rows with Francis and their divorce in 1986. It took its toll on John's marriage and mine as well. Alan and I were going our separate ways. He found somebody else so we divorced amicably in the middle of 1987. I reverted to my maiden name, which Carole decided to take as well. I had told her that Alan was not her father some time before. Alicia was much closer to Alan so she elected to retain his name.

"Emma left John soon afterwards, taking up with a young Greek waiter and moving to Greece with him. John was left to look after Laura by himself. He also had to sell the flat in St. Ives as part of the divorce settlement. He was forced to move to a much smaller place in Penzance. He had been a bit of a cad, but Gillian and I did feel sorry for him. Both Gillian and I helped him by looking Laura some nights so that he could have a break."

Sven could sense that there was something that Jean was not saying. "How did Todd take all this?" he asked.

Jean tensed as she prepared her reply. "Not in the same way. His father was the innocent party in all this and had suffered more than any of us realised. His health had not been good for some time, but deteriorated badly during the break-up of their marriage. He died two months later. Todd was shattered, blaming Gillian, but even more blaming John. It made it worse that he did not say anything. He was only thirteen and not that confident in himself, so he just bottled it up, which was even worse. Gillian got close to a nervous breakdown, so I had Todd staying with me quite a bit around that time. Carole was not very welcoming, but he and Alicia got on very well together. They are more like brother and sister now. Even when Gillian recovered, Todd still kept coming around for Alicia to help him with his homework. She was always bright academically, whereas Todd was more practical. His woodwork and metalwork were exceptional, which developed into fixing bikes, then motorbikes and more recently cars."

"Do you think that Todd still blames his mother?" Sven enquired, keen to understand how history had developed.

Jean's reply was quick and decisive. "Oh no, he was a tear-away at first, but as he got older he realised that he was the man in the house and had to behave like it. He mellowed a lot, settled down and started earning money to help Gillian. He even came to work for me, initially as a porter and handyman, then as soon as he turned eighteen he became a barman. Scarlett Robinson has been a real stabilising influence on him too. Now that he has got the Boatman's Cottage sorted out I expect that they will get engaged very soon. Alicia said that they have made a really good job of it."

Sven nodded, digested the information and then enquired, "What about John? Did Todd mellow on him as well, do you think?"

Jean was concerned about this question and it showed in her face. She knew first hand about the outburst at the party and she was sure that Sven knew of it as well. She was not willing to put Todd on the top of the list of suspects, but knew that she could not just brush this enquiry aside. She weighed up an answer and then responded, "I do not think that is something that Todd will ever really get over. When he first started at the Lighthouse Inn I warned him that he would be out if there was the least sign of trouble with John, but until last Saturday there never was. I am sure that he still bears resentment about the way that his father was treated, but who would blame him? The outburst at the party was testament enough to it, but I think that is as far as it goes. There are other more important things in his life now."

Sven detected an element of finality in that answer. He decided to change the subject. He asked, "Would you tell me about that Christmas Day in 1992? I understand that John and Laura came to lunch with you and the girls."

Again Jean appeared suspicious of the question. "You are very well-informed. I don't think that much of interest happened. It was just a typical Christmas Day with friends."

"Indulge me, please," Sven continued. "It will help me build up background on John and Laura." He decided to keep back the real reason for the question, and in any event, the background information would be useful.

"Very well," Jean began. "I have a little time, so let's see what I can remember. I told John and Laura to come at about twelve, and sure enough he drove into the Lighthouse Inn car park at precisely twelve noon. His 1964 Mark II Jaguar glistened in the crisp winter sunlight. Its maroon paintwork contrasted well with the highly polished chrome, which he told me he had spent hours cleaning only the day before. John was not fastidious about his car, but he did like it to look good for Christmas.

"'My! haven't the girls grown?' was John's opening remark as he walked into the lounge where Carole and Alicia were waiting to greet him. Carole was the first to respond, with a cheery, 'Hello, Uncle John' and the offer of her cheek for him to kiss. Even at that early age Carole was developing her customer-friendly manner. John kissed her, thanked her for her kind comments and then greeted Alicia.

"Alicia shook his hand briefly, greeted him and made an excuse to leave all at the same time by saying, 'Hello, Uncle John; please excuse me, but I must get back to the kitchen.'

"John was very understanding. He told her that that was fine and that I had explained that she was cooking the Christmas dinner. He just asked her to say hello to Laura first since it had to be at least three years since they had met last.

"'Hi, Laura,' was Alicia's reply, made as she was heading for the kitchen.

"Carole, seeing that Laura was not at ease, jumped in. 'Don't worry about her, Laura, she's only comfortable with her pots and pans. Would you like to come up to my room to see my Christmas presents?'

"Even then Carole was always happy to have a dig at her half-sister and show that she was the natural for any front-of-house role that I might have in mind for her. Laura looked at John, who responded, 'Yes, why don't you take Carole up on her kind offer? You can tell her about your presents as well.' Laura nodded as Carole took her by the hand and on to her bedroom.

"That gave John and me some time to chat. He told me that the journey from

Penzance to St Ives had taken only twenty minutes, rather than the hour that it would have taken in the summer. He also explained that Laura was not really happy and had asked why they had to be here. She wanted to have Christmas dinner with her Uncle Edward and Auntie Rose as usual. I say 'asked,' but I understood that it was more of a whine than a question. John knew that she would rather spend all of Christmas with her cousins, but he was going to do something that he particularly wanted to do as well. I appreciated that.

"John did not want an argument on Christmas Day so, as he put it, he used his best sales approach on Laura. He explained to her that her Uncle Edward had changed his job. He was on shifts now and was working that day. His family was having Christmas dinner in the evening, so he and Laura would be joining them for that. John actually worked quite hard to sell the morning to Laura. He said that I was an old friend, so when I invited them to Christmas lunch, he thought it would be good fun. She would have the company of Carole and Alicia, which was much better than just her old Dad playing with his train set. He thought that that was not a bad line, and as he said it appeared to work, at least at the start.

"I was glad to see him even though our brief affair had ended sixteen years earlier. I told him that Laura had grown as well. I remember telling him that she was going to be a pretty girl and that he would have to lock her up if he did not want all the young bucks coming around. 'Take that from one who has twice the problem and is two years ahead of you,' I said. We then sat down for a drink and a chat while the girls were otherwise occupied. John and I shared a passion for malt whisky, which we indulged a little that day. We had agreed that Carole should not know that John was her father, so our albeit infrequent meetings were my way of letting him see his daughter grow up. I have to say that I was not entirely honest with John, because some time after making that agreement I did tell Carole, but told her not to tell anybody that she knew.

"John commented on the fact that I had decided not to open the hotel that year. I told him that it did not seem to be fair on the girls. They deserved a Christmas break as well. Carole had her GCSEs that year and they both worked hard in the hotel in their spare time. It was also very popular with the staff. We re-opened for lunch the following Sunday and we were still doing the New Year's Eve banquet. That was enough.

"John had brought loads of presents, but we agreed on a quick chat before lunch, with the opening of presents being postponed until afterwards. I made frequent checks in the kitchen to make sure that Alicia was getting on all right. Each time, with increasing levels of annoyance, Alicia assured me that she could cope, until I finally realised that she could. Alicia told me that I had half an hour before lunch would be ready so I might as well use it to chat with John. We settled down on the sofa in front of the big log fire.

"'So, how are things going then?' he enquired. 'It must be three years since you took over this place.' I had to count the years in my head before I could confirm that it was actually over four. I took over this place in August 1988 and opened it for the Christmas trade that year. Carole was twelve and Alicia ten. It had gone well. I was getting local trade as well as the tourists. We were sold out for the whole of July and August the following year for the first time. I was turning bookings away. It made me cry to have to pass all that business to the George. They were not that good as us *and* they charged more.

"John was full of admiration. He congratulated me and asked if this meant that I had managed to reduce the huge loan that I took out when I started. I was proud to say that I had. Thanks to the girls pitching in, I had been able to operate with one less receptionist and cook. I had repaid half the loan already and was well ahead of plan. I intended to clear the loan in six years rather than the ten that I took it out for. That was, as I told John, 'unless I expand, of course.'

"It was possibly at that point that the first seed of our business relationship was sown. John asked whether I was seriously considering expansion. I said possibly, but not at that time. I was thinking of building some more rooms here in a couple of years, but only if I could get the planning permission. That was going to be difficult. St Ives is tough enough, but here in Blimford the parish council was, and still is, trying to conserve the whole architecture completely without change. Internal modifications are all right, but they object to anything new being visible from the High Street.

"I asked John about how things had been going with him. There had been quite a few changes. His father, who had been ill for some time, had died the previous month. John said that it was a merciful release really as he had been suffering for some time. Anyway, he had left John quite a large inheritance, so he was thinking of moving. His company was contracting, which gave him the chance of voluntary redundancy. He was considering a move back this way. His idea was that he might buy a little model railway shop in St Ives. There was already one there and he knew that the owner was thinking of selling up and moving to Spain. Since he also knew all the customers through the Model Railway Club of Cornwall, he thought that he would be able to retain the business quite easily. I told him that I was sorry to hear about his father, but it seemed as if things had worked out quite well for him.

"Not wishing to dwell on a sad topic, I asked him what he intended to do about Laura's school. He had been thinking that through, coming to the conclusion that he could either leave her in Penzance Priory or move her during the summer holidays. It would not be ideal because she was half way through her two-year GCSE course, but she would have a full year at the new school. He asked me about the schools around here: where did Carole and Alicia go and would I recommend the school. The girls were both at Hilary Taylor. It's an all-girls school with a very good reputation. It is close to Simon Baker, the boy's school, so they got together for drama and probably lots of other things as well, if truth were told. I had no hesitation in recommending it. John was very pleased to hear that. He did not want the inconvenience of having Laura still in Penzance. 'Hilary Taylor it is then,' he concluded, showing some relief that at least one issue would be easy to resolve.

"It was then that I asked him if he had thought about accommodation. He said that he wanted something with a bit of character this time. He thought that the modern box was functional but had no soul. That got me thinking, so I asked him just how much character he was looking for, because I had the lighthouse in mind. I showed it to him from the window. They were going to turn the light off early the next year and replace it with a new automatic light a couple of miles down the coast. I told him that it was cut off by the tide some of the time, but was easy enough to cross by motorboat. He was clearly interested then, asking about vehicle access and other things. I told him about the causeway that runs directly from the lane, but that he would need a four-wheel drive to use it. The boat jetty belongs to me so that was not a problem, and he could park the Jaguar in my car park. As it happened, I sold him a piece of spare land on the other side of the road where he built a double garage. He preferred to build the garage, to allow him to keep his Jaguar and preserve it from the worst excesses of the Cornish weather and sea-spray, than to buy the four-wheel drive.

"We did not have time to talk much about anything else before Alicia called us all through for lunch. I remember her saying, 'All break off from what you are doing and come into the dining room.' Even in those days she was demanding of our attention when the food was ready. Dinner was quite something. We were all seated there expectantly as Alicia brought in a tray upon which sat a large tureen. 'Parsnip and herb soup,' Alicia announced proudly. 'I don't like parsnips,' Laura piped up. 'Well, you will like this,' Alicia retorted with a smile on her face but in a voice that made it clear she would allow no rebellion. This, coupled with a fast rebuke in the form of raised eyebrows and a glare from her father, ensured that Laura's resistance crumbled.

"The whole lunch was testament to Alicia's abilities. I told her that she could cook for the restaurant any time she liked. I was not sure if the locals were quite ready for Turkey Amerique, Dauphinoise potatoes and Mediterranean vegetables, but I was sure that our tourists would love it. Even Carole was impressed, although her compliment was a bit barbed. If I remember correctly she said, 'Not bad, Alicia, you can do the cooking as long as you leave the staff and the guests to me.' John praised her as well, but I think it was all a little too much for Laura. She said nothing but gave a half smile and looked down on a plate where the vegetables had hardly been touched. John continued, I think to cover his own embarrassment with Laura, by saying that he was glad that Alicia had not gone in for 'this nouveau cuisine,' as he put it. He said that he liked to leave the table feeling that he had had something to eat.

"It did not help when Laura chimed in, 'And something to drink.' John's face began to redden, not least because he knew that she was right. He was looking at two empty wine bottles and was aware that the girls had had little more than a glass each. Even allowing for the three that I had drunk, that left virtually a bottle for him, plus the two scotches before lunch. I had to do a little diplomatic job of my own to keep the peace. I reminded Laura that it was Christmas and she should give her dad a break. Carole helped as well. Before Laura could continue, she grabbed Laura's hand and took her to her room, saying, 'Come on, Laura, you have not seen all my presents yet.'

"John helped Alicia and me to clear away before we all retired to the lounge. Carole and Laura were called back for the present-opening, which was not undertaken until John had a few quiet words with Laura. That assured that it passed without further incident. We all remained in the lounge, John, Alicia and I talking while Carole agreed to play chess with Laura. Since Carole only just understood the moves, and Laura, under her father's guidance, was a member of the school team, it was really no contest. Laura won three games inside an hour before Carole, considering that she had more than discharged her duty, suggested that perhaps Alicia should try her luck.

"After some heavy persuasion from Laura, Carole and me, Alicia consented, thus freeing Carole to go to her room to listen to some new CDs that she had been given. Alicia proved a much tougher opponent, causing Laura to think more and to keep quiet. John told me that he was watching the progress from the corner of his eye, concluding that Laura was heading for defeat when, for no obvious reason, Alicia blundered, allowing Laura to win.

"Elated by her success, Laura piped in, 'Can we go to Uncle Ted's now please, Dad?' It was clear to her that should she play another game she might well lose, and she did not fancy that. John checked the clock. It was nearly four o'clock so he decided that it was probably best to agree rather than have Laura protest. I was not keen on his driving so soon after drinking that much, but he insisted that he was fine and it was time for them to go. I asked Alicia to take Laura to fetch her coat while I said goodbye to John.

"'You have trained a good diplomat there, Jean,' he observed. 'Alicia had her on toast. I'm sure that blunder was deliberate. Anyway, where did she learn to play like that?'

"I knew nothing of the game. It was her father who got her interested. I think they still play when she visits him. They also had a club at school. She played a lot in her lunch hour. She had been asked to play for the school team but preferred to come home to practise her cooking, and yes, the blunder probably was deliberate. She has got a sweet nature and is much more client-friendly than Carole would ever admit.

"John observed that the boy who married her would be a lucky one. I told him that I did not even want to think about that. I had enough on my plate with Carole and her exploits behind the bike sheds. Oh yes, I heard about those things, you know. It's a very small community here in Blimford. And who were the main culprits? It was only my nephew Todd Mitchell and his big mate David Stevens. They were known as the Likely Lads, those two—likely to get a girl into trouble, that is. Still, at least Todd has grown into a responsible, property-owning adult and Carole knows how to look after herself. Alicia has never been any trouble, so I guess I have been very lucky really."

Jean sat back, indicating that she had completed her recollection. Sven had been listening carefully to everything that he had been told. Now was the time for him to probe a little. "You said that it was possibly that day that the first seed of your business relationship was sown. What did you mean by that?"

"Ah yes, that was in relation to the lighthouse. It's a long story from then until now, but it all hinged around John's decision to buy the lighthouse. We had several discussions about it before he eventually phoned to say that he had been successful at auction and the property was his. We arranged for him to come over so that we could take a look at it again and I could help him plan the conversion.

"I remember as if it was yesterday my first visit to the lighthouse after John had bought it. It was the tenth of October 1993, a bright, cold day. I drove John over in the Land Rover almost as soon as the causeway had cleared. We were both very excited to see the challenge that lay ahead. My heart skipped a beat as he turned the large key in the mortise lock of the lighthouse door. It was ten months after I had first suggested that he might wish to buy it, with a lot having happened since.

"As he had hoped, his company had downsized. John hated that word, describing it as 'that nauseating modern term for reducing the size of the workforce by sacking hardworking, loyal staff as a result of senior management incompetence.' John had grabbed with both hands the chance for voluntary redundancy and a most welcome cash injection. He said that for a company that had been so mean with its pay over the past ten years, it had been remarkably generous with its payoff. Some of his colleagues though had been less lucky. Husbands with young families were going to find it difficult to get another job without selling up and moving to London or the Thames Basin, England's Silicon Valley.

"That's a story in itself and quite ironic. John had two good work friends, Len Johnson and Mark Jordan, who were made redundant at around the same time. Len Johnson had been treated really badly by their mutual boss Paul Iage and his boss Mac Allan. He went through a bad time, with Mark and John being really worried about him. He was pleased to report that Len came through it and had fared far better than he ever would have done had he stayed. John and Len were convinced that it all went back to a staff meeting, when he and Len had inadvertently upstaged Mac Allan. John was a good raconteur and could give a humorous presentation, which he did first off that evening. He was followed by Len, an accomplished comedian who did stand-up comedy as a hobby. He was on his best form that night. Mac Allan prided himself that he was good and by rights the star of any evening, but faced with following that performance he dried and was clearly a poor third, which bruised his ego. Len said afterwards that Mac had commented, 'I will get you for that.' Len thought he was joking, but both subsequently became convinced that he was not.

"Mark had done quite well, but there again he deserved to. He was good at his job, far better than either Paul Iage or Mac Allan gave him credit for. He also had great support from his wife. Even though they had just had a baby, they upped sticks and moved to the Thames Valley, where Mark got himself a good job.

"John had little sympathy for Paul Iage, whom he clearly disliked. He called Iage an arrogant young man who thought that all that was required to succeed in selling was to wear sharp suits and invent buzzwords. Not to forget the tie with matching handkerchief in the top pocket, of course! He mimicked Iage's introduction to anybody new in the company, which always included the words, 'It's pronounced "yarge," not "e-arge," old boy.' John ranted on about all the meaningless rhyming pairs that Iage would trot out at sales planning meetings: 'press the flesh,' 'meet and greet,' 'slice and dice,' and 'cut and shut.'

"The three of them never worked out what the heck that last one was meant to mean. He also told me about one meeting where Iage had conceded so much to the client that the deal would never make a profit. He had managed to win some of it back later, but never enough to make the deal worth having. But that was not the worst part of it. Iage was also a blatant shirker. He would turn up late, miss meetings with his own team, go home early and invent non-existent meetings with other managers to get him away from the office early.

"John recalled with delight the day that Iage had come out of a downsizing meeting looking very pale, having been told that he had been made redundant. However, he saved even more vitriol for Mac Allan. He showed even more delight when he too was made redundant. The three of them bought a bottle of champagne to celebrate.

"'Now there is an evil man if ever I saw one. Iage was a shirker and a wimp to boot, but Mac Allan was something else. He was pure evil. He would take your ideas, dismiss them to you face and then present them to his management as his own. He would take any credit that was going and then make life hard on you for good measure.'

"I think that he forgave Iage, because he had some redeeming features and he knew that it was Mac Allan who was the real driver behind his bad deeds. If Mac Allan was your victim then I might have suspected John. In fact, John said to me, 'If Mac Allen is ever found dead in a dark alley with his head beaten in, then you had better come looking for Len, Mark and me. Start in the pubs because we will be celebrating.' It really was not normal for John to be that caustic about anyone.

"However, he needed all that pent-up aggression when the solid door resisted, forcing him to use his shoulder to open it. Not a good start, he observed. Both our minds came back to the present with a start as he opened the door and we stepped into the small entrance area. What had he taken on? He had already paid more than he had planned at a highly competitive auction. Only his determination to get something different had driven him on to spend his lump sum and almost all his inheritance on the property, leaving him precious little to spend on renovation.

"To the left he could see the spiral staircase ascending to the business end of the building, and to the right it descended to the storage basement. I suggested that we start at the bottom and work upwards. He shone the torch down the stairs and led the way. He found the electricity master switch at the bottom of the stairs, flicked it on and then tried the light switch. Nothing happened. He cursed loudly, but I took the more practical approach of shining the torch to the ceiling. It showed the source of the problem very quickly. There was no bulb in the light socket. To John's amazement, I produced a pack of bulbs from a plastic bag that I had bought across. John said that he was impressed by the sheer thought that I had put into the first visit, and why had he not been so well prepared? Remember that I been through it with the hotel a few years earlier.

"He inserted the bulb and was delighted to find that it worked. Examining the basement for the first time, he was pleased to see how spacious it was. There were cardboard boxes full of pictures and other artefacts of lighthouse life. The former owners had shown good manners in offering to remove it all, but he asked them to leave it. He had an interest in local history and intended to learn more about the lighthouse. If possible he would use some of the items to decorate the place to give it authenticity.

"My observation that he could put three bedrooms down there was perhaps a little more practical and certainly so from my point of view. We had discussed the possibility of his providing me with over-spill rooms for the Lighthouse Inn. During July and August I would use his spare rooms as additional guest bedrooms, undertaking all the maid service and cleaning, giving him much-needed income to service the debts that he was bound to incur restoring the place.

"'But there are no windows,' he protested. I told him that Fred Benson would sort that out. He had already done wonders at the inn. I was serious and I knew that I could handle all the issues. Fred Benson was my trump card. He was a local builder who knew the old buildings in the area and how to adapt them to modern use. He had a good reputation for realising his customers' vision and sorting out the planning applications. He probably had relatives in County Hall, but nobody was going to ask as long as they got what they wanted.

"John was prepared to trust me. He had envisaged four bedrooms in the central section of the lighthouse, but this would almost double that capacity. He knew that I could use them all because he had taken the time to investigate my booking requests during the summer. Over July and August I had referred four hundred and twenty-three room-days of custom to the George. They were mostly in complete weeks, so that would have filled seven rooms on most nights.

"He conceded with a note of resignation in his voice, commenting, 'I was hoping for a workshop, but I suppose I can use the new garage that I am going to build on that spare piece of land you have just sold me on the mainland.'

"We went back up the stairs to check out the other rooms. The ground floor had one large room plus basic kitchen and storage facilities. John had already had some thoughts about this area, which he began enthusiastically to share with me. 'I thought of this as my quarters. It is close to the bathroom, which will be useful at night. There is plenty of space for my train set out of the way of Laura and any other potential sources of damage.'

"We continued up the stairs to a very large open space. Looking up, we could see right to the ceiling immediately below the floor of the storeroom, some twenty feet above us. That storeroom was immediately below and led to the lamp room, where the lamp would have spelled out its message of warning to unsuspecting matelots for over two centuries. The lamp and all the associated gear had been removed for re-use elsewhere. To be fair to the former owners, they had warned him of this and the resulting rough area in the floor that it would leave. While we were looking at that, Fred Benson turned up, together with Todd and David, who were working for him at the time.

"Fred immediately endeared himself to John. Ten years of running his own business, on top of the fifteen as apprentice to his father, had not only taught Fred his trade, but also had given him the confidence and manners to deal with new customers and prospects. John liked his manners and welcomed the respect of being addressed as 'Mr. Hamilton' and 'sir.' He knew that I would have told Fred his Christian name, but it would have been impolite for Fred to have used it immediately. John shook Benson's hand warmly, replying, 'Pleased to meet you, Fred, and please call me John.' I knew then that they would be able to work together. He introduced Todd and David. John told me afterwards that he had assessed David as handsome and somebody that he should not leave alone with Laura for too long. The protective father instinct, which was stronger now that Laura did not have a mother looking after her, was coming to the fore. That turned out to be good judgement. It's a pity that John did not pay more attention to it.

"John and Fred virtually sorted out the design of the whole residence that day. John wanted to use the lamp room as a lounge-cum-reading room, keeping the three-sixty-degree view and using the outer access to the windows pretty much as they were, as a viewing balcony. The room below, the old storeroom where all the spares were, he wanted to make into a single bedroom for Laura. He planned to keep the spiral staircase, using screening to close off the rooms. He wanted the remaining area, where we were standing, to be made into four bedrooms by adding in another floor.

"John was concerned to ensure that he could get enough light, which would require extra windows. He decided that he would preserve the existing opening windows for ventilation but add some more for viewing and light. He was going to retain the existing stone walls and paint them all white to get the maximum light reflection. For Laura's room he needed to ensure that she could not lean out of the window, but the four new rooms would need larger windows because they would not have the double aspect. After about two hours of intense discussion and note-taking I had to interrupt their deliberations by reminding them that the causeway was due to flood and they would need to return to the mainland-side. We continued the conversation over supper at the inn.

"Anyway, Fred Benson completed the job for him in about six months. John and Laura moved in during the following April. John had lost a stone through a combination of worry and the exercise going up and down those stairs. I remember visiting him to discuss our arrangements for my use of his rooms for the peak summer season in 1994. It was on a fine June evening with the late evening sun pouring in through the open balcony doors. It fell on the chess set on the coffee table, where John was surveying the pieces. He was sitting back in his chair looking very contented. Even before I had got my breath back enough to ask, he told me that his opponent had resigned one game and just fallen into his trap in the other. He anticipated that collecting the scalp of a high-graded Kent player should assure his place in the UK postal team. He reflected on how retirement had been good for his chess. Although the last six months had been very busy with the conversion of the old lighthouse into a home, there had been evenings available for study, particularly to catch up on his opening theory.

"We reflected on all that he had been through to make the lighthouse habitable. I had been right about Fred Benson and his team. They had been very reliable, turning up when they said and working hard while they were there. They had all worked around the tides, doing fourteen hours a day when that meant they could take advantage of two low tides. Todd and David had done most of the hard work, much of it very heavy going. To cut out for the picture windows, Todd had worked through much of the brickwork by hand, spending several hours at a stretch banging away with cold chisels and a club hammer.

"John lent a hand when they worked the RSJs into place. He told me that he felt his vertebrae closing together under the weight. David too had struggled, but Todd seemed to take it all in his stride. John thought how the lad must have tremendous strength. Not someone with whom you would want to get into a disagreement, he mused. Several evenings he had ferried them back to the mainland in his small outboard. Even Laura had done a turn at ferrying, especially when it was David who had to be taken across by himself. That had not escaped John's attention, but he had been careful not to leave the two of them alone together in the lighthouse.

"Now that the lighthouse refurbishment was complete, the next stage of his retirement plan was about to swing into action. As we had planned, the lighthouse possessed much more space than he required for himself or Laura, so he was in a position to let out the spare rooms to act as over-spill for the Lighthouse Inn during the busy summer holiday period.

"What I had not expected was the research that he had done on the lighthouse. As he said, it would make great reading for my brochure. There was a lot of history in it and even a ghost. Apparently each lighthouse keeper used his spare time to make something that was left to the lighthouse. There were photographs, a stone lamp, a ship's compass and lots more besides. He had even drafted it all out into a brochure for me. I was surprised at the effort that he had put in. It was really good and I knew that my graphics designer could make some splendid advertising material out of it. The ghost was a masterpiece and a must for the tourists."

Jean handed over a copy of the brochure that she had made from John's notes. Sven took it from her, promising to read it when he had a moment. Jean continued, "Anyway, we concluded with a handshake and sealed it all over a glass of scotch. I invited him to have an evening meal with me back at the inn, which he accepted gratefully, adding, 'I must be home by ten, mind; the tide will cover the causeway at ten-thirty and I don't fancy paddling in the dark.'"

Sven reflected on how Jean Young had willingly answered all his questions, been very hospitable and been of help to his investigation. He knew that she was not even obliged to see him since he had no formal recognition as a policeman in England. He decided that further probing about Todd would elicit no further information of any use and could impair later attempts should he need to ask any questions of her or either of her daughters.

He did, however, need information of a less contentious nature, so considered that now was a good time. "In relation to the business arrangement with John Hamilton, could I ask you one thing, please?" he asked, adding hastily, "It's all right, I am not interested in the tax position."

Jean looked a little worried as he asked, "Did you supply the linen and towels for those rooms?"

Jean was surprised by the question, but decided that a straight answer would be best. "That was all arranged by me on behalf of the hotel. We changed linen and towels every day, just like we do in the main hotel rooms."

Sven had to continue to ensure clarity, "Did that include the towels used by John and Laura?"

"No, John was quite meticulous about that. I did offer to provide towels for him, but he felt that was unfair and always insisted on providing his own. We agreed that they would be cleaned using the hotel laundry service because that was the most cost effective way, but he insisted that I deduct the cost from his rental charges."

Sven's next question he knew would be a long shot, but he asked it anyway. "Would you be able to recognise John's towels if you saw them?"

Jean thought for a moment before replying, "I would not, but my housekeeper might. I could distinguish them from the hotel towels, which all have our name on them. I find that marking them is the best way of keeping good towels. I will ask the housekeeper about John's towels and get back to you on that."

Sven continued, "Could I now ask you a question about the hotel, please? I understand that you use poison in the cellars to control mice. Is that correct?"

Mrs. Young immediately understood the purpose of the question, but saw no point in hiding any facts. "Yes, we have had a problem with mice every since our old cat died. We got Topsy as a replacement but he never seems to be bothered to chase them. I guess that he, like the rest of us, is too fond of Alicia's cooking. Anyway, I do use poison boxes to control them. I have four boxes spread around, which I change every month. It's a service that the brewery provides. They send us a fresh set every month and take away the used ones for safe disposal. Of course I now have to ensure that Topsy stays out of the cellar rather that trying to persuade him to go down there."

"Do you know what poison is used?" Sven asked.

"Sorry, I don't," Mrs. Young replied. She reached up for one of her files and continued, "Let's see if the brewery's invoice tells me. Ah, here it is. 'Warning, poison,' but it does not say what type."

"Perhaps we could go and look at the boxes," Sven requested.

Mrs. Young agreed and led Sven down to the cellar. "I only put these boxes down last week so they should still have plenty of power in them. Please make sure you wash your hands well if you touch them," she urged.

Sven picked up the box and read the complete commentary on the side. This confirmed that the boxes did indeed contain strychnine. Sven checked each box for spills, weight or signs of damage. They were all in good condition, felt about the same weight and there were no spills. "Who puts the boxes out and collects the old ones?" Sven enquired.

"It will be whoever accepts the delivery of beer on the day the boxes are due to be changed. That will be one of the bar staff, which means that there are several possibilities. It will be recorded on the invoice. We will check that when we get back to the office, if you wish."

The two of them went back to the office, where Mrs. Young checked her invoices. She found the invoice, confirming, "The last delivery with the poison boxes was signed for by Todd Mitchell. He quite often does it because he is strong enough to manhandle the barrels on his own if need be."

Sven considered that he had exhausted his questions for Mrs. Young, so he concluded the interview with his thanks, adding, "Mrs. Young, you have been most helpful. I have taken up a lot of your time and drunk some excellent coffee. I know that you will have a lot to do, so I will release you to get on with it. Perhaps I could speak with one of your daughters now?"

Jean nodded, took the package of towels and wished him goodbye, saying that she would send Alicia in to see him next.

Chapter 15

The next generation

Barely a minute later, the door on the right-hand side opened and a young red-headed lady entered. She was dressed in a white chef's coat over a long white skirt. She looked hot and her face was flushed. "Hello, Inspector Ffolkes," she said as she smiled and pointed Sven to one of the armchairs. "I believe you would like to talk to me about the terrible events last Saturday." They both sat down together, Sven sitting back in his seat while Alicia perched on the end of hers.

Sven began, "I do hope I shall not be interfering with the guests' meals."

"Oh no," Alicia responded, "everything is under control. The breakfast things have been cleared up and preparations for lunch are under way. Will you be staying for lunch, Mr. Ffolkes? We have rabbit pie, salmon en croute or carrot crumble."

Sven was moved by the genuine warmth of this offer. "Really I do not want to put you to any trouble," Sven replied, but the thought of the rabbit pie had really taken his fancy.

"It's no trouble," was the perky response. "We shall dine together after the main rush is over. I will have to leave you for half an hour in about an hour's time to make sure everything is all right for lunch. We can continue over lunch if necessary. Now how can I help you?"

That arrangement suited Sven fine. He would get the facts before lunch and concentrate on feelings and hunches over lunch when she was more relaxed. He wanted to concentrate on her abiding memories of that night, so set the bounds of the discussion as wide as he could. "I know that you spoke to Sergeant Peters last Sunday morning, but now that you have had a little time to let things sink in, would you talk me through the events of last Saturday again? Please take me from the start of the evening right through to the time you knew that Laura was dead. Do not leave anything out."

Alicia nodded, sat back for a moment to think and then began, "Well, it was some party. Everybody had a lot to drink and at least one person suffered for it during the night. I drank a lot more than I had intended and had a severe headache that morning. It was still thumping when I spoke to Sergeant Peters."

Sven made an immediate mental note that Alicia was the sort to pick up and remember details. That would be very useful to him. He nodded and waited for Alicia to continue.

"I was in the first Land Rover crossing with Jenny, Sarah, Laura, Carole, Scarlett, Todd and James. I had prepared the refreshments for the party as part of my present to Laura. I had done all this earlier and left it over there. As soon as we arrived, Jenny, Sarah and I began to get things under way. Sarah unwrapped the food while Jenny and I got drinks for everybody. The second Land Rover group arrived while we were getting drinks, followed soon after by David and Kyomi, who had walked across. After everybody had been given their first drink, Jenny said that she could cope on her own. I went off to mingle, chatted with a few people and then sat down on my own for a while. I was not with anybody so I was expecting to be alone the whole evening. I had an excellent opportunity to watch the body language of the others. It's something that I enjoy. After half an hour I was thinking about going back to the bar to relieve Jenny, when Nick, who was on his own, offered to do it. Laura gave him a cursory thank you and then left him to it.

"I know that I should not speak ill of the dead, but that was typical of Laura. She really was very selfish. I decided that Nick should be thanked properly so went over to the bar to thank him myself. He and David were at the bar chatting and drinking heavily. I asked him if he was sure that he was happy to do the bar. He explained that he really did not mind and that he would enjoy a bit of people-watching. I understood that, telling him that I was not averse to a bit of it, people-watching that is, myself. He gave me a gin and tonic and had a beer himself. He made it very strong, but I thought, *what the heck, I have nothing better to do so I might as well get tipsy.* I left him to get on with the bar. Jenny came over to say that she was going to retreat to John's room for half an hour. She had agreed with Laura that presents would be opened at twenty-one thirty. Honestly, you police people with your twenty-four-hour clock. Why could she not say nine-thirty like the rest of us?"

Sven smiled at this rather astute observation, making a second mental note, this time to tell Jenny to lighten up when she was not on duty. He nodded to indicate that Alicia should continue.

Alicia duly obliged, beginning, "I started my people watching with Todd and Scarlett, who were talking together. I was sure that they were planning something. Todd went off to chat to James while Scarlett talked to Carole. They did not see me watching them, not that either of them would have minded if they had. A bit later Carole talked to Kyomi, who giggled and gave a knowing smile. Some plot had been hatched. I surmised from Kyomi's giggle that it was to do with sleeping arrangements. Todd and Scarlett may be fooling somebody, but not me. They were planning to sleep together. I don't know why they cannot be open about it like Laura and David were. Who cares anyway? After all, it's entirely their decision. Todd, bless him, saw that I was alone and came over for a couple of dances, then he and Scarlett engaged me in conversation. It was a little bit strained because Todd was doing his duty by his little cousin, but nonetheless it was kind of him to think of me and to get Scarlett come over as well. I like Scarlett, so it was a chance to have a good chin wag with her. She is really very pleasant and is mad keen on Todd, so she gets top marks for judgement. Anyway, after half an hour another one of my hunches was beginning to look right as well. Carole and James went out on to the balcony 'to look at the moon.'"

Alicia made a pair of quotation marks in the air with her fingers to imply that she believed the intent to be different from that stated. She continued, "Todd was being very kind, making sure that every time he went for a drink he brought me one. I hope Scarlett knows how lucky she is to have him. By nine-thirty and present-opening I was beginning to feel a bit tipsy. Laura opened her presents and went around thanking everybody in a showy, but clearly insincere, manner. I gave her a silk scarf. I remember that David gave her a beautiful gold watch, lucky thing. It must have cost him a fortune, although she did not seem to appreciate it. Sorry, but I cannot remember what the other presents were. Is that important?"

Sven shook his head, replying, "No, that's all right, we have got a list. Please continue."

"Soon after the presents, Angela, Andrew, Beth, Brian, Chris and Claire restarted the dancing. David and Kyomi soon joined them. Jenny and Sarah disappeared, to do their studying and marking respectively, soon after that. I was particularly interested in David. He was supposed to be deeply in love with Laura and wanting to marry her, but was spending a lot of time with Kyomi. It was interesting to see how David coped with her coming on to him."

Sven was surprised at this observation. What made Alicia decide that it was Kyomi coming on to David rather than the other way around? All the policemen had told him how attractive she was to men. He was about to ask Alicia why she had drawn this conclusion when she stopped her account to comment, "You seem surprised by my conclusion. Are you wondering how I concluded that it was Kyomi making all the running?"

So she is still body-watching, Sven concluded. *I will have to be very careful if I need to interrogate her.* He smiled to confirm her question and awaited her response.

"Oh, it was Kyomi, all right. I had been watching David and she was giving him the eye. Not that he was putting up much resistance, mind. While they were dancing she moved in very close to him. Not just tightening her arms around his neck but also moving herself forward so that their abdomens were touching— well within what the body language experts call the 'intimate zone,' and I am sure much to the delight of David if the smile on his face was anything to go by. He made the Cheshire cat look positively miserable."

Sven mused for a moment. For someone so observant, Alicia appeared to have forgotten that he was not a mother-tongue English speaker. He flattered himself that there was very little in English, as spoken by the English, that he did not understand, but knew that he had an accent that was sufficient for him to be recognised as foreign. Yet she had ignored this and made a reference to Lewis Carroll. This was interesting. Having turned this over in his mind for a minute Sven realised that in the course of his self-flattery, he had stopped listening to what Alicia was saying, breaking a cardinal rule of his police training.

Sven's mind snapped back into the present in time to hear Alicia comment, "I wondered if anybody else would notice, since it was getting more obvious by the minute. Most of the guests realised, but not Laura, who took another fifteen minutes to start paying attention to it. She watched for a further fifteen minutes, all the time getting more and more irate. I could tell that she was going to blow, when suddenly she stormed over to the dance floor, accusing David of flirting with Kyomi. She went off to her room in a huff. David was clearly angry and just kept dancing with Kyomi.

"By now I was feeling very light-headed and was losing track of time. I remember that soon after Laura left, Andrew and Angela started snogging on the sofa. They seemed only to have eyes for each other and did not take much notice of anybody else. Nick was still running the bar. He appeared to have a drink himself every time he poured a round for somebody else. About half an hour later, I think, Laura came back and started trying to snog with James. She took him out on to the balcony. If that was supposed to make Carole jealous it did not have much effect; and it did not have much impact on David, either. He seemed quite flattered by the attentions of Kyomi. Eventually Carole decided to go out and break it up. I imagine that one look from her and James would have broken off. Anyway, they all soon came back into the lounge."

At this point Alicia went quiet for a moment. Sven thought he could detect a blush. He decided to keep quiet for a minute to see if she would continue. Alicia began again, but her voice had changed. Gone was the detached, matter-of-fact historical account, to be replaced by emotion. "Well, then the big surprise came. Kyomi left the lounge going downstairs, presumably to go to the toilet, when David asked me to dance. I was far too drunk to evaluate his motives properly so I just decided to go with the flow. After a couple of dances we sat together on the sofa and started chatting. He was really quite nice. Once away from Laura he seemed a different person. The mood in the lounge was much quieter, with smoochy songs and lowered lighting. I almost forgot my body-watching, although I did notice Todd and Scarlett go out on to the balcony to look at the moon again. David's watch had just made a single peep, which some do at twelve o'clock if they are not set. It was just before then that Andrew and Angela left the lounge. I assumed that they were heading for the cellar and bed.

"I carried on chatting with David for another half an hour. In that time I remember that Nick abandoned the bar heading downstairs. I was sure that he had had too much to drink since he was staggering quite noticeably. I guessed that his destination was the bathroom. Beth and Brian and Claire and Chris also left the lounge, but for the basement and bed more like. I needed a good excuse to break free of David, who was getting a little too amorous. There was no use our getting into something we would both regret in the morning. I told him that I had to go to the toilet, which was certainly the truth. When I reached the bathroom, I noticed that one of the cubicles was closed and I could smell drink and vomit coming from it. It was really very unpleasant. Somebody, probably Nick, had overindulged.

"I left the bathroom as quickly as I could. When I came back into the lounge I saw David was sleeping on the sofa. I felt quite relieved and looked forward, happily, to a bit more body-watching, but it was really not very interesting.

"It was then that I had an evil urge. It was time to give Laura something to

125

think about. I was by then very drunk, but there again, so was everybody else. I turned on the light and said that it was well gone twelve and that Laura was eighteen now. It was time for her to get the bumps."

Alicia's eyes showed tears as she continued, "I had not idea that only a few hours later that Laura would be found dead." She stopped for a moment, wiping the tears from her eyes with a tissue from the desk, before continuing, "To my amazement, there was immediate agreement and Laura had no chance to escape. Of those left, only David, who remained asleep, did not take part. James was concerned that we should be very careful because she was pregnant. We picked her up and all of us held her very carefully, letting her down to the floor very slowing and only once. Nonetheless, Laura was not amused. She went to her room in a huff, declaring that she had had enough and was going to bed. I remember glancing at my watch to confirm that midnight had passed. It was just past one-thirty. I decided to go to bed soon afterward and retired to the Bodmin Room, as planned, wondering if I would be the only one to sleep in the room that was originally planned for me. I drifted off to sleep quickly. Either that or I just passed out."

Alicia looked up at the clock and was out of her seat with a start. "I must see to the lunch. Do you mind if we finish our conversation over our lunch in about half an hour or so, please?"

Sven was in no mood to be difficult after the help Alicia had given him. She had given him a detailed account of the evening that he could use to validate against what other people had told him. "Not at all," he replied. "I shall look forward to it."

"By the way, what would you like for lunch?" Alicia enquired.

"If your guests have left any of the rabbit pie, that would be lovely, but anything else will be fine, thank you."

"Rabbit pie it is," Alicia confirmed as she left, also saying that she would get her mother to send Carole to him.

Sven took the opportunity to look around the office while he was waiting. The desk was in the bay of the window facing outwards. Out of the window he could see the lighthouse to the right, the car park straight in front of him and the road to the left. A good choice of location, he thought. From here the occupant could see everything that was going on from a very high tide, through theft and vandalism to trouble approaching. Behind the desk were three armchairs arranged around a coffee table. Against the wall there was a filing cabinet and some open shelves. Two doors led out of the office to the left and right of the window. The one on the left, through which he had entered, was half open and led to the reception desk and main lobby of the hotel. The one on the right was shut. Sven imagined that from what he had seen of the rest of the hotel, it led to the kitchens and working areas, and probably out into the delivery bay.

Photographs were displayed on the desk, filing cabinet and open shelves. On the walls there were framed certificates. He read the first one. It proudly announced first prize in the Cornish Tourist Board culinary competition 1995 had been won by Miss Alicia Adams of the Lighthouse Inn. He looked below to see a photograph of a young lady with long red hair being handed a certificate by a large, red-faced man. Sven guessed that this was Alicia with the Tourist Board chairman. He moved to the second certificate, which announced that the Lighthouse Inn had been award a three-star Tourist Board rating.

He looked at the other photographs. The one on the desk was a black and white photograph of a couple who were both in evening dress. He recognised the lady as Jean Young, aged in her early to mid-twenties. The man reminded him of Edward Hamilton when he and Sven had first met. He concluded that this must have been John Hamilton. He looked toward the next photograph, which was a colour picture of two teenage girls, the younger with red hair and the older with dark hair. His glance moved across to a set of certificates that recorded swimming qualifications up to advanced standard, several life-saving certificates and one that recorded the completion of a five-mile swim. They were all in the name of Carole Young. Beside them sat a solitary certificate showing qualification for swimming at intermediate level, awarded to Alicia Adams, aged 11. He was about to investigate further when he became aware of somebody approaching the half open door.

A tall, slim dark-haired girl came in. It was Carole Young. Extending her right hand, she greeted him, saying, "Inspector Ffolkes, Mother said that you would like to talk to me."

"Ah yes, please call me Sven," he replied, gently shaking the proffered hand. Sven was taken aback by the confidence shown by Carole, whom he knew to be only twenty. She was wearing a black trouser suit and a white blouse decorated with an orange and blue striped cravat. This was, he deduced, her working outfit. It was a good choice for her figure, clearly adding to her air of authority. She motioned with her right arm toward one of the chairs, saying, "Sven, please do take a seat."

They sat in two of the armchairs around the coffee table. Sven began by stating that now she had had a little time to reflect on it, he would like Carole to tell him how the party went for her, starting from the beginning.

Carole thought for a moment, then spoke, "Well, taking it from the beginning, it started with drinks in the Sou'wester Lounge. That is the small one facing the sea immediately to the left as you come into the inn. James was early—dead keen, bless him. He came up to chat while I finished dressing. Alicia, Sarah and Jenny were setting up the bar. They press-ganged him into moving a beer barrel, then sent him up, after first making sure that I was decent, of course. We joined the three of them soon after that. I helped serve the drinks as the guests arrived. John was the last to arrive at about quarter to eight. He was funding the drinks for the evening. He and Jean came in to talk, but were soon accosted by David and Laura. The four of them left the room together, to go to Jean's office as I discovered soon after.

"Almost immediately after that Alicia and I both heard what appeared to be a row coming from the bar. Alicia took Todd and they went to sort it out. I was a bit nervous that they would not handle things well, so decided to check things out myself. Scarlett came with me just in case she needed to calm Todd down. Anyway, we soon discovered that the disturbance was coming from Mum's office, so we went in to see what was going on. Todd and Alicia had already arrived and we all witnessed John ranting on at David, who had told John that he wanted to marry Laura. John was having none of it. He went into a tirade because David had said that Laura was pregnant, told him he would have to wait for Laura to finish her studies and that Laura would have to have an abortion.

"David should have left it there and tried to talk to John later, but unfortunately he is a bit of a hothead so he pitched straight in. He said that now that Laura was eighteen they could have gone ahead anyway. That made John worse. He did the 'you will not be welcome here again if you do' bit. As if that was not bad enough, Todd had to pitch in about David stepping up to his responsibilities while John had not. Talk about embarrassing, just imagine having it announced to the assembled company that I was John's daughter. Fortunately, even though John did not know that I already knew, Mum having told me about John several years before, otherwise I do not know what I would have done."

"So how did you react?" Sven asked.

Carole thought for a moment before answering, "I tried to remain dispassionate. It was bad enough with David, John and Todd all reacting without my losing it as well. However, even that was not right."

"How do you mean?" Sven injected.

"The problem was that Alicia did not know about John being my father, so she got upset. I made a remark, which I regret now, about half-sisters. My family background is so weird that I have managed to get a half-sister from both my mother and my father. Alicia was upset anyway, but the remark made her worse. She has always been the sensitive one, whereas I am more laid back about it. Todd sprang to her defence immediately, calling me heartless. He has always had a thing about Alicia. I don't know how Scarlett gets a look-in and for that matter why she puts up with it. Scarlett was rather good actually. She managed to calm Todd down, although not until he had raised the fact that John had slept with my aunt, Todd's mother, as well. John kind of backed off, admitting that he was not proud of what he had done and that he intended to recognise me as his daughter just as much as Laura. He tried to use his experience as reason not to see Laura go the same way. I thought that was a bit rich, but things did calm down after he said it.

"Mum took charge, thank heavens. She got Scarlett to take Alicia to her room to clean up. I was asked to tell the hotel guests and the rest of the party that it was just a minor disturbance in the bar that had now been sorted out. I told the hotel guests first and then returned to the party.

"After telling them that all was well, I decided that I had earned a break so went back to join James. We do not see a lot of each other so we had lots to talk about. I did not get much time with him before Sarah came over. She asked me to outline the sleeping arrangements that Mum had decreed, not that there was much chance of them being used unaltered. Well, being a schoolteacher, she is good at getting people's attention and organising things. Anyway, I did my bit. After that John did a toast to Laura, we all had a couple of drinks and then we went across to the lighthouse."

At that point Carole stopped and looked across at Sven, as if waiting for direction as to what he wanted next. Sven waited to see if she would continue. She did, but only with a question: "What else would you like me to tell you about?"

Sven had hoped that she would be open with her recollections rather than him asking her specific questions. He tried an open question: "Would you take me through the events at the lighthouse as you remember them, please?" Carole's eyes looked to the ceiling as she tried to piece together in her mind the events of that evening.

"Everything was very well organised. Alicia had prepared all the food so that was put out quickly, and that lad from the college—Nick, I think his name is—got the bar going with Todd. There was nothing for me to do so I just took my drink and relaxed. The intrigue started at about nine o'clock, when Scarlett asked me if I would sleep with Kyomi in the Penzance Room instead of the St Ives Room as planned. Miss Goody Two-Shoes wanted to sleep with Todd, so James needed to sleep in the St Ives Room. She said Kyomi had agreed. It did not bother me so I agreed. James had obviously cottoned on, and soon afterwards he asked me if I would sleep with him. It gave him quite a shock when I agreed, but it meant moving Kyomi again. It was no use asking James to do that because he just would not know where to start. I told him to leave it to me. I felt a bit of a fool asking Kyomi to sleep in the St Ives Room after all the other arrangements. Kyomi agreed, but laughed when I suggested it. She is no fool. She understood full well what was going on. Flushed with his success, James took me out on the balcony for a snog. I think that the term *de jour* was 'to have a look at the moon.' Anyway, we were all up to it and I have to say I did enjoy it. There is something about being surrounded by the sea with an attractive man on a warm summer evening.

"Anyway, I digress. The next event of any relevance that I can remember was at about nine-thirty when Laura opened her presents. I gave her two Boyzone CDs. Alicia gave her a silk scarf—very tasteful and generous since she had also given her all the food. James gave her a gold pen and pencil set."

Carole's demeanour changed as she did a sarcastic impersonation of Laura. She put her head to one side and fluttered her eyelids falsely, saying, "James, how sweet." At the same time she pretended to plant a big kiss on the cheek of an imaginary James. She then reverted to her normal demeanour and continued her account in a matter-of-fact manner.

"James started smirking when he realised that she had left a large lipstick mark on his cheek. I allowed him a couple of minutes to enjoy it before I wiped it off. If James was going to have lipstick on his face, it was going to be in my shade. After the presents, we all set about the main business of the party—dancing and drinking, that is. After an hour we were all quite well drunk. I had just watched the tide flood the causeway. Laura had been too busy thanking people for the presents to do much dancing. She rather left David on his own. David, not surprisingly, decided to do a bit of mingling and ended up doing quite a bit of dancing with Kyomi. Laura did not notice for a while, but then became concerned that David had been flirting with Kyomi. She went off to her room in a huff. If she had paid more attention she would have realised that it was Kyomi who had been flirting with David.

"Laura came back half an hour later and started trying to snog with James. She took him out on to the balcony. If that was supposed to make me jealous, it was pathetic, and it did not have much impact on David, either. He seemed quite flattered by the attentions of Kyomi. I decided to go out and break it up in case James made a fool of himself. One look from me and the realisation of what he might lose soon brought James to his senses. David then started dancing with Alicia. He stayed with her for well over an hour. So was this his attempt to make Laura jealous? I can hardly believe that he fancied Alicia and certainly not when he could have had Kyomi. I would not be being honest if I did not admit that she is good-looking and certainly attracts the men."

Carole's face betrayed more than a little envy of Kyomi. She regained her composure and continued, "After that the party started thinning out. Nick staggered out toward the stairs, looking far from well. He was probably heading for the bathroom. Alicia managed to break free from David, whom I next saw passed out on the sofa. The party was down to Todd, Scarlett, Kyomi, James, Alicia and me, with David asleep on the sofa, when Alicia turned up the lights and said that it was well gone twelve, that Laura was eighteen now and it was time for her to get the bumps. I thought, *good for you, Alicia, it's about time you showed an evil streak*, so I was up for it. In fact, there was immediate agreement and Laura had no chance to escape. Only David, who remained asleep, did not take part.

"James was not at all keen because Laura was pregnant, but when he realised that we would do something anyway he took charge. I was surprised; he can be quite masterful when he puts his mind to it. Anyway, we were only allowed to give her one bump, with two of us supporting her in the centre and only from a height of one foot. Laura, needless to say, was not amused. She went to her room in a huff, declaring, 'I have had enough; I am going to bed.'

"Alicia went to bed about a quarter of an hour later. Kyomi went over to David and whispered a few words to him. They had a quick kiss and cuddle before she went off to bed. Five minutes later Todd and Scarlett left. That left me with James and David. It was just past two. I whispered to James to give me time to get ready, to ensure that it was not obvious where he was going, and then come to the Penzance Room. I then told the boys that I was off to bed as well.

"I went off heading for the Penzance Room, but was distracted. As I was passing Laura's room I heard her crying, so I knocked quietly and asked if she was okay. I did not want to embarrass her further, so made sure the others did not hear me. I stayed comforting her for half an hour. I told her that it would all blow over and that she could make it up with David in the morning. There was nothing she could do now as David was already asleep. Also I wanted to borrow something sexy for James to take off. She would not lend me her Japanese silk dressing gown, so I had to make do with her bathrobe, which is very practical but not exactly sexy. I then left so that I would be ready for James. I got back to the Penzance Room at about twenty to three. I wanted to give myself some time to prepare for James.

"James knocked softly on the door at exactly three o'clock. I had just enough time to kick off my shoes, remove my trousers, brush my hair and sit on the bed. Given the time I had, I was pleased with the image that I was able to create. I called him to come in. I am sure I can spare you the details of what happened next."

Sven smiled and nodded, adding, "Please do tell me about anything you heard or saw during the night."

Carole reflected for a moment. "I felt ill during the night, so I went down to the toilet, where I was sick. I remember that being at four thirty-something, because it was getting light and I could read the clock quite clearly. I was sufficiently with it to clean and disinfect the toilet and even opened the window. James heard me come back into the bedroom. He asked me if I was all right. Without going into detail, I admitted that I had had too much to drink and it served me right. He warmed me with a cuddle and I soon fell asleep.

"The next thing I heard was banging on the door. It was Kyomi shouting, 'James, James, wake up, it's Laura.' James was still drowsy as he went to the door. Kyomi dragged him out. Instinctively I looked at the clock. It was eight-thirty. I went out to see what was going on. I went upstairs to find David in a terrible state, with Todd trying to control him. Scarlett came out of the Truro Room and Alicia came up the stairs just behind me. David, sobbing and in a state of shock, said that Laura was outside, dead. Angela, Andrew, Beth, Brian, Claire, Chris and Nick came up from the cellar. I went down to John's room to call Sarah and Jenny. They came back upstairs with me. James came back in with Kyomi. They both looked very pale and clearly shocked. James confirmed that Laura was dead.

"Immediately after that you and Edward Hamilton came up the stairs. At the time I wondered why you had come, but of course I know now."

Carole looked down, appearing to be saddened by the whole recollection. Sven waited for a moment in case Carole was going to add to what she had said, but she remained silent. He decided that the only way to obtain any more information would be to ask his own questions. "Did you see or hear anything while you were downstairs?"

Carole shook her head, but then added, "I did not see anybody, but I recall that when I went into the bathroom I could smell vomit, the other toilet light was on and the door was closed, so clearly I was not the only one who was the worse for wear that night."

"Do you know who that person was?"

Again Carole shook her head, and on this occasion the words gave the same message. "No. I did not attempt to talk to whoever it was. To be fair, I did not even check if there was somebody in there. Whoever had been in there might have just left the light on."

A small pang of hunger reminded Sven both that he was overdue his lunch and that Alicia had suggested that he should join her for said meal. Realising that it was unlikely that he was going to get anything more of value out of Carole, he drew their conversation to a close by thanking Carole for her time. She smiled, shook hands with him and offered to show him out.

Sven explained that he was lunching with Alicia. "I shall tell Alicia that you are ready then," Carole replied as she left him by the opposite door from which she had entered.

Sven resumed his look around the office while he waited. He found a small pile of hotel brochures on top of the filing cabinet. He picked up the top one and sat down to read it. The brochure made much of the rooms in the lighthouse, showing pictures of some of the rooms. He recognised the ship's compass from the Truro Room and the stone lamp from the Penzance Room. Suddenly he felt a light weight on his thighs, together with soft fur rubbing against his left hand. He had got so engrossed in the brochure that he had not noticed the big ginger cat that was now making itself comfortable on his lap. Its front paws pressed alternately into his legs while it purred loudly and contentedly. Sven stroked its head, which encouraged it to purr louder and settle down into his lap. The cat settled down in a seated position with its front paws extended on Sven's knees.

"I see that Topsy has introduced himself then." Sven had been so distracted by the cat that he had been completely oblivious to somebody coming in. He looked up to see Alicia smiling at him. She stroked Topsy, who seemed to take this as a signal that he should not really be there. With that eight sharp claws dug into Sven's knees as the cat jumped off. Sven winced as he moved to get up. Why was it, he mused, that cats had to dig their claws in as they jumped off your lap? His own cat did exactly the same.

Alicia noticed his wince, commenting with sympathy, "Oh dear, did he use his climbing boots?" The question really did not require an answer. "Come to the dining room and I will try to make it up to you with some lunch."

Alicia led him through to a small function room with a large table laid with two places. "I thought that you might prefer not to dine in the main dining room, since we will want a private conversation."

"Very thoughtful," Sven remarked as he pulled a chair back for Alicia to sit down.

She sat down, saying, "Thank you, Sven. Such manners are so rare these days." Sven blushed as he realised that although he was being old-fashioned, he had been brought up that way and would always remain so. Alicia had noticed and returned his compliment with equal good manners. Clearly nothing passed her attention, confirming his assumption that any observation that she reported was very likely to be accurate.

As they sat down a waitress came over to fill two glasses with water. Alicia began the conversation by asking Sven if he would like wine or anything else to drink. They soon agreed that alcohol was probably not appropriate for either of them, both having a lot of work to do after the meal. Alicia began, "Now where were we when I had to leave?"

The question was clearly rhetorical, so Sven waited quietly for her to continue. "Ah yes, I was going to describe what happened after I went to bed. I will tell you now that everything I tell you I genuinely believe to be true and would be prepared to swear to it in court, despite what the others might tell you."

Sven wondered what was coming. In his long service as a policeman he had heard all sorts of outlandish things, many of them either untrue or with explanations different from those propounded by their tellers. Should he reassure her? He hesitated and then decided as she began to speak again that reassurance would not be required.

Alicia started her recollection. "I had had a lot to drink and felt tired so went straight to bed. I fell asleep quickly. I woke with a start in the middle of the night. The Bodmin Room has fairly thick curtains so it was in semi-darkness, but for a small pencil of light coming through a gap in them. I felt freezing cold, much more than I should have been in the summer. I sat up and looked across the room. What I saw terrified me. There was a tall bearded man carrying a lantern standing by the door. He was dressed like one of those old-fashioned sailors you see in the *Mutiny on the Bounty* that is playing in St Ives. Although the door was closed he appeared to be standing in the doorway. He beckoned to me to come over to him.

"For reasons that I doubt that I will ever be able to explain, I looked at my watch. It has an LED display so I was able to read the time clearly. It was four thirty-eight. I looked back to the door, but the man had gone. I turned on the light to look around, then went over to the door, where I felt even colder, and then went back to bed. I head the sound of somebody being sick in the bathroom below, followed shortly afterwards by footsteps on the landing outside and then a door open and close. I lay there for a while trying to comprehend what I had seen."

Sven enquired politely and earnestly, "What did you conclude?"

Alicia drew breath and responded, "When I came into the office I saw that you were reading our brochure. Did you get to the story about the lighthouse ghost? We put it in to attract the tourists, especially the Americans, but I can now genuinely claim to have seen it. I can give you no other explanation. The description was an exact match right down to the lantern. I do not expect you to believe me, nobody does. Carole and Laura used to make fun of me because I have seen ghosts before, although not this one. Even though they would never say it, Todd and Scarlett do not believe me either. They say that I am more sensitive than they are and am capable of picking up vibrations that they cannot, but that's just Scarlett being kind."

Sven was at a loss as to what to say. This was a situation that he had not met before. Should he tell her he believed her or that he did not believe her? These deliberations served to confirm in his mind that he did not know whether or not he did believe her. He fell back on his police training, asking, "You said that the room was in semi-darkness but for a pencil of light coming through the curtains. Did that light illuminate the man in the doorway?"

Alicia closed her eyes to play back the scene in her mind. "No, it could not have done, because the window is at an angle to the door rather than opposite. I saw the man in the semi-darkness. The pencil of light fell on the felt pictures above the dressing table." She opened her eyes again and nodded as if to confirm what she had just said.

Sven continued his questions, attempting to analyse the incident. "For how long was the man visible to you?"

"Only from the moment that I woke up and saw him to the time that I glanced at my watch. That was probably no more than a couple of seconds." This time Alicia's answer was more certain.

"During that time was the door open or closed?"

"It was closed the whole time. That is what made me so scared. He appeared to be on either side of the door at the same time." Again Alicia spoke with confidence.

Sven concluded that he could gather no more about the incident. He also realised that he was preventing Alicia from eating her lunch, which had been served while they were talking. "I will stop asking questions now so that you can enjoy this excellent lunch," Sven said, since he was also thinking of his own rabbit pie, which looked very appetising and smelled even better.

Alicia thanked him and began her meal. They both ate in silence for a few minutes until Sven felt it appropriate to restart the conversation. "Was anybody smoking at the party?"

Alicia's face showed her disapproval, which was reinforced as she responded with an immediate, "Yes, regrettably. John should have banned it, at least inside the lounge. Some of them were considerate and went on to the balcony to light up, but others smoked in the lounge. Nick was the worst with his roll-ups. The trouble was that most of Laura's classmates were getting him to roll cigarettes for them too. They smelt horrible. To make things worse, Nick lit an incense candle on the bar. He said that it was to cover the smell of the cigarettes, but it was much worse. It made me feel so sick that I avoided going to the bar to get drinks."

Sven realised that Alicia had no idea that these might not be ordinary cigarettes. He decided to probe further, but by a roundabout route. "But didn't you say that you got rather drunk?"

"Oh yes," Alicia replied, clearly recalling how bad she felt the next morning. "Todd got me the drinks to start with, then after he started chatting and dancing with me, David fetched them."

"They were not affected so badly by the smell then. Were they smoking as well?" Sven intended the question to sound innocent. He was pleased with the way that it had come across and even more pleased with the response.

"Todd certainly was not. He gave up several years ago after I had nagged him constantly. He made me a promise that he would never start again. I am sure that he has kept that promise and is likely to continue keeping it as long as he is going out with Scarlett. She is even more anti-smoking than I am. I can be almost certain that David was not smoking either. If he had have been I would have smelt it off him when we were dancing. No, it was the pharmacy set and their boyfriends—excluding Scarlett and Kyomi, who do not smoke—who were the main culprits."

Sven made sure that Alicia was not intending to add anything further before querying, "You did not exclude Laura from that list?"

Alicia responded cautiously, "I know that Laura did smoke, although I did not see her smoke that evening. She kept it hidden from her father, who was dead against it. When I went up to her room last week to discuss what food she would like for the party, she had a couple then. She smoked near the window to keep the smell down and also had air fresheners in her wardrobe."

There was a natural hiatus while the waitress removed the plates. Sven had enjoyed his rabbit pie, completely clearing his plate of food. Alicia had more picked at her food, giving up way before it was exhausted. Sven, feeling guilty, apologised for making her talk too much and preventing her from enjoying her lunch. Alicia would hear none of it, saying that she rarely finished her plate. She put it down to the hours that she spent in the kitchen. They both declined sweets, electing only coffee.

Despite Alicia's assertions that there was no need and that mother would be cross, Sven insisted on being billed for his lunch. He explained that he knew that Jean Young meant it only as a gesture of hospitality, but that he was forbidden from accepting such offers for fear of police officers appearing to be bribed. Sven used the break while they waited for the coffee to continue his questions. "Did you often visit Laura in the lighthouse?"

Alicia shook her head. "No, Laura and I were not close. She and I moved in different circles at school and still have different sets of friends. In fact I was quite surprised to be invited to her party."

"Why do you think she did invite you then?" Sven enquired.

It was obvious that Alicia had already posed this question to herself and was able to give an immediate response. "John Hamilton probably suggested that she should, although I am sure that the main pressure came from Todd, via Scarlett and/or David. Todd always looks out for me. He knows that I like going to parties but get relatively few invitations, so he would have made sure that I did not miss out on this one. I also got to know David quite well when he helped Todd to restore the Boatman's Cottage."

They were just finishing their coffee when the waitress brought the bill for Sven. He glanced at it briefly to determine what he needed to pay, which was considerably less than he was expecting. Jean Young had ensured that only his meal was included and that a hefty staff discount had been applied. "I must thank your mother for her kindness," he observed as he placed a five-pound note on the dish.

Alicia smiled, commenting, "Well, you know that we would rather not have charged you at all. All of us here at the Lighthouse Inn would like to see you catch the person who killed Laura. I will of course pass on your thanks to Mother."

"Indeed, that is my earnest wish too," Sven replied as he got up from the table. "Thank you, Miss Adams, for your time and help this afternoon."

As they were about to leave, Jean Young appeared carrying the parcel containing the towels that Sven had brought with him. "Just caught you," she said, handing the parcel back to Sven. "Mrs. Barnes, our housekeeper, says they are definitely the same type of towel that John used. She has checked her lists to see how many towels of that type there should be in the lighthouse. She could not check out whether there were any towels missing because the police have sealed off the lighthouse, so she wrote down the numbers on this list for your boys to check."

Sven took the list, thanked Mrs. Young again and left to return to the police station.

Chapter 16

Routine police work yields results

Having completed the account of his day, Sven turned to Sergeant Peters to report next.

Peters began, "Interesting day today, Sven. The first thing that I did was to visit the bank where those spare keys are kept for the Penzance College poison cabinet. The manager there is a bit of a stickler for protocol. He did not want to show me anything. I thought I was going to have to get a bit heavy, but he said that he would phone the college principal for permission.

"Anyway, the principal gave the all clear, so I got myself taken down to the vaults rather than have the bank staff bring the keys to me. I wanted to see if anything had been disturbed. The keys are held in a safe dedicated to the holding of customers' property within the bank's strong-room. They showed me the records. The keys have not been requested in all the time that they have been held there, which is since November '94.

"The safe has been accessed regularly for other customers, five times in the last two weeks, to be precise. They showed me the records. For each access, the client and a member of the bank's staff have to sign a book for the opening, and a note of what is taken out and what is put in is also made in the book. I even had to sign the book for this inspection. They were also able to show me the original entry for when the keys were deposited, by Dr. Jones on 14th November 1994 at 1:14 p.m. Well, I took a good look at the keys to check for traces of wax, which might indicate that they had been copied, but there was nothing. Both keys were bright as new pins. If you were to ask me, Sven, I would say that had not ever been used."

Having described his visit to the bank and convinced all present that the keys held there had not been used illegally, Peters went on to describe his next piece of work. "I telephoned Inspector Corke in the drugs unit about Nick Dean. He was quite happy to pull Dean in again to give him a bit of grief about his drug dealing. He said we were welcome to attend and that his boys would bring him in. I agreed that he should do that and that I would attend the interview. He phoned me again about an hour later to say that they had been to Nick's place but he was not there. His mother said that he had been strange ever since he got back home on the Sunday afternoon after the party. He went straight to his room and stayed there until he went to bed that night. He refused any supper, which was unlike him. He went out on the Monday morning for ten minutes, then returned, had breakfast with his mum and then went back to his room. He went out on his motorbike in the afternoon and has not been seen since. She was getting worried because he had not taken any overnight things and she was expecting him back for supper. Normally he phones her if he is not coming back. Inspector Corke said they would look out for him. I know that he intended to have a word with Big Porky Jewell and a few of his boys. He said that he would keep me informed and of course I agreed to do the same."

Sven thought for a moment before replying, "Well, there is nothing that we can do until the drugs unit find him. However, just in case anything untoward has happened to him, we should, in all our future interviews, find out where our suspects were on Monday afternoon and evening. Anyway, please continue, Sergeant."

Peters got out his notebook and began, "We divided up the interviews. I talked to David Stevens and James Cross while the lads visited the remaining pharmacy students and their boyfriends. I wanted to make sure that we got each girl and her boyfriend together so that we could interview them separately at the same time, if you see what I mean." As he spoke, Peters replayed the last sentence in his mind and realised that it had sounded rather complicated.

Sven nodded in reassurance and Peters continued, "I saw Stevens first. He came into the station voluntarily this morning. He still seems to be in shock, not really accepting that Laura was dead. We went over his whole story again. He was consistent about what had happened up to the time he passed out on the couch. It was the period after that I was most interested in and where I probed the hardest. His story was completely consistent with last time. Summarising, he was nodding off to sleep on the couch in the lounge when he heard a commotion with cheering, which we think was Laura getting the bumps. Next was Kyomi offering him some food to soak up the alcohol, her kissing him and telling him to come to the St Ives Room when the others had gone, and then her going off to bed. After that was James coming over to check him out and put a blanket over him, followed by Kyomi coming back to tell James that she would look after him and that James could go to bed.

"After James left, it was Kyomi snuggling up to him, the disastrous attempt to make up with Laura and then off to Kyomi for an hour of lovemaking. Finally it was back to the lounge, seeing somebody in a sleeping bag behind the sofa, but he still did not know who that was. The one extra piece of information he recalled was when he felt the icy blast coming up the stairs. Previously he had made a joke about it being the famous ghost. I asked him whether this had disturbed the person in the sleeping bag. He said it had. He could definitely recall movement, possibly the person actually getting out of the sleeping bag and then getting back in a couple of minutes later. Since he had snuggled further down under the blanket, he could not be sure.

"That was all he recalled until waking up again at eight-thirty with a thumping headache. He went to the kitchen to look for an aspirin but could not find one, so decided to get some fresh air instead. As he went outside he saw something on the rocks. It was Laura lying there motionless. He felt sure that she was dead, but had to get James just in case. He ran into the lighthouse and banged wildly on the door of the Truro Room, calling out for James. As we know, from Todd's testimony, he went to the wrong room and encountered Todd instead."

Peters paused at that point, but Sven remained silent because he realised that Peters intended to continue, which he did soon after. "Having confirmed the facts, I talked to him about his state of mind and what had caused the row with Laura. David said that he had been going over that in his mind time and time again. He felt miffed that Laura had accused him of flirting with Kyomi when he had done no more than Laura had asked him to."

Peters could see the surprise on the faces of the rest of the team at this remark. He continued, "Yes, that surprised me too, so I asked him how he worked that out. He said that he picked up Kyomi because Laura had requested that he should. Kyomi had started coming on to him and, although he remained polite to her, he did not respond. Then came the presents, when he was expecting Laura to be really grateful, because the watch that he gave her cost him a fortune and he was still paying for it. Instead she just opened it, gave him an insincere thank you and went on to the next present. That really did upset him, so he accepted Kyomi's invitation to dance almost out of spite. When Kyomi continued coming on to him, he started enjoying it and reacting to her. That was what sent Laura off in a huff, and he felt that she was being childish so he just let her go. Even when she came back she seemed dead set on provoking him, so he just kept going with Kyomi, although not without some conscience. He claimed that he demonstrated that conscience with two attempts to break away from Kyomi. The first was asking Alicia to dance when Kyomi went to the toilet, and the second the disastrous knocking on Laura's door. He admitted that he did not fancy Alicia and danced with her to spite Laura whilst at the same time keeping away from Kyomi. As he said, Laura was doing the same thing with James until Carole stopped her."

Sven came in, "Yet despite all that he still went back to Kyomi and made love to her. Did you discuss that with him?"

Peters smiled as he responded, "Yes, he admits it was a spur-of-the-moment thing after the refusal by Laura even to answer the door. He did not, however, at any time say that he regretted it. He said that he enjoyed it and was surprised that Kyomi had let him come to her after his public protestations about Laura. It is obvious that he likes Kyomi and I would not be surprised if he attempts to continue the relationship."

Peters stopped consulting his notebook to look across to Sven, who replied, "I suspect you may be right. I think perhaps we should keep an eye out for that. Assuming you have nothing more to add on your interview with David Stevens, perhaps you would move on to James Cross?"

Peters began, "Difficult bloke to get any time with. I finally got hold of him at the end of his shift at the Penzance General Hospital. He was pretty tired but still managed to confirm everything that he told us before. I spoke to him about his relationship with the rest of those at the party. He had come with Carole Young, a girl he had been dating since last Christmas. Although that meant that they had been going out for six months, they had seen relatively little of each other because they both worked very odd hours. He had been pleased with himself for engineering a whole weekend off for the party and very sad that it had turned out so badly. He said that he knew most of the guys vaguely because they had all gone to Simon Baker School. He was older than the rest, so encountered them mostly in his role as a prefect, controlling them and punishing their misdemeanours.

"He knew none of the girls apart from Carole. At the time he was surprised at the way Laura had flung herself at him, but had enjoyed it because the amount of drink he had consumed had dulled his brain to any consequences. He had failed to realise that she was just using him to try to make David jealous. Those were his words, but he also said that Carole had warned him at the time and told him not to make a fool of himself. He backed off out of respect for Carole, but mature reflection told him that Carole had assessed the situation correctly."

Peters closed his notebook and looked up at Sven, saying, "That concludes my interviews for today. Would you like to hear how Jenkins and Orchard got on?" Sven nodded and looked toward the two constables.

Jenkins was the first to speak. "We were interviewing the three girls from the pharmacy college who did not already know Laura through the Hilary Taylor School. That is Angela Palmer, Beth Goodheart and Claire West, and their boyfriends Andrew Pitman, Brian Whitehead and Chris Fisher. As Sergeant Peters suggested, we got them to come to the station in pairs. We already had the statements taken on Sunday morning so we went through the details again. All their accounts were consistent with the previous statements and with each other.

"The three girls knew Laura, Scarlett, Kyomi, Nick and each other and had at least met each other's boyfriends. The boys knew all three girls, Nick Dean and again had at least met each other. They had a passing acquaintance with the other pharmacy students. They all seemed to get on well, with the exception of Nick Dean. All three girls said that he had tried and failed to date them. They found him 'too smooth by half,' as Miss Goodheart put it. She did say that she thought Laura had gone out with him once or twice."

Jenkins appeared to have completed his report, so Sven came in with a question: "Would you go over what they told you about happenings after they went to bed, please?"

Jenkins looked over to Orchard, who began, "Yes sir, we are getting a consistent story here. Angela and Andrew went to bed in the St Austell Room at midnight. They confirm that they heard the other four coming to bed about half an hour later. They did not actually see them but recognised their voices. We then have reports of three incidents during the night. The first is a thud, heard by two of the girls but none of the boys. Neither of them can put a time on it, but they both said that it was still dark at the time and that it happened soon after they fell asleep. We have checked the interview notes from the other guests but nobody else has reported a thud. We deduced that this is because the thud would be more audible at the bottom of the lighthouse, especially when all three couples were sleeping with their windows open.

142

"The second incident was reported by Angela and Andrew and occurred when it was getting light. It was the sound of a door opening and a cold draught under the door. We have similar reports of this incident from David Stevens and Jenny Hamilton. Jenny looked at her watch and put the time at four-thirty, which is consistent with it occurring while it was getting light.

"The third incident, of somebody being sick, was reported by Claire, who said it was light when she heard it. A similar incident was reported by Alicia and James and is consistent with the time that Carole said that she was sick."

Orchard looked over to Sven in case he had any further questions. Sven thanked the team and suggested that they call it a night and report back at eight sharp the next day.

Chapter 17

Unusual holiday accommodation

Before he left, Sven picked up the mail in his in-tray and headed back to Edward's house. After supper he excused himself to check his mail. There were two pieces that interested him. The first was a message from Carlton Forbes, the leader of the forensic team working at the lighthouse. He had checked the towels in John's personal stock against the number predicted by Mrs. Young's housekeeper. A smile came to his face as he read the note left by the team secretary:

> *Mr. Forbes reports that he checked the towels in the lighthouse. There are four fewer than you said there should be. The four are two bath sheets, one bath towel and a hand towel. Only one bath towel and one hand towel of the type stated were present. Please call Mr. Forbes if you require any further information.*

Sven's pleasure was further enhanced when he read the second letter, which was the laboratory report on the towels. It confirmed that the red stains were indeed blood and that they had obtained a DNA match to prove that it was Laura's blood. He now knew that Laura had bled profusely before she fell from the lighthouse and that somebody had cleared up the blood. This was conclusive proof that Laura had been murdered.

Before retiring for the night, Sven decided to read the brochure that Jean Young had given him. He pulled it out from his jacket pocket, settled back into the chair and began reading.

Welcome to the Lighthouse at Blimford. We hope that your stay will be a pleasant one. First and most importantly may I remind you about the tides. The lighthouse is at the end of a causeway and is only accessible on foot for twelve hours a day. We **do not** *recommend crossing the causeway in the dark, nor do we like taking the launch out at night other than in an emergency. Please consult the tide times to make sure you are back in time at night. The tide tables are displayed in the lighthouse lobby and at the inn. Crossing to the hotel at high tide in daylight is no problem. Just call the switchboard (dial 0) and we will send the launch for you.*

Blimford Lighthouse is fifty-five feet high with an outside base diameter of thirty-four feet. Its walls are five feet thick at the base, tapering to two feet at the top. It was built and opened in 1788 and remained in constant service for over 200 years until it was replaced by an automatic light at Blimford Head, two miles west along the coast. The light was turned off on the 8th July 1991.

The lighthouse was bought by John Hamilton, who converted it into a home for himself and his daughter Laura. John has maintained the look and authenticity of the lighthouse, both inside and out. On the outside the only difference between now and when it was a working lighthouse is that some windows have been enlarged and others added. To preserve the lines of the building, all the windows align from top to bottom in two columns that are diagonally opposite each other. One set looks back across the causeway to the Lighthouse Inn, whilst the other looks out to sea.

Inside, the original spiral staircase has been retained. All the lighthouse storerooms have been converted into bedrooms, which the hotel uses for guests in the summer. The enlarged windows in the guest bedrooms now open to let in the natural light and fresh sea air that is such a benefit of life in Cornwall. Even the cellar has been converted into rooms that can be used for the occasional night's stay.

Lighthouse-keeping was a solitary, lonely business that required a man— there have been no women keepers—happy with his own company, who could amuse himself. By tradition each keeper used some of his spare time to create something for the lighthouse, a lot of which remains with it to this day. These artefacts, which range from a collection of photographs of the lighthouse taken by keepers over the years to a solid stone table lamp crafted from rock outside the lighthouse, are displayed in the rooms of the lighthouse. They give each room its own character. We have given you a taster of this in our virtual tour below, but in order to appreciate the true nature of the lighthouse you must spend a day and night in it, cut off from the rest of the world.

Come with us now as we take you on virtual tour of the lighthouse. Our tour starts with the lounge or observation room. This room, situated at the top of the lighthouse, is the old lamp room. We have retained the original balcony and put in an observation deck where the light was. It is a fine spot for an evening read or for just looking out to sea. You will find a selection of novels in the lounge and a set of binoculars for observing the shipping. On the walls there are pictures of Blimford and the lighthouse from 1800 to present day.

Taking the stairs down one floor brings you to Laura's room. This room occupies the whole of the third floor, with the exception of the stairwell. The room is used by Laura Hamilton, the landlord's daughter. It is private, but guests may use the stairs to get to the lounge and balcony. It is the original lighthouse store for lamp parts.

Descending another level brings you to the first pair of guest bedrooms. Room 1 on the landward side, known as the St Ives Room, is a cosy single room with views to Blimford and St Ives. Lands End can be seen on a clear day. The felt pictures of a tiger and a giraffe were made by Trevor Nunes, the lighthouse keeper from 1976–1988. Room 2, the Truro Room, is a twin-bedded room with fine views of the sea. It is decorated in the style of a ship's bridge. The compass and housing were recovered from the SS Queen of Sheba, which sank nearby in 1922, but with all hands saved. The compass was the gift of a grateful captain to the lighthouse keeper, Peter Stefford, who raised the alarm and helped in the rescue.

Continuing on down to the next floor brings you to Room 3, the Penzance Room. This is the larger double bedroom with a fine view out to sea. It is decorated in the traditional lighthouse style. The white solid stone walls and varnished wood floor show off the Persian rugs and wall hangings to their best effect. The bed is an original four-poster full-tester, dating back to the late 18th century. We have added a modern sprung mattress for your comfort. The stone table lamp was made by Thomas Becket, the lighthouse keeper from 1904–1909. Adjacent to it is Room 4, the Bodmin Room. This spacious single room also has a fine view of Blimford and on to St Ives. There is a picture of the view to St Ives painted by Alan Peters, the lighthouse keeper from 1934–1959.

Continuing on downstairs brings you on to the ground floor near the entrance hall. Located on the landward side are the bathroom and toilets. The bathroom is fitted with an electric shower. The lighthouse does not have mains water. The toilets and bathrooms are serviced by purified sea water. This is fine for washing and will not harm you if you swallow a drop, but do not drink it. Bottled water for drinking, tea and coffee is provided in the kitchen. The kitchen is opposite the entrance hall.

The room to the seaward side is used by the landlord and is private. The stairs continue on down to the cellar, where we have three additional rooms. The cellar rooms are only used when everywhere else is full. They provide the basic comforts, but do not have the luxury of the other rooms. The windows are situated high up on the walls, since most of the cellar is cut into the rock. Guests usually only stay in these rooms for a single night. Rooms 5 and 6, St Austell and Mousehole, are twin-bedded, and Room 7, the Looe Room, is single-bedded.

If you are lucky, you might even meet our ghost. The lighthouse logs record several sightings of a keeper running through the lighthouse with a lantern and beckoning to someone to follow him. Other sightings are by people who wake up with somebody tugging at their shoulders and find a man standing over them.

The description fits that of lighthouse keeper Peter Finch, who was drowned on the 4th September 1892. Records show that he dived into the sea to save a child who had fallen overboard from a passing boat. Unusually for the time, there was somebody else, his brother James, staying in the lighthouse. James's account stated that he was sleeping in the afternoon when his brother woke him. Peter said that a child had fallen from a pleasure yacht, but that the parents had not noticed. He called James to signal with the lantern while he attempted the rescue. James, in a daze and not knowing his way around the lighthouse, stumbled about as he tried to follow his brother, who stood there beckoning him. When James got outside he successfully signalled the boat, which turned to pick up Peter and the child. Before they could reach the pair, the strong tide dragged them both under the waves to their deaths. They were washed up in St Ives bay the next morning. There is a plaque honouring Peter's heroic effort in the hall just to the left of the entrance.

Sven put the brochure and the remaining papers back into his briefcase. Things were beginning to come together in his mind. He knew that Laura had been murdered in the lighthouse, and very conveniently he had a detailed mental map of it, which gave him some clues. With that thought in his head he decided that he had earned a night's rest.

Chapter 18

A bad day at the office, 4th July 1996

Sven was up early with a feeling that he was getting somewhere. As usual, Edward joined him for breakfast, which was an excuse to get an update on how things were getting on. Today's conversation was different in that it was Sven who was likely to learn more, since Edward had obtained copies of both John's and Laura's wills.

Edward passed the copies to Sven and explained the reason why it had taken so long to get them. "I got the wills from John's solicitors, Jones, McInally and Harbour, yesterday. Laura's will was quite simple, poor thing, but there was a complication with John's will. He changed it on the evening that he died. In the original will, which he made in 1989, he left eight thousand pounds to Carole and five thousand pounds to Todd. The rest of his estate went to Laura. There was a clause relating to Carole and Laura stating that each had to survive him by thirty days to achieve their inheritance, otherwise everything due to the one went to the other. The money would be held in trust until each girl was eighteen. There was also a note with the will explaining why he had left money to Todd. He recognised that his liaison with Todd's mother had caused the break-up of Todd's family and the money was by way of apology to, and compensation for,

Todd. The only other point of interest was a request on the beneficiaries to continue to allow Jean Young to use the rooms in the lighthouse that she currently uses at the same rent that applied at the time of his death. Since it is only a request, I doubt that it is legally enforceable. The change is more interesting, since it is a witnessed instruction rather than a new will."

Edward passed a copy of the fax to Sven, who examined it carefully. Although a fax, it took the form of a letter addressed to Alan McInally of Jones, McInally and Harbour. The letter was signed by John Hamilton and witnessed by two members of the Ship Hotel's staff. The contents read:

I wish to change my will in relation to my daughters. After the payment of £5000 (five thousand pounds) to Todd Mitchell, I wish to divide the remainder of my estate equally between my daughters Carole Young and Laura Hamilton. They must survive me by 30 days otherwise, after the payment to Todd Mitchell, i) If one fails to survive me all my estate goes to the other; ii) If both fail to survive me all my estate goes to my twin brother Edward and iii) If both my daughters and Edward fail to survive me then all my estate goes to the RNLI.

Both girls are over 18 so I need no trustees.

Please will you make the necessary changes and let me know when it is ready. I will pop in to sign it next time I am in Truro.

The paper stated that it had been faxed by the Ship Hotel, Truro, Cornwall, at 20:58 on 29th June 1996.

Edward continued, "Of course, legally it makes no difference which will prevails. Carole will benefit providing she survives another twenty-six days. However, as a detective, it makes a lot of difference. Although he did not know it, John was already dying when he sent that fax, so whoever murdered him certainly did not know of that change in the will."

Sven listened in silence to what Edward was saying, and then, as he scanned the papers that had just been given to him, asked, "Does Laura's will add anything?"

The question was clearly rhetorical since Sven was already reading Laura's will. Edward allowed him time to digest it and comment. After reading it, Sven looked up. "She leaves everything to her father as next of kin, or if that fails then it goes to her mother. That was logical for one so young, but I do not expect that to amount to much now that her father's estate is not included. By the way, are you still in touch with Emma Hamilton?"

Edward shook his head as he replied, "No, I lost contact when she went to Greece. I asked the solicitors if they could help. They have an address in Greece so they are going to see what they can do for me. They won't give me the address, of course, but they will get a message to her if they can."

Sven arrived at the police station in time for his team meeting at ten o'clock. Peters was already there. He gave Sven just enough time to sit down before he said, "I have just had a call from Inspector Corke, sir. He has found out that Nick Dean has started to use heroine. He was suspicious, so he got a warrant to search Dean's room and his locker at the college. They found a used syringe and twelve Ecstasy tablets hidden in a vacuum flask in his locker. The tablets made them suspicious, so they also searched the lockers of all the other pharmacy course students. They found cannabis in the lockers of Angela Palmer and Claire West. They brought both of them into the station for a formal caution yesterday afternoon. That's not all, though, sir. They have found Nick Dean's motorbike in the Acres Heath cliff top car park, but there was no sign of Dean. They are still looking, of course, but he thought that maybe we would like to take this one over. It's at least a missing person now and could be more."

Sven agreed and asked Peters to inform Inspector Corke. While they were talking, Orchard and Jenkins appeared. Sven was keen to get down to business. "Right, Peters and I are going to check out the car park where Nick Dean's bike was found. Would you two please chase up the forensic team in the lighthouse? Go over there and get the preliminary findings if the final reports are not ready. Are there any questions?" The tone of Sven's voice made it clear that he expected none, and he got none. Sven continued, but only to close the meeting, "Right then, let's get to it."

The sun shone brightly as Peters drove himself and Sven into the Acres Heath car park. A uniformed officer guided them to a suitable parking space facing the sea. While Peters went to talk to the CID staff on site, Sven reviewed the location. It was on the cliff path between St Ives and Zennor. He stood facing the sea, with the town of St Ives to his right. The path to the left headed out west along the cliff path toward Zennor. Directly in front of him a path led down to a beach in a small bay. A second small path ran off at forty-five degrees to the left to a viewpoint with a bench. He walked along to the bench, looking around as he went. The views over the cliffs and out to sea were spectacular, but he could not see the beach.

He checked under the seat and in the surrounding undergrowth but found nothing out of the ordinary. He went back to learn what Peters had discovered. Peters introduced him to a constable from the traffic unit. "Sven, this is Constable Harris, he was the officer who found the bike."

The constable greeted Sven with a cheerful "Good morning, sir." Sven returned the greeting, asking the constable what he had discovered. "I should say that the bike has been here for a fair time, sir. The exhaust pipe is cold and the seat is quite wet. It has not rained since early Tuesday morning, so I reckon that it was there then. It is too wet for simple condensation. Also there are no tyre tracks, suggesting that the bike was parked here before it rained. Of course that is just an amateur opinion, which would need to be validated by an expert."

The constable appeared pleased with his analysis, which had also impressed Sven, who decided that an acknowledgement was appropriate. "Thank you, Constable Harris, that looks like a fine piece of deduction." Turning to Peters, he added, "I am going down to the beach to take a look. Would you please make the arrangements for the bike to be checked over by a forensic unit?" Peters nodded as Sven left to go down the path to the beach.

The path descended steeply, finishing in a set of steps that led on to the beach. The beach was enclosed on both sides by headlands running down to rocks. It was late afternoon and the tide was high, making access across the rocks almost impossible. He guessed that there would be passage around the rocks at low tide. The beach was sparsely populated with a mixture of families with small children and young couples. Some were swimming, others sunbathing and one dedicated father was building a sand castle with his two young sons.

As he stood there taking everything in, Sven noticed two young couples, who had been playing in the water, walk back to where they had left a pile of clothes and towels on the beach. He instantly recognised the small, dark, attractive girl in the blue swimming costume as Kyomi Taylor. A second look confirmed that the others were Todd Mitchell, Scarlett Robinson and David Stevens. They soon spotted him as well, with Scarlett giving him a wave of recognition, which he answered with a smile. Sven thought, *No time like the present*, as he crossed the beach toward them.

Todd was the first to speak. "Morning, Inspector. It's a nice day for the beach, but aren't you a little overdressed?"

Sven looked down at his polished shoes, tweed trousers, crisp blue shirt and tie. Even holding his jacket by its hook over his right shoulder did not disguise the fact that he did look very much out of place. "Work, I am afraid," he replied, "but it's nice to take a break with a little sun and air. Do you guys come here often?"

Scarlett responded, "It's a favourite of ours outside of the main holiday period of July and August. We come here most days when it's fine."

Sven saw his chance to check something without raising any alarm. "That could be handy for me. Were any of you here either yesterday or Monday?"

Again it was Scarlett who responded, "Yes, we were all here in the afternoon on Monday. We met Kyomi and David at about one and left at…." Scarlett hesitated for a moment and then, looking to Todd for confirmation, continued, "About five, I guess."

Todd nodded, adding, "Yes, give or take ten minutes anyway. How can we help you, Inspector?"

Sven asked, "Did you see anybody else that you knew?"

Scarlett smiled as she responded, "Yes, we pharmacy students get Monday afternoons off in the summer term, so we all—well, all the girls anyway because Nick never comes—used to meet here with as many of our boyfriends who could make it. We called each other and decided that we would go ahead, both as a tribute to Laura and as a way of trying to get our lives back in some sort of order. We were all here. Kyomi even phoned David to make sure that he came along as well."

Sven did a mental count before confirming, "That was ten in total, then: the four of you, Angela Palmer, Beth Goodheart and Claire West and their boyfriends Andrew Pitman, Brian Whitehead and Chris Fisher."

He waited for confirmation, which came from Scarlett, before continuing, "Did you see anybody else that you knew that day?"

Three of them shook their heads, but David recalled something. "Now you come to mention it, I did see somebody else that I recognised. It was a guy who was at the party. I cannot remember his name but he was on the pharmacy course with Laura."

Scarlett came in, "That has to be Nick Dean. He is the only boy on the course. You know, David, the one who spent most of the party behind the bar and drank a drink for every one that he poured?"

A spark of recognition went across David's face. "Yes, that's him, Inspector. Nick Dean. He was walking across the beach toward the cliffs over there." David pointed toward the cliffs at the west of the bay.

"Can you remember when that was?" Sven enquired.

"Oh, soon after we arrived, I think. I saw him while we were all in swimming. We got here at about one-thirty so I guess it would have been about two o'clock, give or take ten minutes."

"And can you remember what he was wearing?"

David shook his head, thought for a moment and replied, "Jeans and a tee-shirt, I think. He was barefoot and carrying a pair of trainers. I remember thinking that it was odd that he did not have a towel with him."

Sven said, "Thank you, David, that is very helpful. Oh, just one other point, was the tide in or out while you were there?"

Todd came in straight away, "It was coming in. Low tide was at ten forty-seven on Monday."

Sven thanked them all for their help, wished them an enjoyable day and left to return to the car park. The forensic team had already arrived. They were busying themselves in the cordoned-off area around Nick's bike.

"Anything interesting, Sven?" Peters enquired as a somewhat out-of-breath inspector reached the top of the cliff. After he had caught his breath, Sven asked what was accessible from the bay at low tide. Peters looked down, pointing out features as he spoke. "To the right it runs round behind St Ives to Carbis Bay, but you cannot get there by foot, even at low tide. To the left you can get around the headland and along a bit, but you would soon run out of beach. There are a couple of caves but they do not lead anywhere. The lads plan to search them when the tide goes down. That'll be in about four hours' time."

Sven pondered for a moment before asking, "Is there any other access to those caves, Sergeant?"

"I suppose that you could scramble down the cliff, but there is no path and I would not recommend it without climbing gear. A good swimmer could get round from Nid beach; that's the next bay along. It has been known for people to swim round at high tide and do a bit of nude sunbathing before the tide falls enough to allow access from this side. We don't bother about it because they cannot be seen from the land."

Sven responded immediately with another pair of questions. "Is there a path leading off the cliff path that goes down to Nid beach?"

"Yes, it's a couple of miles that way," Peters replied, pointing to the cliff path on the left.

"Is there a car park as well?"

"No, Nid beach is for pedestrians only. This would be the nearest vehicular access."

Sven appeared pleased with these answers. He thought for a moment, then said, "We should join the team that is searching the caves. Would you please tell them that we are coming? Before that I shall use the opportunity to take a look at Nid beach. Oh, also would you please get Jenkins and Orchard to check out where James Cross, Carole Young and Alicia Adams were on Monday afternoon? I will ask the whereabouts of Sarah and Jenny Hamilton when I see them this evening. I think that covers everybody. I will meet you back here in about four hours. Why don't you take the opportunity to go home for a meal and a rest because it could be a late night."

A Labrador came bounding toward him with her tail wagging furiously. Sven was just able to catch two muddy paws before they landed on his trousers. The dog settled back, allowing Sven to pat her but, more importantly, keep her from leaping upon him again.

"Honey, come back here." The voice came from a lady of ample proportions in her mid-sixties, wearing a thick roll-neck sweater, tweed suit and "sensible" shoes. "I'm sorry; I still haven't managed to train her not to do that. She is only being affectionate. I hope she did not get mud on your nice trousers."

Sven, as always, remembered his manners. As the dog planted a muddy paw on his highly polished shoes he smiled and assured the lady that no harm had been done.

"Lovely day," the lady added more to cover her embarrassment than in any attempt to make genuine conversation.

"Indeed it is," Sven replied. "There can be nothing finer than a coastal path in England on a sunny day. Do you get the opportunity to walk it often?"

"Oh every day, my dear. Honey must have her walk, mustn't you, Honey?" She reached down as she spoke to stoke the dog's head. This had the effect of making the dog jump up again, but this time, to Sven's relief, the paws landed on her mistress's skirt. Sven took the chance to wish her well, disengage from the conversation and continue his walk of discovery.

A little later Sven checked his watch. He had left the Acres Heath car park an hour previously and had not found any sign of a path leading down to the sea. Had Peters really meant two miles or was "a couple of miles" just a local term for something much farther? Clearly Peters expected him to be able to get there and back within four hours, so it could not be much farther. As he was pondering his dilemma, a man in his sixties, complete with walking socks, boots and a stick, came striding around the corner. To Sven's relief, he was not accompanied by a dog. A brief enquiry of this man elicited the fact that the path was about one hundred yards farther up and that it was unmarked and a little overgrown.

The man warned him, "There is room to get through, but be careful of the nettles, especially at this time of year." Thanks to this description, Sven found the path with little problem. He was sure that without this advice he would have ignored it. He followed the path, which descended steadily down to the sea. He surveyed a deserted beach about fifty yards wide, with about ten feet of dry sand followed by a further twenty feet of wet sand. The tide had been going out for about an hour. A solitary pile of clothes, a towel and a pair of shoes lay on a rock on the right-hand side. He looked out to sea, where a man who was definitely a strong swimmer was heading out to sea. Sven surmised that he might be one of the nude sunbathers that Peters had mentioned. He estimated that the swimmer would need to go another hundred feet out to sea before he could turn right and access the caves. A quick look at the rocks on the right confirmed Peters's assertion that access across them would be extremely difficult without climbing gear. There being nothing else of interest to him, Sven returned to the cliff path and back to Acres Heath car park.

Peters greeted him with some urgency. "Ah, there you are, Sven. That's good because we are about ready to go." It was clear that he had been holding the rest of the team back. Sven joined Peters and two members of the drugs squad on the walk down to the beach. As they rolled up their trousers and removed their shoes and socks, the same thought of lack of dignity went through Sven's and Peters's minds. Peters was the first to articulate it. He observed, in a style that mocked a nineteen-fifties *Pathe News* reader, "The intrepid British bobby is prepared for all eventualities."

All four men broke into laughter almost simultaneously. The thought of what he expected to find then crossed Sven's mind, but he did not share it with the others. He restricted himself to thinking that he hoped that they could all still laugh after they had inspected the caves. The group trudged across the white sandy beach, over the wet sand recently covered by the high tide, and around the rocky headland to the first and larger of the two caves. They entered, inspected it using a torch provided by one of the drug squad officers, and were surprised to find only a small amount of litter at the far end of the cave.

Somewhat relieved, they all proceeded to the second, smaller cave, where their mood changed rapidly. The torch, once lit and shone into the cave, cast its light on the pasty white body of a man lying chest-down in the sand. His head was turned to one side, revealing his face, which all present immediately recognised as Nick Dean. He was naked, with his clothes thrown with a high degree of abandon around the cave. The body and all the clothes were soaking wet. Sven surmised that this was from the previous high tide. He had received two heavy blows to the back of his skull. Blood had run out of these wounds and on to the sand in the cave. All four men stopped any further advance into the cave in order to preserve the crime scene for the forensic team. One member of the party was despatched to get the forensic team. There was clearly no time to lose, as they needed to gather as much evidence as they could and remove the body before the tide returned to cover it again.

Sven looked around the area in the mouth of the cave that the team had reached before they discovered the body. He noted that the sea had done a fine job of cleaning everything off the sand to, he surmised, the back of the cave. To one side something glinted in the sunlight. He bent down to examine it at the same time asking Peters for a sample bag. It was at that point that he realised it was a syringe with a hypodermic needle still attached.

"Best not to touch that, Sven, it would be better to leave it to the forensic boys. They have the implements to make sure it and they do not get damaged." Peters's concern was genuine, but he need not have worried.

Sven covered the hypodermic with the bag, placing stones on either side to keep the bag down. "Just marking it and protecting it from the gulls," Sven observed as a large, squawking bird dropped a message near him before flying off.

"They remind me of our visiting top brass from Scotland Yard, they do, sir. Fly in, eat your food, squawk a lot, dump all over you and fly out again."

Sven laughed at Peters's observation, confirming that he had similar types in Norway and congratulating Peters on his refined choice of verb for their penultimate act. "Thank you, Sven, that was out of respect for you, sir. We normally say that the advice we get from Scotland Yard is correct, reasonable and practical, although we just use the acronym. You, on the other hand, Sven, have rolled your sleeves up and got on with it."

Sven's mind went into overdrive trying to work out the joke that he knew was in there somewhere and to assess whether the compliment that followed was genuine or delivered with a tinge of sarcasm that marked the understated nature of Peters', humour. Concluding that the compliment was probably genuine and wishing to hide his embarrassment, he commented, "Well, I do not think that there is much more for us here; let's get back to the car."

Peters was at the top of the cliff well before Sven and had the car started and ready for the off by the time Sven reached it. "Where to now, Sven?" Peters enquired as he drove to the car park exit.

Sven responded with reservation in his voice, "I told the drugs sergeant that we would break the news to his mother, so I guess that we should do as soon as we can. I will radio the station to get a WPC to join us. I don't care even if it is not strictly required; those girls are ten times better at coping with the results of somebody being given bad news than I will ever be. With a bit of luck she might even get there first." With that Sven reached for the radio.

"You are right there, Sven, I'm the same," Peters replied, adding, "To Nick Dean's place it is, then."

By the time Sven and Sergeant Peters arrived, WPC Hayes had already broken the news to Mrs. Dean. A lady in her mid-forties wearing a nurse's uniform greeted both men, who promptly identified themselves with their warrant cards.

The nurse introduced herself in a pleasant, professional manner. "Good afternoon, gentlemen, I am Brenda Wells, Julia Dean's sister. Julia is keen to help you as much as she can. I assume that you would like her to talk to you straight away?"

Sven was keen to get information quickly, but was not prepared to put any further strain on Mrs. Dean. "Yes, I would," he replied, "but only if she is sure that she is up to it. I promise that for now I will be brief."

Brenda Wells confirmed that her sister would answer questions. She gestured both men to sit down while she went to fetch her sister. While he was waiting, Sven looked around the room. It was the lounge of a typical two-up, two-down cottage built at about the turn of the century. The two policemen were sitting on a settee immediately behind the front window. Behind them and to the right was the front door, which was in the corner of the room. On the right-hand wall was the staircase with a cupboard underneath it. The stairs rose from right to left, starting opposite the front door. To the right of the opposite wall an open door led out to the kitchen. To the left of that wall was a small television sitting on a stand with a video unit beneath it. On the television was a framed photograph of a small boy on a tricycle. Sven guessed that the boy was Nick Dean. The left-hand wall was dominated by a fireplace with a gas fire in the grate. A carriage clock sat in splendid isolation in the centre of the mantelpiece. Above that was a large mirror fixed flat to the wall. The only other piece of furniture in the room was an armchair placed against the staircase to give a good view of the television.

Sven's observations were distracted by the sound of footsteps coming down the stairs. Julia Dean, a tall, well-built lady, came in to the room on the arm of Mrs. Wells. Sven estimated that she was younger than her sister and probably in her early forties. It was clear that she had been crying, but at least for the moment the tears had stopped. Both men got to their feet immediately.

Julia Dean responded in a faltering voice, "Please, gentlemen, do sit down. We do not need any formalities. Now, how can I help you?"

Sven expressed his condolences and confirmed with her that she felt strong enough to answer some questions. He had decided to keep the conversation short, so he got straight to the point. "Did Nick go to the beach at Acres Heath or Nid often?"

Julia Dean's response made it clear that she had been told that Nick had been found in that area and had been pondering upon it. "No, he never went to the beach. He did not swim and he was not one to sunbathe."

Sven probed gently, "Perhaps he had some other reason to go to the beach, maybe fishing for shellfish or lobsters or even just collecting shells?"

Mrs. Dean thought for a moment before replying, "I suppose he just might have done. If he thought he could make money from them he would have done. He was quite an entrepreneur, always buying and selling things."

Sven decided that she was able to continue. "Thank you, Mrs. Dean. I have one more question. Did Nick have a regular girlfriend?"

"Nick had lots of girlfriends, but as far as I know, nobody special. He often went out for the evening but he never brought anybody back. There are pictures of plenty of different girls in his room."

Sven thanked her for her help. She was going to be taken to the mortuary to identify Nick's body. Despite Sven's suggestion that perhaps it might be better left to her sister, Julia Dean insisted on going as well. Sven obtained her permission to look over Nick's room before he left.

Nick's room was upstairs at the back of the house. As he entered, Sven was greeted with a small, untidy room with a single unmade bed, fitted wardrobe, chest of drawers and desk with a desk light. The floor, bed and desk were strewn with clothes, compact discs, tapes and books. A hi-fi unit, television and a video unit sat on top of the chest of drawers. Two speakers were mounted on the wall above the bed. Posters of female pop stars and motorbikes filled most of the walls, with the exception of a small area above the desk where there was a notice board. Sven recognised the largest poster, which had pride of place opposite the head of the bed, as Kylie Minogue, but he could not identify any of the others. He moved over to the notice board, which had several photographs pinned to it.

There was a set of four from a photo booth. Two were of Nick and a girl while the other two were of the same girl by herself. Sven recognised the girl as Laura Hamilton. He looked at the rest of the photographs. There were a couple of the pharmacy class and several of a younger-looking Nick, which Sven assumed to be from his school days. In the desk drawers he found more compact discs and tapes, textbooks and Nick's own lecture notes and coursework. At the back of the drawer he found several well-thumbed men's magazines. He looked at the coursework that had been marked. The pieces were graded between C+ and D, which Sven took to be passes but showing no great flair for the subject. Of the seven pieces that Sven examined, three had been annotated, "submitted late."

Peters called up from downstairs, "Anything of interest, Sven? Would you like me to come up?"

"No, nothing," Sven replied as he came down the stairs. "I had hoped to find a diary but no joy there. Let's get back to the station."

Peters dropped Sven off at Edward Hamilton's house sharp at six o'clock. Rose had given him strict instructions that he be home in time for evening meal because both girls were also dining in. They wanted to make it a bit of a family occasion. Sven handed her the bottle of white wine that he had remembered to purchase on the way home.

"Oh Sven, how kind, but you really shouldn't," Rose said, thanking him and planting a kiss on his cheek at the same time. "Still, since you have, I will put it in the fridge to cool."

This remark confirmed what Sven had thought: that her resistance was only token. He knew that both she and Edward enjoyed a glass of wine with their meal and were limited by the number of occasions when driving prevented one of them from indulging.

A voice behind him said, "Hi, Uncle Sven, busy day?" Sven turned just in time to receive another peck on the cheek, this time from Jenny.

"Yes, thank you, how about you?" Sven replied, deciding that he was not going to spoil the mood by giving them details of the tough day he had just completed.

Jenny beamed. "I've had most of the week off; so today I decided to take Sarah off to the beach. We went to Carbis Bay."

Sven looked surprised. "I thought Sarah was at work. Has term finished already?"

"No and no," Jenny replied, making her answer totally precise and then explaining, "Poor Sarah could not face work after Laura's and John's deaths. She has been on compassionate leave ever since. Her headmaster has been great. He has told her to take all the time she needs and he does not expect to see her back this term. So anyway, I have been trying to take her out of herself. Today, since it was such a beautiful day, was the beach, yesterday I took her walking on the moors, and on Monday we went to St Ives for a bit of retail therapy. I made her do some walking that day as well, though. Since you can never park in St Ives, we drove to the car park at Acres Heath and walked in along the cliff path from there. I bought this top, do you like it?"

Sven looked at a top that was tied behind Jenny's neck and halfway down her back. That was the extent to which it covered her back. At the front it covered the essentials but little more. The uncovered parts had tanned to a deep brown with no trace of redness. Sven struggled for a suitable reply. "Very nice, and it looks like it achieved its objective. That's a fine tan you have got there."

Jenny smiled, thanked him and went upstairs to change. Edward came to meet him carrying two glasses, each filled with a generous measure of whisky over a solitary ice cube. He thrust one into Sven's hand with the comment, "A quick snifter before supper, Sven."

Chapter 19

Evidence, but not enough of it

Inspector Pinks walked in just as Sergeant Peters was about to start the daily meeting. He nodded to Peters and then turned to Sven. "Sorry, Sven, the super is visiting today so I need to understand what is going on in case he asks. I am not sure that Ron Graves has let him in on our local arrangement. I have had regular meetings with Sergeant Peters, who tells me that the team has gelled well and that all the lads are pleased to be working with you. For my part I am pleased to be leading such a well-run team, even if it is in name only. I should like to take the opportunity to thank you, Sven, for the effort that you have been putting in on what is notionally only a fact-finding visit. I will make sure that the super feeds that back to your superintendent in Oslo. Now, Sergeant Peters, would you carry on as if I was not here—that is as normal, please."

Sven blushed at the compliment that he had been paid. He had known Edward Hamilton for some time and had been gaining increasing respect and confidence in the team, under Sergeant Peters, that he had been leading. Inspector Pinks was, however, an unknown entity. He had met Pinks only the once when he was introduced to the team at St Ives. As he was mulling this over Peters began, "Thank you, guv. Constable Orchard, would you tell us what you found out about the whereabouts of Carole Young, Alicia Adams and James Cross on Monday afternoon when we believe Nick Dean was murdered?"

Orchard opened his notebook, cleared his throat and began, "I decided to visit them all, Sarge, so that I could see their reactions to my questions rather than just call them. I visited James Cross at the Penzance General first. He has been on night shifts this week starting last Sunday night. Notionally they are twelve-hour shifts but he did not get away until eight o'clock on Monday morning because he was dealing with a major road accident. I checked it with Traffic Division over in Penzance and they confirmed the accident. Even spoke to one of their guys who took statements. He remembers seeing James Cross on duty at about seven that morning. Anyway, Cross says he finished at eight, went straight back to his quarters and went to bed. He says he slept until about four o'clock Monday afternoon when he got up, had breakfast, read the papers in the common room and then went back on duty. I checked the signing-in records. They confirm what he said. He has his own room at the residents' house, so there was nobody to confirm his whereabouts when he said he was sleeping."

Orchard stopped talking to await questions, but none came. He turned over the page in his notebook and continued, "Next I visited the Lighthouse Inn. Mrs. Young was a bit surprised when I called to make the appointment. She said that she and her daughters had told Inspector Ffolkes everything only the day before. I explained that there had been developments that necessitated further questions, without actually telling her what those events were. Anyway, she accepted that and I interviewed them all yesterday afternoon. She was at the Lighthouse Inn all day. She said there were plenty of staff who could verify it if needed. During the course of my interviews with Carole and Alicia they did both confirm that their mother was on duty on Monday. That was the only reason why both of them were able to get out in the afternoon.

"Carole said that she worked until twelve when her shift ended and then she went out. She went for a walk, a swim and some sunbathing. She parked her car at Acres Heath and took a walk down the cliff path to Zennor. She has a favourite beach that she uses down there. It's called Chard beach, just to the east of Gurnard's Head. I know it well, it's very pretty. She took the cliff path west, past the track down to Nid beach and the next one to Pen beach until she reached the third track that leads down to Chard beach. That is a very pleasant walk of about four miles. Anyway, she said that she got there at around two o'clock, swam and sunbathed at Chard until about five, walked back to Acres Heath beach and then home. She added that she fell asleep for a while and burned her back. I could not verify that because she was dressed in her working clothes, but her face did look well-tanned. She said that she got home at about six-thirty to go back on duty at seven. Mrs. Young confirmed the times of Carole's shifts and the fact that she was on time for her evening shift."

Again Orchard stopped to take questions, but again there were none. He turned over a page in his notebook and continued, "I also spoke to Alicia. She finished lunch at about two-thirty, but had to be back at five-thirty to get the dinner under way. She too decided to go for a walk, but thought that she did not have time for a swim. She did take her sketch pad, though. She showed me a sketch of the lighthouse that she said she did at Navax point. It was really very good. She went east along the coast path to Navax point, cut back across country and then returned to the hotel from the other direction on the coast path. That's a distance of about a mile and a half, I reckon, so she would have had plenty of time to do her sketch. She told me that she saw Carole at just before twelve when Carole brought through an early lunch order. Carole remarked at the time that she was off to Chard for the afternoon. Mrs. Young saw Alicia come back on duty at five-thirty for the evening meal. I could not corroborate this with any of the kitchen staff, though. There were two of them who were working Monday evening. Both came on at five and picked up written instructions that Alicia had left for them. They commented that this was quite normal and that the first hour of preparation was always very busy. They also said that just because they did not see Alicia did not mean that she was not there. Apparently she is not one of those chefs who shouts at everybody. Instead, they said that she just gets on with her work and is a pleasure to work for. Unless, that is, you get sloppy and do not present the food exactly right. Then she is on to you like a ton of bricks, but that's quite rare. It seems that after one warning they do all they can to avoid another. For completeness, I asked Carole about the times that she saw Alicia. She confirmed that Alicia was there when she went to collect her first wine order just after she had started her shift. That would be just after seven."

Sven sat back in his chair, dejected. "So from what we have learned, any of our suspects had time to kill Nick Dean, or do any of you have any insight that I have missed that identifies who did kill him, or for that matter, who could not have killed him?"

They all looked blank. Peters was the first to speak. "I certainly cannot, Sven. I have also been trying to think of a motive. We appear to be assuming that Dean was killed by the same person who killed Laura, presumably because he saw something. But is there another possibility? We know that Dean was dealing in drugs. Could it be that one of his customers got desperate and killed him for what he was carrying? Perhaps it is time for me and a couple of the boys to pay Big Porky a visit?"

Sven nodded with his demeanour showing signs of resignation. "Yes, Peters, that is a good point. Please see if that line of enquiry gets us anywhere. In the meantime, how did we get on with the post-mortem results?"

Jenkins spoke up, "That was my task, sir. I started with Laura, whose post-mortem was conducted at the College Hospital in Penzance. The formal report only serves to confirm all that the pathologist told us in the preliminary report, with no additional facts. Shall I just summarise those for us all, sir?"

The question was really directed at Inspector Pinks, but both he and Sven agreed to the idea. Jenkins scanned his notebook for the salient facts, beginning, "There were several injuries consistent with Laura having fallen a long way, including a fracture to the left cheekbone, two fractures to her left upper arm and the single fracture to her collar bone. Her body had multiple bruising on the upper left side, suggesting a fall with impact in that area, probably face-first.

"One injury, a depressed fracture to the right side of the skull, was the one that interested him most, since it was inconsistent with the fall. The amount of blood around this wound was greater, which strongly suggested to him that it was made first. The pathologist said that although he could not be sure, it is likely that the blow to the right rear of the skull preceded the injuries from the fall. He confirmed that this blow knocked her unconscious but did not kill her. Neither did the fall kill her. She died later from multiple injuries. He also recorded abrasions to the stomach, abdomen and fronts of the thighs consistent with the body having scraped against a hard, probably metallic surface. Estimated time of death was between two and four-thirty on the morning of the thirtieth of June. His best guess was that she died fifteen minutes to an hour after she fell. The pathologist notes that Laura Hamilton was about twelve weeks pregnant. He found no evidence of any drugs in her system."

Peters was the first to respond. "So now we know for certain that it was murder and a callous one at that. First the murderer bashes the poor girl over the head, knocking her unconscious, then throws her off the lighthouse and leaves her to die. Well, at least she was unconscious and did not suffer."

Sven responded with reservation, "I hope that you are right, Sergeant, and that she did not regain consciousness. Anyway, let us continue with Constable Jenkins's report of his day's work. Please continue, Constable."

Jenkins nodded, turned over a page in his notebook and continued his report. "I then talked to the pathologist who examined John Hamilton. It's the same thing again, sir, with the formal report confirming the initial conclusions.

Death was caused by heart failure, induced by the intake of strychnine poison. Blood analysis showed a level about that normally considered lethal for a healthy adult. The poison would have been ingested up to five hours before death. The heavy meal would have slowed the effect, so the pathologist estimated the latest time of ingestion to be three hours before, with four hours before being the most likely. Blood analysis also revealed an alcohol level of one hundred and fifty milligrams per millilitre, which is equivalent to having twelve to twenty standard drinks. The pathologist also noted that the condition of the liver and analysis of the liver cells indicated that Mr. Hamilton was a heavy drinker, but that this condition was not life-threatening and did not contribute to his death."

"So now you have two confirmed murders with different MOs and a suspected third. Do you suspect one, two or three murderers?" The tone was not critical but just factual.

Sven turned to Inspector Pinks, who had made the enquiry. "That's a fair question, but I hate speculation. The facts tell me that three people who are connected to each other have died within three days but in different places and by at least two different methods. The fact that they are related suggests a connection, pointing to the same murderer or murderers. I need more facts. I need to know why they were killed, I need to know if they have anything more in common and I need to know if anybody else is at risk."

Sven put greater emphasis on the word "need" each time he used it, betraying the increasing frustration that he was feeling about this case. He sat back in his chair and waved his hand by way of apology for his outburst.

Pinks's face flushed with embarrassment, from which he attempted to talk his way out. "My dear chap, I am so sorry. I had no desire to put pressure on you and I intended no criticism. I was wondering if you needed any more help."

Sven recovered his composure, replying, "Thank you, Inspector. I assure you that I took no criticism from it. I am frustrated with myself for not seeing the death of Nick Dean coming. You have provided me with an excellent team and I will not take any more of your precious resources. We will get to the bottom of this, but also look to protect any more potential victims. I include all those who were at the party in that category. This is what we will do. Firstly we will phone all these potential targets to warn them not to meet anybody in a one-on-one or to go out alone into a deserted place or in the dark. We will also offer police protection to any of them who wish it. We will do that before we go home tonight. Secondly we will interview all those who were at Acres Heath beach on Monday. I want to know if any of them could have slipped away without the others knowing it. Thirdly, we will go back over the backgrounds of all our suspects and victims to dredge out any more possible connections. That includes police records, club memberships, interests and anything else that might give us a clue." Turning to his team, Sven added, "Gentlemen, we have a busy time ahead of us."

Chapter 20

Co-operation and confession, 5th July 1996

Inspector Corke had planned this raid meticulously. Peter Paul Jewell, known to his friends as Big Porky, lived in a large detached house set in a wooded plot backing on to the cliffs at the end of Nags Lane. It was surrounded by a ten-foot-high brick wall with broken glass set into it. The front entrance had radio-controlled electric gates operated from the house. There was only one other way through the wall: a heavy wooden gate bolted at the top and bottom and set into the wall at the back of the property. This led out to the cliff path running along the rear boundary of the property.

Security cameras surveyed the front entrance, the rear gate and all around the wall. They even surveyed the footpath that ran from the end of the lane along the side of the wall to the cliff path. At night guard dogs patrolled the grounds. There was no way that an intruder could get in undetected and, the unsuspecting observer might think, no way that anybody could get out undetected. Inspector Corke was, however, not unsuspecting. He had heard of several police raids that had failed to catch Big Porky so he had done some homework. He had viewed plans of the house lodged at the time that an extension was built. He had discovered that the house had an old priest's hole. But that was not all. Aerial photographs taken from a police helicopter revealed a suspicious line leading out under the garden and extending fifty feet beyond the wall to a small clearing in woodland on the cliffs. An earlier examination of the clearing revealed a concealed exit to a tunnel leading from the house. Three of Inspector Corke's team now patrolled that exit while another two waited behind the back gate. It was four o'clock in the morning, the trap was set and he was about to spring it.

Two police cars pulled up at the front gate with their lights flashing. Corke's assistant, Sergeant Bill Jones, spoke clearly into the intercom. "Open up! Police!"

Fully half a minute later a woman's voice responded, "Come in, please." At the same time the electric gates swung open and the trap door in the clearing opened. Three policemen jumped on a burly man who struggled violently. The man screamed, "Police!" into the mobile radio that he was holding.

As two of the policemen began cuffing the restrained man, the third policemen yelled into his own radio, "It's not Porky; it's Freddy Russell, one of his henchmen. Send back-up."

Four policemen from the second car rushed down the footpath as the first car containing Corke, Jones, a WPC and two constables reached the front door, which opened as they arrived. An attractive girl in her early twenties held the door. Her eyes appeared glazed as she hung on to the door to prevent herself from falling over. She was stark naked and made no attempt to cover herself. The two young constables stopped in their tracks in amazement.

"Well, we know where some of Big Porky's drugs have gone," Corke observed. He then turned to the WPC, adding, "Cover her up and book her, will you, Morgan. You two guard this door." He headed straight for the priest's hole, followed by Jones. He found the secret door very quickly and opened it anticipating a struggle but found nothing. "Keep watch," he yelled to his sergeant as he began tapping the sides of the priest's hole.

As he tapped he heard a yell of "There he is!" from his sergeant. Corke turned to see the two constables wrestling a large man to the ground. Sergeant Jones jumped on the man from behind, ensuring that he remained on the ground while one of the constables applied handcuffs. Seconds later four policemen came up the stairs from the basement.

Corke was enjoying his moment of triumph. He had caught Big Porky and one of his henchmen and knew that he had the evidence to put him away. "Going for an early morning jog, were we then, Porky? It is a pity for you that you did not make it. The only exercise you are going to get for at least the next ten years is a prison yard."

"You got nothing on me, Corky. Just you wait till my lawyer gets to hear about this." Porky's response was spat through clenched teeth as the three policemen manhandled him into the nearest chair.

Inspector Corke thumped the palm of his hand against a side wall of the priest hole, which caused a concealed door to click open. He pulled the door back to reveal a cupboard piled high with brown paper packages. "I suppose this is your stationery cupboard, is it. Let's have a look, shall we?" Corke removed one of the packets and opened it carefully. It contained at least twenty small plastic packs, each with white powder in it. "Oh sorry, it must be your pantry. Little lady do a bit of baking, does she? That's an awful lot of baking powder even for wacky biscuits. Take them away, lads."

Freddy Russell shifted uneasily as Sergeant Jones and Sergeant Peters entered the room. Jones switched on the tape and announced the beginning of the interview. He asked Russell why he had fled the house through the tunnel and why he had resisted arrest. He also asked Russell if he knew that there were drugs in the house. All Russell's answers were non-committal. Jones warned him that he was looking at a long prison term, but that had no effect either. He tried a different tack. "You know what we really want to know, Freddy. Who supplied those drugs to Big Porky? If you co-operate we might be able to get your term reduced."

"No comment, Mr. Jones." Freddy's reply was firm and calm. It was obvious that he had accepted his fate.

"Okay, Freddy, but just before we finish, Sergeant Peters would like a word with you on another matter." A faint flicker of concern showed across Russell's face.

Peters asked, "Do you know Nick Dean, Freddy?"

"Yes, he has visited Porky at the house a few times. He is one of Porky's poker school."

"Really, is that what Porky calls it? Who else belongs to this poker school then?" Peters made no attempt to disguise his sarcasm.

"Dunno, Sarge, I don't play myself. I just look after the boss."

Peters's voice hardened. "Where were you last Monday?"

Russell fidgeted uneasily on his chair. "I can't remember. What's this all about anyway?"

"Well, you had better start remembering quickly because Nick Dean was found dead yesterday. He had been murdered, and you are our chief suspect. We will leave you to think about it for a while." With that he concluded the interview on the tape recorder and left the room with Sergeant Jones.

Sven met with Jenkins and Orchard for their midday briefing. He asked for the results of their morning's work interviewing the pharmacy set and their boyfriends about their Monday at Acres Heath beach. Jenkins summed up the interviews. "We called all ten of those on the beach that afternoon. We could not get hold of Todd Mitchell or David Stevens so we left messages for them to call the station. Scarlett Robinson invited us to come to the Boatman's Cottage this afternoon and Kyomi Taylor is coming to the station at three.

"We interviewed Angela Palmer, Beth Goodheart, Claire West, Andrew Pitman, Brian Whitehead and Chris West this morning. Their stories tally very well. This group met in Penzance at twelve-thirty and travelled to the beach together in two cars driven by Andrew Pitman and Chris West. They arrived at about one-fifteen. Todd Mitchell and Scarlett Robinson were already there. David Stevens and Kyomi Taylor arrived together about ten minutes later.

"They went in swimming for about half an hour, after which they all settled down to sunbathe for another hour. Chris West had bought a volleyball net that he then set up. They all played for a while, boys verses girls, but Kyomi and David soon dropped out. They went back in swimming while the others continued playing. It appears that they played for another hour before they all got tired and decided to sunbathe again. That lasted until about four when they went back into the water. It was there that David and Kyomi rejoined them. Nobody knew where the two of them were between three and four-fifteen."

"Then we must find out," Sven replied purposefully, "but first I shall tell you about my morning with the pathologist who was examining Nick Dean. Sergeant Peters has gone with the drugs team to pay a visit to Big Porky Jewell, so we will catch up with him later. Nick Dean died from a blow to the head, probably from a rock. The force of the impact was too great to be explained by a simple fall, so it seems that we are looking at murder. He died sometime between one and five o'clock on Monday afternoon, but we know from David Steven's statement yesterday that he was alive at two o'clock. Also there was heroine in his blood, which the pathologist suggests might have been injected at or about the time of death. That would explain the syringe and needle that I found in the cave. It is therefore very important that we know where Kyomi and David got to when they left the group. I know that Constable Jenkins has booked holiday for this afternoon, so if you, Constable Orchard, would interview Miss Robinson and Todd Mitchell if we can find them, then I shall take care of David Stevens and Miss Taylor."

Although disappointment showed on Orchard's face, his reply was immediate and positive. "Certainly, sir, I will get on to it right away."

Kyomi was sitting at the table in the interview room when Sven arrived. A woman police constable whom Sven did not recognise was sitting on a solitary chair against the wall of the room. Kyomi got up and approached Sven, extending her right hand as she came over. "Good afternoon, Sven, how are you?"

Sven shook her hand gently and motioned her back to the chair. "I am fine, thank you, and you also, I trust. Please do sit down." He chose to sit beside her rather than face her, so that she would not feel that she was being interrogated.

Kyomi responded with the confidence that Sven had come to expect. "I am, thank you. Now how can I help you?"

Sven wanted her to be relaxed so that she would remember events better. He sought to settle her with his opening remarks. "It's just a couple of points about your trip to Acres Heath beach last Monday. Do you remember when you arrived?"

Kyomi thought for a moment, then responded. "We normally meet between one and two, so David said that he would pick me up at about quarter past one. He was on time and I was ready for him so we left straight away. It takes about ten minutes to get to Acres Heath beach from my house, so David and I would have arrived at about one-thirty."

Sven nodded, then continued, "Thank you, Kyomi, that agrees with what the rest of the party have told us. Can you tell me what you did and where you went that afternoon, please?"

Kyomi looked up to the ceiling, paused for a moment, then began, "Let me think now. All the others we were expecting were already there. We joined them at a spot close to the rocks on the St Ives side of the bay. Fairly close to where you met us last Wednesday, in fact. We stripped down to our swimming costumes straight away and then went for a swim. I guess we must have been in there for about half an hour before we all came in to sunbathe. I could have stayed there all afternoon but Chris had bought his volleyball net so we were all forced to play. I was not enjoying it much so I gave up after ten minutes. David volunteered to break off as well to keep the teams even. He said that he knew of a very small bay, only accessible by swimming, where we could go to sunbathe on our own."

Kyomi drew a pair of imaginary quotation marks in the air as she emphasised the word "sunbathe." "I told him that too many people now knew about the caves and beach around the headland toward Nid and we would not be alone. David said he did not mean there. He knew of a very small cove on the other side going toward St Ives. He and Todd had found it one day when they were swimming. There is only beach there for three hours either side of low tide and you have to be a strong swimmer to reach it. Anyway, we went for it, although I have to admit that I was pretty tired when I got there."

"Did anybody see you there?" Sven asked his question without really having fully assessed what Kyomi had said until he had completed the question.

Kyomi smiled as she replied coyly, "Well hardly, that was the whole point."

"Quite so," Sven replied, trying to cover his embarrassment for having asked such a silly question.

He was considering his next question when Kyomi spoke again. "Sven, I know that you have a murder investigation to complete and I will help you as much as I can. Laura and I were good friends so I would like to see her murderer caught and punished. You have always been straight with me and have not appeared to judge what David and I have done. I know better than most the impact of losing somebody close. It took me six months to get my life back into shape after my brother's death and David was one of the friends who really helped me. That was far too long and I don't want David to have to do the same. He has to get over Laura and get on with his life with somebody else, and if that somebody else is me then I am happy with that. However, there are those who are more narrow-minded and will not see our friendship that way. I am sure there are even some who think that David and I killed Laura so that we could be together, but it is just not true. I will answer any questions that you ask of me but I would be grateful if you could keep as much of it confidential as you can."

Not for the first time in his conversations with Kyomi, Sven was taken aback by her statement. She had remained calm and spoken with measured tones throughout. This was no outburst or tantrum, so how should he take it? She could be telling the truth or attempting to put him off her trail. Facts were in short supply. He had no witness placing Kyomi and David on that deserted beach, if it even existed. He could and would check on the existence of the beach, but for now all he could do was probe her story and check it against what the rest of the party had already told the police team and what he would hear from David.

He responded to her cautiously, saying, "Kyomi, thank you for being so honest with me. I shall be equally honest with you. Police investigations are confidential, and all the time that I am supporting the Cornwall and Islands police force I shall abide by its rules. When we make an arrest and bring a case against the murderer or murderers, which we surely will, relevant statements may be presented in evidence and witnesses called to tell in open court what they have told us in our investigations. Some of what you have said may fall into that category and you may be called as a witness either by the prosecution or even the defence, who will have access to our evidence. I shall not hold back anything that is germane to the case, but neither shall I use anything that I do not consider to be relevant. Do you understand that?"

Kyomi nodded, but Sven wanted her to say that she understood. He remained silent, looking her straight in the eyes. She picked up the unspoken signal, replying, "Yes, Sven, I understand that, thank you."

Sven continued his questions. "How long were you on that beach?"

"I would have to guess, because I did not have a watch with me, but probably half an hour. We had taken a long time to swim there, so most of the beach was covered when we arrived. We stayed there until the tide covered the beach, then we swam back."

Sven decided to test how far her openness would extend. "What did you do while you were there?"

Kyomi blushed, but answered straight away. "I could tell you that we sunbathed and to a point that would be true, but I did say that I would answer all your questions and I will make that answer complete. We made love. I trust that you will not need to bring that up in evidence."

"Let us hope not," Sven replied, "although as I have told you, I cannot guarantee it. Thank you again for your help. That will be all for now."

As Sven left the interview room the desk sergeant handed him two messages. The first said that David Stevens had called.

He was back in the interview room with David within fifteen minutes of Kyomi having left, so he was sure that David had not had the opportunity to talk to her. He asked David the same questions about their time of arrival and where he and Kyomi were when they left the group. David confirmed the time of arrival as one-thirty, swimming for half an hour after arriving, the hour's sunbathing and the short period of volleyball before they broke off.

Sven had now come to the crunch question, which he posed in as calm and unthreatening a manner as he could. "What did you and Kyomi do when you left the others?"

David replied, "We went for a long swim."

Sven probed carefully, asking, "How long were you away from the rest of the group?"

David's reply was again limited. "I cannot be sure, but about an hour and a half, I guess."

Sven probed further, "Were you in the sea all that time?"

David shifted in his chair and then appeared to relax. "No, we swam around the rocks to a small cove, where we stayed for a while sunbathing and chatting."

"Where is that cove, David?" Sven probed.

"It's around the rocks to the eastern side of the bay. Very few people know about it. Todd and I spotted it when we were out fishing. It has a small beach that disappears as the tide rises. We stayed there until the sea covered the beach and then swam back. It's a long swim. It took about half an hour to get there and a little less to get back because the tide was with us most of the way."

Sven decided that David had told him all that he was prepared to and to probe further would be pointless. He terminated the interview and thanked David for his co-operation.

Sven took the note containing the second message out of his pocket. It was from Dr. Adrian Jones to say that he had completed the audit of the poisons that he had promised to undertake. He was pleased to report that he could account exactly for all the snake poisons, but there were some discrepancies with the other poisons. In some cases he had slightly more than his records showed and in other cases slightly less. For each poison the discrepancy was never more than a gram. Jones admitted to being concerned at even these low levels of inaccuracy, which he put down to weighing errors at the time of issue for poisons that were measured out from a container holding a larger content. He intended to introduce tighter controls as a result and thanked Sven for having brought the problem to his attention. Sven checked the list of those poisons that showed less than expected volumes. He found to his dismay that the list included strychnine, which was 60 milligrams short.

There was an air of excitement as Peter Pinks walked into the team briefing at six o'clock. "It sounds like you boys had some success today. So tell me the news."

Sven looked perplexed until Peters came in. "I think the inspector is referring to the drug bust, Sven. I have only just come away from the interrogation of Freddy Russell, one of Big Porky Jewell's minders. He is singing like a canary. With that information they should be able to send Jewell down for a long time. He might even get life. I am really pleased for the drug boys because they have been working on this one for ages. It was our case that tipped the balance. My telling Freddy Russell that he was our prime suspect for Nick Dean's murder really put the frighteners on him. He admitted that he was with

Jewell collecting a shipment of drugs on Monday afternoon. Not only has he implicated Jewell, but they will get his supplier as well. As I said, great for the drugs boys, but as far as Nick Dean's death goes it only rules out one of our suspects."

Sven tried to be pleased, but his expression portrayed that his own case had not really moved forward from this. He put as much enthusiasm into his voice as he could muster as he turned to Pinks, who was also looking somewhat dejected. "Thank you, Sergeant. Well, at least it narrows our suspects down. Constable Orchard, perhaps you will tell us how you got on with Todd Mitchell and Scarlett Robinson."

Orchard, detecting a mood of dejection, began brightly. "Yes, guv, I interviewed them both at Mitchell's cottage. I did them one after the other so they would have had no time to confer. They were the first to arrive at Acres Beach, at about one o'clock, so they picked a spot near the rocks on the St Ives side. They confirmed all the times that the others gave us this morning and also the disappearance of Kyomi and David during the volleyball. Mitchell says he saw them both swimming out to sea and guessed that they were heading for the little cove that he and David knew about. He surmised that they might have been intending some 'rumpy-pumpy,' as he quaintly put it. Miss Robinson confirmed all the times but did not see where Kyomi and David swam."

"What now, Sven?" asked a rather dejected Pinks.

Sven knew that he had to keep the momentum going through this low patch. "Firstly we must check if this cove exists, and if it does whether it is visible from the cliff path. Would you get Jenkins to work on that tomorrow please, Sergeant? With his contacts in the department of oceanography at Plymouth that should not be too difficult. Also would you walk that cliff path tomorrow afternoon to see if you can see any bays from it and also check for people who walk it regularly? Dog walkers are always a good bet. I will check how our forensic team is getting on with the lighthouse. Right, if there are no more questions, we will call it a day."

Chapter 21

Forensic evidence, 6th July 1996

A small, dapper man in his early fifties wearing a tweed jacket and flannels greeted Sven outside the door of the lighthouse. "You must be Sven Ffolkes. I saw you striding across the causeway fully ten minutes ago. It's amazing how far you can see from the balcony. I am Carlton Forbes, forensic scientist in charge of this investigation. Please do come into the tent for a coffee before we start. You will have to get kitted up as well, I'm afraid."

As both men donned protective suits, Forbes began describing progress on the investigation. "Bit of a logistic nightmare, this one, since nobody could really tell us where to look. Sergeant Peters said to check everywhere, but to start with the balcony, lounge and Miss Hamilton's room. Of course we had to do the hall and stairs first to make sure we did not destroy anything there going in and out of the place. They gave no surprises. There was hair, fibres, mud, sand, salt and plenty of fingerprints, but nothing suspicious. There was no blood to be found anywhere. Several of the fibres matched Miss Hamilton's pyjamas. They were found on the stairs outside her bedroom and going down two flights. Had she been walking up or down the stairs in her pyjamas, or even been carried, that is what I would have expected to find. From the lack of fibres elsewhere on the stairs, I can say with some certainty that she did not reach the rocks via the balcony or the ground floor door that night. Anyway, come up to the lounge and I will talk you through what we have found up there."

Forbes allowed them both to get their breath back before he took Sven out on to the balcony to see the broken rail. "This is the most interesting thing by far," Forbes said as he pointed to the broken rails. "As you can see there are three horizontal rails fixed to vertical supports that are set into the stonework of the lighthouse at three-foot intervals. The upper and middle horizontal have broken away near one of the vertical supports and bent outwards. The joints to the vertical supports have significant amounts of rust, which extends into the horizontal rails. The rails fractured near the joints as a result of horizontal outward pressure, leaving the rails bent outwards. Somebody could fall from there, but not as a result of leaning on the rails, either backwards or forwards. They would have to have been pushed after the rails were broken, and if they had, then I would expect evidence of fibres and blood on the jagged rail breaks, but found neither. I do not think that anybody has fallen from here."

Both men went back into the lounge, where Forbes continued to describe his findings—or, to be precise, the lack of them. "We have taken this room apart," Forbes began, shaking his head as he did so. "There were lots of fingerprints, fibres and hair, but no blood and no fibres from her pyjamas. I do not think that she came in here in those pyjamas. Now let's go down to Miss Hamilton's room."

They took the single flight of stairs to Laura's bedroom, where the door had been left open. The room had been stripped bare. "Here we found fibres from Miss Hamilton's pyjamas and also from the clothes worn by Carole Young and Sarah Hamilton. We also found hair from each of them, but again, no blood. That is about it, really. We still have the other rooms to go over. Would you like us to tackle them in any particular order?"

Sven could detect the exasperation in Forbes's voice. He was a professional trying to do the best job he could but he was not getting the support he deserved. Sven also knew that he could not guide him now. Any room would be as good as the next, with the possible exception of the basement rooms, and even they might yield something. "Probably best to continue from the top downwards, and thank you and your team for the thoroughly professional job that you are all doing," Sven replied, trying to appear as positive as he could. He left feeling very dejected.

Sergeant Peters was having no better luck trying to find David's secret beach. In the two miles that he had walk from Acres Heath he had passed several headlands that could well have held a beach between them, but he could see nothing. The cliff path had drifted inland, leaving bracken between him and the headland, which made it difficult to find any vantage points from which to look over. He had been thorough, cutting through the bracken where there was any semblance of a path to follow and had the scratches to prove it, but still nothing. He stopped at the point where the path began to descend into St. Ives. On the headland opposite he could see the St Nicholas Tower, and looking down the path, the bright green square of the bowls club stood out two hundred yards ahead. From the bowls club the path ran into St Ives and its series of beaches. On the other side of St Ives, the coast path continued past St Nicholas Tower to Carbis Bay and Blimford Head, which was immediately above the Lighthouse Inn. He reasoned to himself that if he had been able to see any beach down below, he would have seen it by now. If there was a bay then it was not accessible or even visible from the cliff path. Peters turned around and started back. *Might as well be thorough*, he demanded of himself. *Something might be visible on the way back.*

Sven opened the daily wash-up meeting in the most optimistic tone he could muster. "I expect that you are all wondering why I have called our meeting at three o'clock today instead of the usual five."

Jenkins and Orchard both nodded, while Peters put it into words. "Yes, guv, I think we all are. Are you going to give us all an early night then?" The tone of Peters's voice made it clear that that was the last thing he expected.

"Actually, I am and I am not," Sven replied to allow a bit of mystery to build up. "But first, let us see if any of you have had any more luck than I have today. Who would like to start? And please make it somebody who has discovered something."

Both constables remained silent, looking to Peters to open proceedings, but Peters just looked down and shook his head. Jenkins began hesitantly, "Well, yes, I can report something positive. I went to see my friends at Plymouth oceanography department and they confirmed the existence of that secret beach. In fact there are two of them visible from the sea at low tide. The one closer to Acres Heath beach is uncovered for three hours either side of low tide, and the one farther away is only uncovered for an hour. Given the time that you said Kyomi and David left the rest of the group, it must have been the closer one that they went to."

Sven managed a small smile as he said, "Well done, Jenkins, at least that gives us something. Can you brighten our day a bit more, Constable Orchard?"

Orchard smiled as he opened the now-familiar notebook. "I think so, guv.

As you know I interviewed Dr. Williamson, the pathologist who is examining Nick Dean. He called first thing this morning to say that he had discovered more since he talked to you, Sven. He told you that he had found heroine in Dean's blood, but further tests revealed strychnine as well. There was a second recent injection, not in the crook of the arm where the heroine had been injected, but in the left biceps. Dr. Williamson thinks that it was injected while he was unconscious and possibly when he was already dead. It was the blow to the head that killed him, not the strychnine."

"Well," said Sven, "you lads certainly did better than Peters and I did today. Now I should like to get back to the reason for this early meeting. You may not know this, but my period on secondment from the Norwegian police force comes to an end tonight and I fly back to Oslo tomorrow. I can say without any reservation that I have enjoyed my stay immensely and I could not wish to have worked with a more professional and committed team. I only regret that we have not been able to identify the murderer or murderers before I left, but I am confident that you will soon get a result and I look forward to a call from Inspector Hamilton telling me that you have made an arrest. Anyway, I have booked a private room at the Lighthouse Inn tonight and I would like you all to join me for dinner by way of a thank you. I have also invited Inspector and Mrs. Hamilton, who have made their home my home for the past two weeks. I will see you all there at seven o'clock then?"

Chapter 22

A matter of timing

Sven was hardly out of the taxi before Carole came out to greet him. "Good evening, Mr. Ffolkes, and welcome to the Lighthouse Inn."

Sven noticed immediately how her work persona differed from the Carole he had interviewed on more than one occasion. She was confident then, but now she radiated self-assurance. That she looked immaculate in her clean, finely pressed uniform went without saying, but it was as if her presentation had been given the same excellent finishing. She continued her well-rehearsed process, which while being totally efficient still carried a warmth that put him and his guests at ease.

"Please come through to the Snug. Your other guests are already here." Carole led Sven, Edward, Jenny, Sarah and Rose into a small room where Peters, Orchard and Jenkins were already waiting. The three men jumped to their feet simultaneously to greet them. Edward introduced the ladies to them as they all settled down to talk together. Carole took the orders for drinks and handed the menus around.

As they all began their consideration of what to have, Sven spoke. "I thought of the Lighthouse Inn because I have already had the pleasure of tasting the meals here. The owner's younger daughter Alicia is the chef. I had lunch with her after I had interviewed her about the tragic events in the lighthouse last week. She is a very fine cook, especially for one so young. I expect to hear of her being associated with a top London hotel before too long. Anyway, enough of my chatter, please choose whatever you fancy and let's enjoy the evening."

A waiter brought the drinks and began placing them in front of the guests. Nobody took much notice of him until he said, "Good evening, Mr. Ffolkes, ladies and gentlemen. Enjoy your evening."

Sven looked up to see Todd Mitchell smile, nod his head and make to leave. "Todd, of course, I had forgotten that you worked here," Sven said. "How are you?"

"I'm fine, thank you, Mr. Ffolkes. You will probably see a few more of us that you recognise tonight as well. David and I are working here today, but we finish at ten. Scarlett and Kyomi are going to join us then to have supper with Alicia."

"Well, I wish you all a pleasant supper as well," Sven replied. Todd thanked him, then left to continue his duties.

Edward raised his glass. "Here's to you, Sven, wishing you a safe trip home."

Everyone echoed the toast and drank to Sven, who appeared embarrassed by the attention. "I just wish I could have finished this investigation first," he replied. "I hate leaving things half done."

Peters responded immediately, "But you have achieved an incredible amount in a week, Sven. That will give us a firm basis on which to finish it. After all, we have not even had the full forensic details from the lighthouse yet."

Jenkins and Orchard nodded their agreement. Rose added, "It was just a matter of timing, Sven."

Sven went silent for a moment before saying, "Pardon, Rose, what did you say just then, please?"

Rose looked a little surprised, fearing that unwittingly she had offended him. "I said that it was just a matter of timing. I meant if you had been given this case at the start of your visit rather than in the last week of it then you would have had enough time to resolve it, that is all."

"Timing," Sven repeated quietly as if to himself. "Timing, timing is the key. That is what I missed."

A voice called from behind him, "Ladies and gentlemen, dinner is served." In his confusion Sven had not noticed Todd reappear to make his announcement. The party followed Todd obediently, moving into the small dining room where Sven and Alicia had had lunch only a few days earlier. The room contained a single round table laid with eight places. Sven was seated facing the window and his back to the door. The first course was already on the table, allowing the guests to start as soon as they sat down.

Sven was very pensive, saying nothing throughout the whole course. He remained quiet, hardly touching his wine, while that course was cleared away and, after a further five minutes, the main course was served. Edward was the first to raise the subject. "You are very quiet, Sven. Is there something on your mind?"

At first Sven said nothing, but after another prompt from Edward, he began in a slow, deliberate tone, "What we have here is three murders. The first is the poisoning of a middle-aged man whose immediate family is one legitimate daughter and a second illegitimate daughter whom latterly he had decided to recognise. He was a man who had several affairs and did not mind whom he hurt by them."

Sven looked up, realising that it was Edward's brother he was describing in terms that were not flattering. Edward was clearly saddened, but he recognised that the description was fair. He nodded for Sven to continue.

"His own marriage broke up when his wife left him for a younger man, leaving him to bring up their only daughter. He was fond of his drink and was prepared to drive whilst over the limit. We know this from the evidence of his former lover and business partner, Jean Young, and also from his present lover, Julia Rowntree. But why was he killed? He was a quiet man who kept to himself. He was a model railway enthusiast and chess-player. I cannot see gang warfare arising in the model railway fraternity with cartels forcing up the price of model locomotives, or even a rival chess club taking out one of the opposition. No, it was either vengeance for his killing Peter Taylor in that accident on New Year's Day—if indeed it was John Hamilton who was the culprit—or it was for his money.

"So therefore, who had a motive? Laura clearly did. She was a selfish girl who would not relish the thought of another person muscling in on her inheritance. She knew from her pharmacy course what the effects of strychnine were. She would know that it would take several hours to take effect, putting her well away from him at the time of John's death. We know that the Lighthouse Inn kept strychnine as a poison to eradicate rats from its cellars, but did Laura? If it was Laura, then who killed her? Two independent murders on the same night affecting two related people are so improbable as almost to be discounted. It is far more likely that the same person had a reason to kill both victims. However, I do not discount the possibility that the murderer killed one victim to disguise the fact that the other was the only real target.

"We know from the post-mortem that Miss Rowntree could not have killed John Hamilton. He had already taken the poison before he met her that night. Jean Young could have slipped the poison in his drink, but she could not have killed Laura unless she crossed the flooded channel in the dark, evaded observation by any of the partygoers, killed Laura and then returned also undetected. But what motive would she have? There is none that I can find. No, ladies and gentlemen, our murderer was a guest at the party.

"Before continuing to examine motive, we have to understand how Laura died. Let us go through the events after Laura went to bed at just after one-thirty. At that time, Angela and Andrew, Beth and Brian and Claire and Chris were already in bed. Alicia went to bed twenty minutes later, at one-fifty, followed by Todd and Scarlett at five past two.

"Carole left five minutes after that, planning a clandestine meeting with James in the Penzance Room. She had fifty minutes to spare, just less than half an hour of which she reports spending with Laura. She went to borrow a dressing gown but found Laura in distress so stayed to comfort her. She left, with Laura feeling better, at about two thirty-five.

"James left the lounge after Kyomi returned to David and before David left to go back to Laura. We know that to have been at a time between two-ten, when Todd and Scarlett left, and two-forty, when David went to Laura.

"The next thing we hear of Laura is when she refuses to let David into her room. We have both David and Kyomi putting the time of that encounter at two-forty or thereabouts.

"That is the last we hear of Laura until David discovers her body at eight-thirty. The pathologist says that she was hit with a blunt instrument, then fell a long way and died fifteen to sixty minutes later. He puts the time of death at between two and four-thirty, with the blow being struck up to an hour before then. From the evidence we have here, then, Laura was struck and fell from the lighthouse any time between two forty-five when David left her door and four-fifteen, which, according to the pathologist, is the latest time she could have been struck in order to be dead by four-thirty.

"What reports of activity do we have during that time? David said that he heard activity in the lounge soon after he returned there to sleep. He went back to the lounge at about quarter to three and then to Kyomi at five past three, so whoever went on to the balcony did so between those times. David confirms that the door to the balcony was opened and closed, so at least one person went out there.

"Was that Laura and her murderer going out on to the balcony? If it was, then why did Laura go on the balcony and unbutton her pyjama jacket? We can be sure that the jacket did not come open as she fell because the buttonholes were undamaged. Did she go out there expecting to be seduced? Perhaps, and if she did, then we are looking for a boy whom she would wish to seduce her. Certainly two candidates fit that role: David, whom she had just rejected, and Nick, with whom she had had an affair earlier. There may have been others whom she fancied. James, the boy she took out on to the balcony, for example. Was a rendezvous agreed before Carole came out to break up their little encounter?

"Would Laura be fickle enough to reject David when he came to her room and go to him five minutes later? From what we know of Laura, that is possible, but we have Kyomi's statement to prove that David was telling the truth about knocking on Laura's door five minutes earlier and was back making love with Kyomi twenty minutes later. Therefore I think Laura was not with David for two reasons. If David had been that close to Laura just fifteen minutes before going to Kyomi, then Kyomi would have known. She would have smelled Laura's perfume on him and not her own. The second reason I will discuss in a minute.

"Could James have been in the room with Laura and killed her? Yes; he is unaccounted for from the time that he left the lounge until Kyomi finds him in the St Ives room—a maximum of thirty minutes and probably significantly less. But if he was with Laura, why would he kill her, and how would he have managed to dispose of her body? We know that the window was too small to get a body through, because John Hamilton made sure of that. John was frightened that Laura might lean out of the window and fall. Kyomi found James in the St Ives room at two-forty and we know that he stayed there until three, when he met Carole. If he had been a murderer trying to dispose of a body, then he would have used those twenty minutes more usefully to do precisely that, rather than killing time awkwardly with Kyomi.

"So did Nick get up from the toilet, go to Laura's room and persuade her to come to the balcony? He certainly had a motive. The fear of realising the responsibility of fatherhood might have driven him to desperate measures. But if he did, then what did he use as a weapon to hit her? Also nobody, with the exception of David when he was in the lounge, reported hearing any noise outside his or her room at that time, although we have plenty of reports of disturbances at other times.

"Let us look at those disturbances chronologically. When David and Kyomi were together, which was between three and four o'clock, they reported footsteps outside coming from below passing the landing and continuing up. This is consistent with Nick's statement that he left the toilet at three-thirty to return to the lounge. Nick said that he settled down to sleep in a sleeping bag in the lounge. On his return to the lounge, at about four-ten, David reported somebody sleeping in a sleeping bag in the lounge, so Nick's statement is supported. That would have given Nick forty minutes to go to Laura, persuade her to come out on to the balcony, hit her, throw her over the rails and go back to the lounge to sleep. If Nick killed Laura, he would have had to strike the blow with a blunt object after three-thirty. That is toward the end of the time that the pathologist said that the blow could have been struck. He put the time of death at between two and four-thirty, with her fall occurring fifteen minutes to an hour earlier. So she fell between one and four-fifteen.

So was Nick our murderer? If he was, then we have to answer the following questions." Sven started counting the points on his fingers.

"One: if Laura thought that Nick had come to seduce her and she wanted him to, then why did she go to the balcony with him? Would it not have been easier just to invite him into her room? Perhaps she did and Nick struck her in her room, knocking her unconscious, and then carried her to the balcony where he threw her off. If he did that, then how come we found no traces of blood on the carpet in Laura's room or on the stairs going up to the lounge or in the lounge?

"Two: if Nick killed Laura, with what did he hit her?

"Three: even if Nick did manage to kill Laura between three-thirty and four-fifteen, then who did David hear go out on to the balcony between two forty-five and five past three? Nobody has come forward to say that they were there. If this was an innocent encounter of love, or even somebody going out for fresh air, then why didn't anybody say so? And how did the railings get damaged?

"Four: if Nick killed Laura, then who killed Nick and who killed John? I have no good answers to these questions, so I conclude that Nick did not kill Laura. Furthermore, since whoever went out on to that balcony has not come forward to identify himself or herself, we can assume he or she was up to no good and was probably the murderer.

"The next disturbance is at around dawn. The most accurate estimate is Alicia's clock, which read four thirty-eight. Claire and David reported hearing vomiting, and Angela, Andrew, David and Alicia report a cold draught, with Alicia adding that she saw an apparition consistent with the ghost described in John's brochure and for which the lighthouse is famous. Angela and Andrew also report a door opening. Kyomi reported footsteps above or below her, but not on her landing. If the outside door was opened, then this would certainly explain the draught. What are we to conclude from this? It occurred at the same time that Carole reported going downstairs to be sick, so all the evidence points to Carole's statement being true.

"The last disturbance, reported only by Kyomi, was after it was light. She heard somebody going to the toilet. This is consistent with Alicia's account of going to the toilet at five o'clock. Alicia also reported disinfectant, confirming what Carole said about her earlier trip to the toilet. So everything is neatly accounted for, and anyway, these last two incidents occurred after Laura was known to be dead. So how, where and when did Laura die and by whose hand?"

During the whole of this explanation everybody had listened in stunned silence. They had all expected Sven to identify the murderer. Edward could contain his frustration no longer. "Then we are no further forward, are we, Sven?" he protested, but more in resignation than in anger.

"On the contrary," Sven replied. "I have related the events to you as the murderer wishes us to see them. There are two other pieces of evidence that I have not related that we cannot ignore. Both Angela and Beth reported hearing a thud soon after they had fallen asleep. Neither could give an exact time, but we know that it was still dark, so it was before Carole went downstairs to get some air.

"That thud was, I believe, Laura's body hitting the rocks. It is the only report we have of anything falling down outside. If it was not Laura, then what was it and when did Laura fall? These two unanswerable questions support my conclusions. We were meant to believe that Laura fell from the balcony, either accidentally or deliberately, whilst romancing with a boy. This would point the finger at David, or possibly Nick or James, any of whom had opportunity, although in the case of James I can find no motive.

"But why then did Laura have scratches on her breasts, stomach, abdomen and fronts of the thighs? If she fell from the balcony, she would have to have been leaning on it either looking out or looking in. Even then if the balcony fence gave way, she would only be scratched if the handrail was rough, which it was not, or from where the horizontal supports had broken away. In that case she would have been almost impaled on these supports and would have had fewer, much deeper wounds. Either way the abrasions should not have occurred above the waist. No, the *murderer* broke those railings to make us think that Laura fell from the balcony. It was the *murderer* whom David heard go on to the balcony before he went to Kyomi. It was the *murderer* who did not expect David to be there and who did not see him in the dark, trying to confuse us."

Sergeant Peters, looking perplexed, interrupted, "So do you know who killed Laura, Sven?"

186

"Indeed I do," Sven replied and then continued his explanation. "Neither Beth nor Angela could be definitive about when they heard that thud, but both said that it was soon after they got to sleep. A lot earlier, I suspect, than the events that we have already discussed. As Rose said, inadvertently, it was all a matter of timing. So we return to the evidence of our pathologist that Laura fell between one and four-fifteen. We have just shown that Nick could not have committed the murder at three-thirty, that David did not kill her between two-forty and five past three, and that the murderer was on the balcony soon after two forty-five. We must therefore conclude that the murder took place between one and two-forty. Even though we know that James did not kill her between two-ten and two-forty, somebody else did."

"But we know that Laura locked the door on David at two-forty," Peters protested.

"Do we?" Sven asked, his voice suggesting not. "We know that *somebody* locked David out, but how do we know that it was Laura? David did not say that she answered him, but only that the door was locked from inside the room. Surely Laura, this highly emotional girl who never hid her feelings, would have said something? No, it was the murderer who locked that door.

"We can now place the murderer in Laura's room between two forty and two forty-five and on the balcony at two-fifty. This also means that neither David nor Kyomi could be the murderer, as they were outside the room at the time. We can also confirm that James can be excluded since Kyomi found him in the St Ives Room when she returned.

"Let's return now to the murderer, whom we know to have been in Laura's room at two-forty. So what then was the murderer doing in Laura's room, and how long had he or she been there? Carole said that she stayed talking to Laura for a little less than half an hour before leaving her to go to the Penzance Room to await James. We know that she left the party at about two-ten, so she must have left Laura fit and well at about two thirty-five. James found Carole in the Penzance Room at three o'clock, just as they had arranged."

Edward summed up, "So you are saying that Laura let the murderer into her room between two thirty-five and two-forty. The murderer then knocked Laura out by hitting her over the head with a blunt instrument and locked David out immediately afterwards. When David had gone he unlocked the door and carried Laura up the stairs, through the lounge past David, whom he knew would be there, and then to the balcony where he threw her over? I say 'he' because I do not believe that a woman would have the strength to do that."

"That is possible," Sven admitted, "but if it were true, apart from the murderer knowing that he was highly likely to be caught, we have more unanswered questions. One: what was the murder weapon?; two: why did we find no traces of blood in Laura's room, on the stairs going to the lounge, in the lounge or on the balcony?; and three: why did the murderer break the balcony rails?

"No, my friends, our murderer was cleverer than that. Those railings were bent back to make us think that Laura was leaning against them when she fell or was pushed. This means that the murderer went on to the balcony deliberately to break the rails and furthermore went out on the balcony alone, because Laura was already lying on the rocks, although probably not yet dead."

Edward looked more perplexed. He queried, "Then if Laura did not fall over the balcony, how did she end up on the rocks? As you stated yourself, the window in her room is too small to get a body through, because John had ensured that it would be that way."

Sven nodded. He was about to tell Edward how Laura died and by whose hand. This was going to be painful enough for Edward without inflicting on him the suffering of realising that he had failed to work out what happened when Sven had. He began carefully, intending to emphasise that it was meticulous police work in which Edward had been prevented from taking part that had solved this crime. "You are quite right, my friend, she could not have fallen from the window in her room. She must have fallen from another room before David ever knocked on her door. It was the murderer, *alone* in Laura's room, who locked the door on him."

At that point the penny dropped for Edward. He started uneasily, "But this means that Carole was lying."

Sven waited silently for Edward to continue and also stopped Jenkins, who had worked it out, from coming in.

Edward continued, "So Carole must be the murderer." He then hesitated before asking, "But how did she do it?"

Peters's eyes moved toward the door and his expression changed to one of alarm. As Sven was about to speak, Peters raised his hand to stop him. Despite being in full flow with his explanation, Sven had sufficient presence of mind and understanding of Peters to know that there was something wrong. Peters was already halfway out of his chair and looking toward the door. All eyes followed his to discover that Carole had just entered the room. Peters broke the silence: "Miss Young, please do join us in a drink to wish Sven farewell. Please take a seat for a moment."

Carole was about to protest when Peters took her gently by the hand and led her to his chair. He picked a fresh wine glass from the sideboard and placed it in front of her as he sat her down. Orchard sensed what was going on so he half filled the glass with wine for her. "This is very kind of you," Carole began. "Just a small glass to wish you well, then I must be off to look after my other guests. A safe journey to you, Mr. Ffolkes."

"Oh, we can do better than that, Carole; Sven has just told us who murdered Laura." Edward's voice gave no hint of the venom that was to come.

Carole shifted uneasily in her chair, but she retained her composure. "Why, that's wonderful news. Are you at liberty to say who now?"

"Oh, most certainly," Edward responded, "but you already know don't you, Carole, because it was you." This time Edward's voice was full of hate for somebody whom he knew had killed his niece and, he guessed, had also killed his brother.

Carole shook her head gently in denial, but a slight blanching of her face confirmed to Sven that he was right. Sven reflected on the sheer coldness of her reaction. Not for her a loud and passionate denial of her involvement. That might give something away. Instead she chose cool and belittling silence to discredit Edward's accusation.

Sven was relieved that Edward had identified the murderer for himself, but he still had to proceed gently. "That you killed Laura," he began, "we will only prove with forensics, but this is what I conclude happened.

"After leaving the party Carole went back to the Penzance Room as she said. She rolled up the rug, leaving just the varnished wood floor and white stone walls, and then opened the bedroom window as wide as it would go. She waited until all was quiet before going around to Laura's room and knocking quietly on the door. She did not want to wake anybody else. When Laura came to the door Carole asked her to come to the Penzance Room because, she said, 'David was very upset and threatening to kill himself.'

"She told Laura to keep quiet because they did not want the others to know that David was making a fool of himself. Laura came straight away. As Carole opened the door Laura saw the open window and no David, just as Carole had planned. Laura rushed over to the window. Carole came up from behind and hit her with the stone table lamp. Laura fell unconscious. Carole took off her dressing gown and slippers and unbuttoned her pyjama top. She wanted it to look like Laura had been on the balcony with David when she was pushed or fell over. Carole did not mind which. She then pushed her out the window. That would explain all those shallow scratches on Laura's chest, stomach and thighs. As I said, the walls of the Penzance Room are white painted stone and the floor is varnished wood, so it was easy for her to clean up the blood that had spluttered on to them. We would see nothing even with a thorough search, but be sure that our forensic team will find it. She used some towels that she got from the bathroom earlier in the evening. She put the towels in a bin bag and threw it out of the window as well. She then replaced the rug so that nothing looked out of place.

"That would have been at about two-forty. She then checked that the coast was clear and went back to Laura's room to put the dressing gown and slippers back in her wardrobe. Just as she was about to leave, there was a knock on the door. She heard David say 'Laura, open the door. I want to talk to you.'

"Thinking quickly, she said nothing, but walked over and locked the door. Note that she did not run over, because she wanted to mimic the deliberate footsteps of an irate Laura. David called out again, 'Laura, please open the door.' She waited until David left and then another five minutes before creeping out and up to the lounge. It was in darkness. She crept past David, who was by now asleep, and on to the balcony. She probably did not even see David. Using the moonlight she found the broken rails that she had spotted earlier in the evening and bent them back. She then went back to the Penzance Room, arriving just before three o'clock—in time for the arrival of James, who would be her alibi for the night.

"But she did not stop there. No, this girl was thorough. At four-thirty Carole went downstairs pretending to be unwell, but in reality to check that Laura was dead. That was when Alicia was woken by the draught from the open door and the creaking. She did not dare move because she thought it was the ghost. Carole went outside and confirmed that Laura was dead. She also found the bin bag full of towels and threw it out to sea, unfortunately not far enough for it not to be washed up down the coast the next day. To cover her tracks she went into the bathroom, pretending to be sick. She put bleach down the toilet and wiped it around with disinfectant. Content with her night's work, she returned to the bed of her innocent and unsuspecting alibi.

"Unfortunately for Carole it was her thoroughness that led her into more complications. Unknown to her, Nick Dean had gone on to the balcony for some fresh air and he saw her. He would still have been very drunk at the time and would not have understood what was going on. It would just have appeared strange. However, when he learned of Laura's death the next day, he would have worked it out. But Nick was not the sort to share his observations with the police when he might be able to make something of them himself. Blackmailing Carole was his preferred option, but he did not know what he was taking on.

Remember that Nick had just acquired a very serious drug habit that would require feeding, so easy money would appeal to him.

"Carole agreed to meet him. She set the venue as the caves, knowing that he would access them from Acres Heath beach. She picked her time such that the tide was rapidly coming in, so any innocent sunbathers who might have decided to go there would be on their way back by then. She also knew from Laura that the pharmacy students met there on a Monday so she could divert suspicion on to one of them. Meanwhile she chose to access the caves by swimming from Chard beach on the west, which is the Nid beach side. She is a strong swimmer, as all the certificates proudly displayed in her mother's office will testify. That way nobody would place her anywhere near Nick at the time of his death.

"So picture the scene now with Nick Dean waiting in the cave for Carole. Remember that Nick does not swim or sunbathe and is ill at ease in that environment. He takes a shot of heroin to calm his nerves. He then spots Carole striding in from the sea wearing only some form of swimwear. This is an attractive girl whom he would like to seduce and she knows it. She plays on his desires by slowly removing her swimwear as she approaches him. By the time she is within ten yards of him she is naked, her swimwear left well behind her on the beach. He thinks that this is a payment that he is more than willing to accept. He strips off his clothes as quickly as he can, throwing them all about him and leaving them where they fell, waiting expectantly for Carole's embrace, which he probably gets.

"However, Carole has something other than sex on her mind. She does not want to get his blood on her swimsuit when she strikes him ruthlessly on the back of the head with a rock that she has picked up while Nick is undressing and his attention is distracted. Nick was hardly likely to have seen it because he would not have been looking at what was in her hand. He was probably rendered helpless by the first blow and killed by a second. But just in case that was not enough, she injects him with strychnine to make sure. As I have said before, she is not one to take chances. Carole would then have washed the blood from her body in the sea, put her uncontaminated swimwear back on and swum back to Chard beach. Having murdered twice before, this was probably much easier for her. There was far less chance of being seen."

Sergeant Peters had already moved behind Carole, just in case she attempted to escape, but his precaution was unnecessary. As Sven fell silent, his gaze and that of the assembled company fell upon Carole. She calmly returned his gaze before responding, "As you say, Mr. Ffolkes, that is your theory, which may or may not be given any credence by further forensic analysis. While you are in the mood to speculate, perhaps you would care to give a motive as to why I should kill my friend Laura? I did not make her pregnant or seduce her fiancé, and I certainly was not going to compete with her for her precious father."

Even Sven, a hardened murder detective, was taken aback by this callous attempt to sew discord and shift the blame away from herself.

"Indeed I shall," he began, "and at the same time resolve the murder of John. Your motive was money, specifically the inheritance from John. You have known for some time that he was your father, even though he did not know that you knew. Your mother told you a long time ago. She confirmed that when I spoke to her earlier this week. To get that money, you knew that you would have to kill both John and Laura. Killing John was easy for you. You knew that your mother kept strychnine to control the rats in the cellar. You just put some in his glass during the reception, before you all went across to the lighthouse. You gave him just sufficient to kill him in a few large measures of whisky to disguise the taste. After that it was the party where you disposed of Laura. While everybody else was getting drunk you just drank tonic from a glass dipped in gin to give the smell—a trick that you no doubt learned from some unscrupulous barman. It was easy for you to pretend to be just as drunk as the rest of them."

Carole smiled as she moved to play her ace. "So," she began, "you are saying that I poisoned my father before he changed his will, in the hope that he would change it in my favour before the poison took effect? Perhaps you propose to suggest that I hypnotised him into changing it?"

Edward and Sergeant Peters looked perplexed, but not Sven. He had done his homework better than that. "Oh no, Miss Young," he countered, "John's change of will was just what you wanted to avoid, so that suspicion did not fall on you. Once it was known that John had recognised you and left you half his inheritance, you would be a suspect. Any suspicious death of John and Laura had to occur before he changed his will, or at least before you *knew* that he had changed it. It was a clause in his original will that you sought to utilise. Anybody might assume that if he died before Laura, then his bequest to Laura would fall within Laura's estate. But there was a caveat that many use to cater for the risk of dual inheritance tax in the event of a main beneficiary dying very soon after the testator, for example in a car accident. Laura had to survive John for thirty days before she inherited from him; otherwise her inheritance would go to you. And you knew that. When I interviewed Miss Taylor, she told me that her brother Peter was training to be a solicitor. She also told me the chambers at which he worked. It was Jones, McInally and Harbour in Truro—the same chambers that handled John Hamilton's will. And that, Miss Young, is how you knew what was in your father's will and its significance for you. Peter was your boyfriend and he told you. Little did the poor unfortunate lad know what use you would make of that information."

Carole's face portrayed everything. She knew that she had been found out. Sven nodded to Peters, who with the help of Jenkins led her to a waiting police car that Orchard had called while Sven was talking.

The journey back to Edward's house passed in complete silence. Edward and his daughters were too shocked to speak, and Sven did not wish to disturb their reflections. Rose, Sarah and Jenny decided to retire early, leaving Sven alone with Edward. Sven could tell that Edward had turned the whole saga over in his mind several times and was still wondering. "Is something still bothering you, my friend?" he enquired.

Edward hesitated for a moment. "Yes, I am still amazed at how you pieced together all the events of that fateful evening, but can you explain what Alicia saw that frightened her into immobility?"

Sven smiled ruefully as he answered, "I am a policeman who can deduce what happened from the facts that are presented to him and then present proof. What I cannot prove then I neither accept nor reject. Clearly the young lady *thought* she saw the ghost of the lighthouse and I, for one, will not say that she was mistaken."

Printed in the United States
R2253000001B/R22530PG49179LVSX00001B/1}